# THE
# LAST DINNER
## AT
# WISTERIA
# HOUSE

# BOOKS BY SUE ROBERTS

STANDALONE NOVELS

*My Big Greek Summer*

*My Very Italian Holiday*

*You, Me and Italy*

*A Very French Affair*

*As Greek as It Gets*

*Some Like It Greek*

*Going Greek*

*Greece Actually*

*What Happens in Greece*

*Take a Chance on Greece*

*There's Something about Greece*

*All You Need is Greece*

*The Greek Villa*

*Not My Greek Wedding*

CHRISTMAS NOVELS

*Christmas at Red Robin Cottage*

*The Village Christmas Party*

*Home This Christmas*

# THE
# LAST DINNER
## AT
# WISTERIA
# HOUSE

## SUE ROBERTS

*bookouture*

Published by Bookouture in 2026

An imprint of Storyfire Ltd.
Carmelite House
50 Victoria Embankment
London EC4Y 0DZ

www.bookouture.com

The authorised representative in the EEA is Hachette Ireland
8 Castlecourt Centre
Dublin 15 D15 XTP3
Ireland
(email: info@hbgi.ie)



ISBN: 978-1-80550-376-7
eBook ISBN: 978-1-80550-375-0

*To friends old and new.*
*'Every friendship begins with a simple connection. Only*
*the courage to open your heart can make it grow.'*

UNKNOWN

# PROLOGUE

As Alice Bennett stood across the road from the handsome Victorian building a slow smile spread across her face.

The rather grand entrance had half a dozen stone steps flanked by wrought-iron railings that led to the shiny black front door. Above the doorway was an arched, stained-glass window that Alice used to love. The colourful glass had a fairy-tale quality to it, like something you would find in a prince's castle, and it would fire up her childhood imagination.

Adjacent to the door an intercom system displayed the numbers for the four interior flats the house had been split into since she was last here.

Taking in the red-bricked residence stirred up memories for Alice. It was like looking through her old photographs that were kept in a treasured leather-bound album.

Wisteria House, built around 1880, still had all the hallmarks of a grand Victorian residence, its well-maintained exterior spanning the decades, and proudly displaying the natural elegance and grandeur of days gone by. Days that used to be filled with parties and laughter. But it was all too quiet now.

Glancing around the familiar wide, tree-lined street, lost in memories, her eyes rested on the 'To Let' sign on the ground-floor apartment. It overlooked the well-kept front lawn but there were some climbing plants making their way up the corner of the building.

Following them upwards, she spied the window boxes outside the upper apartments, the one on the left displaying vivid pink and red flowers, the one on the right some slightly wispy greenery that may have been an attempt at growing herbs. As Alice wondered what the herbs might have been, a young woman appeared at one of the windows. She did a quick double-take at the older lady, before pulling it shut.

Her attention was pulled back to the front door as a tall, well-built man came out of the apartments. He looked lost in his own heavy thoughts, but even so Alice realised that she probably shouldn't attract any more attention. She must look odd watching the building like this.

As a light drizzle of rain began to fall, she put up her large black umbrella, walking away from the apartments with determined steps.

It was time to bring Wisteria House back to life.

# ONE

## DECLAN

## Flat 4

Declan drummed his fingers on the arm of the black leather tub chair in the waiting area at Jarvis and Green, Accountancy Services. When he glanced down at his leg, that was clad in the grey trousers of a sharp designer suit, he realised it was twitching. He wondered why the hell he felt so nervous. Wasn't he a brilliant accountant, award-winning even? Just recently he had successfully allocated money to council services that had received praise from the locals, who were now enjoying a brand-new park with their children.

Working for the council was not exactly giving him the buzz he desired, though. Declan needed the thrill of a big company in the city centre and maybe a chance to make some serious money. He had no desire to stay in his rented apartment forever.

Declan cleared his throat as he entered the room, where two people sat behind a polished wooden desk. The woman, an attractive redhead, greeted him with a smile; the dark-haired older bloke was twirling a pen around in his hand, his face expressionless.

'Take a seat, Declan,' said the bloke, who had not introduced himself.

Declan was asked about his various accomplishments, as the interviewers' eyes flicked over his CV. They asked him the usual stuff, including his future ambitions and asked him to name some of his biggest achievements to date. That was easy for Declan, but he was distracted by the vibe in the room. He got the feeling that the pair in front of him, especially the bloke, were just going through the motions. Either they had someone else in mind for the job, or had decided at first glance that he was not a good fit.

The final straw was when the bloke put his feet up on a nearby chair. The redhead glanced over and shifted a little uncomfortably in her seat, before plastering a smile on her face.

Declan felt the anger rise inside him, just as the guy's phone rang. He took the call without apologising for the interruption.

'Have you finished with that?' Declan gestured to his CV on the table with a snap of his fingers.

'What, oh yes, sure,' said the redhead, glancing across at her colleague, who ignored her.

Declan reached over and picked it up, just as the guy finished his call.

'Thanks for your time. Well, yours anyway.' He smiled at the woman. 'You gave a good show of at least pretending to be interested in what I had to say. Unlike you.' He eyeballed the bloke, who quickly removed his feet from the chair, and gave a little cough.

The bloke attempted to say something as Declan headed for the door, but the tone in Declan's voice made him think again.

Clutching his CV, he counted to ten as he descended the lift to the reception area, where he made his way across the highly polished floor of the glass-fronted building.

He breathed deeply and pushed down his anger. Maybe he ought to escalate a complaint to HR. Who the hell did that guy think he was, putting his feet up like that and taking a call in the middle of an interview without a sniff of an apology? He half expected him to pull a sandwich out of a drawer. What a tosser.

His irritation was still bubbling away, but Declan patted himself on the back for restraining himself. There was a time when he would have flattened him, no question.

Not that he ever went looking for trouble. He was easy-going by nature, but he had learnt to look after himself. He grabbed a takeaway coffee from a nearby café and decided to walk the ten minutes back to the train station, rather than take a taxi, to calm himself down.

A late morning sun finally broke through some grey clouds as he walked and, feeling warmer, he removed his suit jacket. By the time he finally arrived at Wisteria House, he was almost in a good mood. That was before an old lady came hurtling out of the front door and he knocked her off her feet, and into the bush in the front garden. Shit. Bugger.

'Are you okay?' he asked the silver-haired lady in the red jacket.

'What? Oh, I'm fine, dear, don't worry.' She leapt up with a youthfulness that belied her age and smiled at him as she brushed herself down. She was tall and elegant looking with a ready smile, and a slash of red lipstick that matched her blazer. An attractive lady, who was the type that stood out in a crowd despite her age.

'Are you sure?' asked Declan, a little uncertainly.

'Oh fine.' She waved her hand. 'Do you live here, then?' she asked him.

'Yes, first floor.' He nodded upwards.

Now he knew she was okay he just wanted to get inside, take his tie off and grab a beer from the fridge. As well as peruse the job vacancies once more. At least he still had a job, even though it was less than exciting these days. He was still surprised by the rudeness of the guy at the interview but was determined not to dwell on it.

'I see. Oh, where are my manners,' said the elegant lady. 'I am Alice. I moved into the garden flat last week.'

'Declan.' He shook the hand she had extended.

'Nice to meet you, Declan. And may I say, you look very smart. Have you been somewhere nice?' she asked him brightly.

Bloody hell, was he ever going to get inside?

'A job interview. I don't think it went too well, though,' he said, which was most definitely an understatement, with a shrug.

'Oh dear. Would you like to have a drink and tell me about it?' she asked.

'I thought you were on your way out?' He frowned. He wasn't in the habit of making small talk and drinking tea with the neighbours.

'That can wait. It is far more important to get to know my new neighbours, I think. Come on.'

She gestured for him to go inside, and, to Declan's surprise, he found himself following Alice into her ground-floor flat.

He glanced around the neat as a pin lounge, the tastefully furnished room dominated by a large brown leather sofa with velvet embossed cushions. The wooden dining table and chairs at the far end of the room looked expensive. Mahogany maybe? As Alice disappeared into the kitchen, he expected to hear a kettle boiling, but to his surprise, she returned with a bottle of single malt and two tumblers with ice.

'I will join you. It's no fun drinking alone.' She winked.

As Declan sipped his smooth as silk malt – the lady certainly had taste – he found himself telling her all about his disastrous job interview.

'Oh dear. What a dreadful man.' She shook her head. 'I'm afraid the world is full of them these days.'

'You're not wrong there,' agreed Declan. He had met enough of them.

'What was the role?' she asked good-naturedly.

'An accountant post at Jarvis and Green,' he told her.

'Ah, so you're an accountant? Interesting.'

'Not that interesting at times, although I do enjoy it, and I'm bloody good at it,' he stated proudly.

He apologised then for swearing, feeling a bit like he was sitting in front of his gran.

Declan would never forget the pride he felt when he passed his exams and was tempted to take his certificates to his old school and wave them in front of his teacher, who had told him he would never amount to anything. Apparently, the old codger was still teaching there, counting down the days to his retirement, no doubt still churning out the same old lessons in the jaded tone he had all those years ago.

It was a terrible school. No wonder the kids played up. They were tolerated rather than nurtured at the school on the wrong side of town, the pupils bored and unchallenged. In a way, though, his teacher's remark had spurred him on to prove him wrong. Okay, he had to do a bit of growing up first and attend a night school to get some qualifications, but against all the odds he did it.

'So, if you're so good at what you do,' said Alice, 'why don't you work for yourself? Then you wouldn't have to endure any more humiliating interviews, although you would be unlucky to encounter another man as rude as that.' She shook her head.

'Set up by myself?'

'Yes, why not. If you are as good as you say you are.' She took a sip of her whisky.

'Erm. Well, I don't have an office for a start, and I know what you're probably thinking, I could work from home, which I did consider but that doesn't create the right impression, does it? Not if I want to attract some decent clients.'

'I see. Well, I might be able to help you there.' Alice looked thoughtful as she sipped her drink.

'Help me, how?' The old lady had his attention now.

'I own some office space in Liverpool Road. Do you know it?' she asked.

'I do, yeah.'

Liverpool Road was a popular area with offices, restaurants and fashionable coffee shops popping up more frequently these days. It would be beyond his wildest dreams to have an office space in that location.

'So, what do you think? Would you like to look at the office? There is a desk there already. We could go tomorrow if you like?' Alice offered.

'I will be in work, but maybe afterwards?' He could hardly take in what was happening. Why would this woman who he had known for all of five minutes be so generous towards him?

'It's a date. Shall we leave here about six o'clock?' suggested Alice as she finished her drink.

'Great. Is the rent much, though? I already have the rent on the apartment here,' Declan reminded her.

'When I said I might be able to help you out, I meant exactly that. There will be no charge. Obviously if you become very successful, you might like to buy me a small gift.' Alice smiled at him, nodding towards the bottle of whisky on the small table beside her.

'It's a deal. But why are you doing this? You barely know me.' Declan thought it all sounded a bit too good to be true.

'You are my neighbour, and we are meant to help each other out, aren't we? Love thy neighbour.' She smiled again. 'If more people did that, the world would not have half as many problems.'

That was true enough. He thought of the tales his mother would tell him about her childhood and how everyone helped each other out. Clothes and toys would be passed around the neighbourhood so that no one went without. A lady who worked at the toilet roll factory would barter biscuits with the lady who worked at Jacob's, all purchased for pennies at the staff shop. There was no such thing as a food bank back then, she had told him.

'Fair enough. And if that's the case, I would be happy to return the favour, if you ever need anything,' he offered, although he had no idea what that might be.

'As it happens, there is.' She swirled the remains of her whisky around in her glass.

'Go on.'

'You could come to a dinner party on Friday evening,' she said to his surprise. 'I am making my coq au vin, which is quite delicious, if I say so myself,' she declared. 'I haven't decided on dessert, although I imagine it will be banoffee pie or an Eton mess. Do you have a particular preference?'

Declan thought of the Eton mess he'd eaten after his Sunday carvery at the local pub with a few of the lads after football.

'That's a tough one. I like them both. I'd say the Eton mess just edges it, though.'

'Wonderful. I'll make both.'

'Make them? You know you can buy fancy desserts from Waitrose.' Declan grinned. Alice seemed like the type of person who would shop at Waitrose.

'Yes, but it's a little bit of a trek to the nearest one in Formby and I do enjoy cooking. Although, I may buy the meringue for the Eton mess but don't tell anyone.' She smiled.

What Declan didn't know was that Alice had stopped driving her car a couple of years ago as her long-distance vision was not quite what it was, but she was proud she had been able to drive well into her eighties. She could hardly believe she was ninety-one years old and other people found it hard to believe too. She still did her morning stretches, a habit from her dancing days, and could still almost touch her toes.

A dinner party. Declan hated those things. He preferred the local pub with a few mates, especially at the weekend. He had been single for longer than he cared to remember, but his life was full enough right now, and he was relishing the freedom. Alice's food did sound good, though, and she had just offered him some office space, after all.

'I have invited the other two tenants in the building who both live alone, I believe. I thought it would be a lovely way to get acquainted with my new neighbours. In fact, I have posted you an invitation too.' She smiled.

She had only been here a short time, yet she seemed to know that the other tenants were also living alone. Declan was beginning to think she was a nosey old bugger. He wasn't sure he wanted someone poking their nose into his business. He preferred to keep himself to himself, apart from those in his carefully selected circle.

'Oh. Um, sure, okay then, thanks,' he said after a long pause. If it would make the old dear happy, then why not? He had no plans this coming Friday.

It occurred to him that he didn't really know the other occupants of the flats, apart from the occasional nod if they crossed paths. Did anyone really know their neighbours these days? He had noticed the pretty woman with the kid opposite him, though, who always seemed to be in a hurry. Perhaps this dinner party was a good idea after all. Maybe it was time to let his guard down a little.

'Lovely. I will see you tomorrow then after work to view the office premises,' she said, standing to indicate he could leave. 'See what you think.'

He thanked Alice and felt a mellow feeling as he headed to his upstairs flat. Inside, he picked up the red envelope and opened the dinner invitation.

# TWO
## JESS

## Flat 3

'Come on, Maisie, we are going to be late.' Jess sighed as she scraped her long, dark hair into a ponytail, before shoving her feet into her white trainers.

She had already put a wash on, popped a casserole in the slow cooker, and hoovered the lounge. In the long hallway that had grey flooring and white doors leading to the other rooms, she had wiped away a smudge of paint from one of the doors. Maisie must have had it on her fingertips after she had been painting. Jess smiled to herself as she rubbed the stain away with a cleaning wipe. Before she knew it, those little signs of a young child living here would have disappeared. She dreaded the thought.

'I can't find my pencil case,' moaned her six-year-old daughter, Maisie.

'They have pencils at school. Go and grab your reading folder.' Jess didn't have time for this today; she was due in work in just over half an hour.

'But I want my pencil case.' Her daughter folded her arms defiantly.

The pink fluffy pencil case in question, featuring a shiny unicorn, was entirely inappropriate for school. She wished the headteacher would ban the kids from bringing such things in from home, instead of her being the bad cop when she forbade her daughter from taking them. She wouldn't be surprised if some of the kids had designer pencil cases these days.

There was a subtle competitiveness amongst some of the parents at Maisie's school. She had lost count of the conversations she had overheard between them on the playground, comparing their children's reading levels and various other accomplishments. One child had worn a pair of designer trainers to school on dress down day for Comic Relief, their parents clearly missing the irony of raising money to alleviate child poverty. Thankfully, not everyone was that way, though.

Jess remembered at the last minute the money in the brown envelope Maisie was to hand in to her teacher for the school trip.

The cost was forty pounds for a full day at Chester Zoo, including a café lunch. The price also included the hire of the coach, so although it was reasonable it was a lot for Jess to pay all at once. When she had mentioned it to Jess's teacher, she had suggested paying the balance in two instalments. Most of the parents would not have a problem, as forty pounds was hardly a fortune, but it was a bit much to stump up all at once for a single parent. Jess liked Maisie's teacher, who always tried to find solutions discreetly.

It might have been helpful if Maisie's father could contribute to the practical things more regularly, such as school uniforms and trips, rather than overblown gestures, like the five-foot unicorn he appeared with after working away.

Her ex would alternate between being unemployed and

working in a hotel or similar establishment, often on the other side of the country, sometimes abroad.

He was generous on his pay days, but they were sporadic. She never said too much, though, as he did regularly pay a modest amount of maintenance whatever his financial situation.

'Have you brushed your teeth?' Jess grabbed her bag and slung it over her shoulder.

'Yes. But I want my pencil case.' Maisie wasn't budging.

They had precisely two minutes before they needed to leave. It was a ten-minute walk to Maisie's school, and a two-minute walk to the bus stop afterwards, where Jess would wait for five minutes – if the bus was on time – before making the journey into town to her job at the M&S Food Hall in the city centre. At four thirty exactly, she would leave and make the journey back in time to collect her daughter from after-school club. She didn't want to think about the next school holidays and prayed that the school would be running a summer holiday club, which they had recently been considering, or she had no idea what she would do for childcare.

Her mother had recently upped sticks and moved to Cumbria with a bloke she met at one of those school reunion dances and even though her mother reassured her that it was only an hour and a half drive away and promised to still see her and Maisie regularly – which was fine, it was her mother's life after all – she missed her.

She was happy for her mum, though. She deserved to have someone nice to spend her later years with, after Jess's dad had left her for another woman a couple of years ago.

After scanning her daughter's bedroom, Jess spotted the horn of the unicorn on the fluffy pencil case poking out from beneath the bed, that was covered with a princess duvet. This was the last bloody time. She was going to have a word with the school about banning such things. When she had the time.

As she approached the front door, she spotted a red envelope on the mat. A glance at her watch told her she needed to get a move on, so she stuffed it into her pocket.

'Right, go.' She ushered her daughter out of the front door, as she handed the pencil case to Maisie, who dropped it into her school bag triumphantly. No wonder Jess never had time to speak to the neighbours in the block, as she was always in such a rush. Not that she encountered them much anyway. It would appear the other tenants led busy lives too.

Jess liked the walk to school, especially when they were not in a hurry. She loved how her daughter commented on just about everything, a chatterbox from the minute she was able to talk.

Halfway down the road was a duck pond surrounded by railings, a somewhat unusual sight in the middle of a busy city road and one that they often lingered at on the way home from school, along with lots of other families. Sometimes Maisie would feed the ducks the remains of her packed lunch, and Jess was sure she was saving things deliberately, but as it was generally just a few bread crusts or a handful of crisps she didn't mind as she did not want to discourage her kindness. Besides, they always had a hearty evening meal, which was often discounted food items from the M&S Food Hall.

'Love you lots.' She kissed her daughter, who was a mini version of herself, goodbye on the playground outside of the classroom where the children were lined up.

'Like jelly tots,' replied Maisie as the teacher appeared then and led them into the classroom.

Jess caught a glance of her reflection in the window of the bus stop, and her pretty, lightly tanned face stared back at her, but there was no disguising the bags beneath her green eyes. She would kill for a lie-in, but Maisie's routine lately was waking at around six thirty, even at weekends.

Once seated on the bus, she fished the little red envelope

out of her coat pocket that had mysteriously appeared on the mat behind the door this morning and opened it.

A dinner party invitation for this coming Friday at seven o'clock. Jess could not recall ever being invited to a dinner party. House parties sure, where you would take a bottle of something and eat from the home-made buffet in the kitchen, but a dinner party? She wasn't sure if it sounded a bit too formal. Not only was she unsure of what to wear, but who would watch Maisie? Unless, of course, she was allowed to bring her along. The invitation was from a lady called Alice in the ground-floor flat.

The flat had stood empty for a while, and she had not realised anybody had moved in. She would call in after work and ask if her daughter could come along. It might be fun, she mused, as the bus trundled along its familiar route to the city centre. It was hard to juggle a social life being a single parent, so maybe it would do her good to get to know her neighbours a little more. Besides, what else would she be doing on a Friday evening?

# THREE

## MARK

### Flat 2

Mark was sitting in his neat lounge in Wisteria House reading the sports section whilst sipping a mug of tea. He'd walked down the tree-lined avenue to the Co-op for his newspaper and was now thinking about having the chocolate muffin he had bought. He resisted, though, as he'd already had a bowl of cereal.

He was trying to lose a little weight, but it was difficult in your mid-sixties. Besides, it was only a small paunch, and at six feet two he carried any extra weight quite well. He knew he would have to up his exercise to keep fit with the advancing years, though. Maybe he ought to leave the car behind and walk the couple of miles to the marina where he often spent his days on his sailing boat that was moored up there.

He was definitely more conscious of his health than his looks, though he was grateful to still have a full head of sandy-coloured hair that had only greyed at the temples. There were one or two women at the sailing club who had shown an obvious interest in him lately, but romance was the last thing on his mind.

He flicked the television on and found himself watching a repeat of an American sitcom that always put a smile on his face. Until he thought about Diane. His wife wasn't keen on American comedy and used to spend that time reading or watering the potted plants and shrubs in the garden outside.

He missed her terribly.

They had sold their three-bedroomed house and downsized with the intention of travelling the world. They had rented the apartment as a base, and on the days when they were not away somewhere, they might stroll down to the beach, taking a rug and a flask of coffee with them if the weather wasn't too blustery. If it was, they would have coffee at the Marina Café. Life was good. They did thankfully get some travelling in before she became ill.

And then she was gone, the late diagnosis of her cancer giving her so little time. Their daughter had come over from Australia then, asking Mark to move over there with her so she could look after him. She was a good daughter, but his life was here, along with all his memories, and her life was there.

Mark was comforted by the fact that Diane had visited all the places she had dreamt of visiting before she became ill, a highlight being the Taj Mahal. She loved how the emperor had built the mausoleum for his favourite wife, such was his love for her.

'Would you do that for me?' she had asked him as she rested her head on his shoulder and took in the view of the mesmerising palace. He had reminded her that he once built her a bookcase and she'd laughed, telling him an IKEA flat-pack didn't really count.

They laughed a lot together, even after thirty-five years of marriage. It was one of the things he missed most, the sound of her infectious laughter. They just got each other, and he could not imagine how anyone else could ever take her place.

He tried to turn his thoughts to the present. It was a good day to go to the marina, but he was in a restless mood and toyed with the idea of heading into town and maybe catching a train somewhere. He'd gone off before, just randomly picking a place and taking off.

Last time he had ended up in York where he spent a thoroughly enjoyable three days, having to nip into a department store and buy a couple of items of new clothing as he had only intended it to be an overnight stay. He had tried to ignore the hammer blows that occasionally hit him in the chest when he was out sightseeing and saw something that he knew Diane would have loved. They had never been to York together, which he regretted, especially when he wandered along The Shambles, an historic, narrow street full of timber-framed medieval buildings that faced each other across the cobbled street.

He was pondering his next move when he heard a knock on the door. When he opened it, a smartly dressed old lady stood in front of him on the landing.

'Hi,' said Mark, smiling. 'Can I help you?'

'Forgive me for knocking, but may I introduce myself,' said the woman. 'My name is Alice and I have recently moved into the ground-floor flat.'

'Oh right, yes, hello. Good to meet you,' he replied.

Damn, he had forgotten to reply to the invitation he had received in the little red envelope that had landed on his mat yesterday.

'Nice to meet you too.' She smiled.

'Sorry, my name is Mark.' He extended his hand then, and warmly shook Alice's thin, papery hand.

'I just wondered, before I write my shopping list, whether you will you be coming to dinner on Friday evening?' enquired Alice.

Feeling put on the spot, Mark hesitated before he responded, wondering if she might be lonely.

'Yes, sure, why not? Sounds good. I can't remember the last time I had a home-cooked meal,' he confessed. He thought of his sister Lynn's Sunday lunches then, the smell of roast chicken filling the house and the afternoons spent playing board games with his nephew, but pushed those thoughts to the back of his mind.

'Splendid.' She smiled. 'Oh, and you're not vegetarian, are you?' she asked.

'No. I don't mind the odd veggie curry, but I'm not a vegetarian.'

'Right. See you Friday,' said Alice, before she turned and headed across the hall to her flat.

'Looking forward to it,' Mark called out, realising he actually might be. He would take a couple of bottles of decent wine. He knew a thing about USA wines, after he and Diane had toured a winery in the Napa Valley.

As Alice left, Mark heard the strains of another episode of *Frasier* starting on the television, so that was his mind made up. He would settle down and watch several episodes that were showing on a loop.

He found himself mulling over Alice's invitation, and wondered whether he had been a little hasty in accepting it. His life was ticking over nicely without the company of neighbours, although he occasionally wondered if it was healthy to distance himself from those who lived nearby.

In his old neighbourhood, he and Diane would sometimes socialise with neighbours, especially around Christmas time when it was open house, Diane welcoming everybody inside for a drink and a mince pie. She had been the driving force, the one who found events to attend, circling things on the calendar. Left to his own devices he would never have sought out company.

The invites from friends still came after Diane passed away, but over time they stopped, and he would instead receive the occasional text asking after his well-being.

He was comfortable being alone these days. Too comfortable maybe.

Mark eyed the crime novel on the coffee table that he kept meaning to start, so perhaps he would do that this afternoon. He had had a poor sleep last night, so despite his slightly restless mood, a day taking it easy was probably on the cards. Tomorrow he might venture down to the marina and take the boat out.

# FOUR

## JESS

'Have you got a minute?' Maisie's teacher, Miss Jenson, asked Jess when she arrived to pick Maisie up.

'Sure,' said Jess, even though she probably didn't really. 'Is everything okay?' This was slightly concerning. Not just because she wondered what Maisie had gotten into.

She followed the teacher into the classroom, and the smell of Play-Doh and crayons hit her nostrils.

'There was a bit of an incident,' said Maisie's teacher, tucking a strand of dark hair behind her ear.

'An incident?' Jess frowned.

A child ran back into the classroom then, grabbing her blue cardigan with the school badge, that was hung over the back of her chair, before running back outside to her mum.

'Yes. Another girl has the exact same pencil case as Maisie, and there was a mix-up,' Miss Jenson continued. 'Maisie insisted the other child had hers as her own had gone missing. Anyway, she found it in the end. She'd taken it to the toilet with her and left it there.'

'So what was the problem if she found it in the end?' asked Jess. 'I hope she apologised to her classmate, though.'

'Maisie pushed the other child over at playtime quite force-fully, and she grazed her knee,' explained Maisie's teacher. 'Her mother has just been on the phone to the headteacher complaining.'

'And is the head still here?' asked Jess.

'Yes, she's in the office, but she might be busy, I...'

Jess did not wait to hear any more; she grabbed Maisie's hand and strode purposefully, the teacher following, her heels clipping on the wooden floor. She always taught Maisie right from wrong, and found it out of character for Maisie to react the way she did. She needed to hear the whole story.

'You might need to make an appointment,' Miss Jenson said, as she struggled to keep up with Maisie and her mum. When they reached the headteacher's room, Jess rapped on the door.

'Come in,' came a voice from behind the door.

The cropped-haired headteacher, somewhere in her forties, glanced up from her laptop.

'I'd like a word, please,' Jess said firmly but calmly. 'About the incident today with Maisie and the pencil case.'

'Ah yes. Please take a seat,' said the head, removing her glasses. She gestured to a nearby chair, and the class teacher took a seat opposite her as Maisie stood silently beside her mother.

The room with magnolia painted walls and office-style seats was soulless, thought Jess, who wondered why it had to look so corporate. But then, that's what schools were these days, busi-nesses. Results published for all to see and parents making deci-sions based upon them. If they lived in the right catchment area, of course.

Jess thought it might be more inspirational to the children if some of their work was displayed on the walls of the head-teacher's room, or at least something that gave it a personality. She recalled her own primary school, and how the headteacher had some exceptional artwork pinned to a board in his office, and how the reception area proudly displayed clay sculptures and cardboard vehicles made during science lessons.

'I hear the child's mother has complained to you about Maisie pushing her daughter over,' said Jess.

'That's correct. I had a call from Mrs Evans about what happened to Lottie.' The headteacher closed the lid of her laptop. 'I was hoping this was something Miss Jenson could have dealt with.'

Jess thought she detected the faintest hint of annoyance in the headteacher's voice.

'Maybe, but the thing is, and I'm not excusing Maisie's behaviour for a second, don't think I am,' said Jess evenly. 'But I'm not sure children ought to be allowed to bring things in from home that are basically toys. I know budgets are strict, I get that, but surely you still have pencils in school?'

'I would argue that a pencil case is not really a toy,' said the head.

'Maybe a clear, plastic one, no. But half of them have bells and whistles. Look at this.'

She raised the pink, fluffy case with the silvery pink unicorn protruding from it. The one that had caused so much fuss when Maisie had misplaced it yesterday morning and ultimately ending in a fight with another child today. She did not need another morning like that.

'You can see how this might distract children from their work,' Jess continued. 'And thinking about it, maybe it's even a little divisive.'

'Divisive? Really? How so?' asked the head.

'Not everyone can afford these things,' Jess explained. 'Me included. I am a single parent. This was a gift for Maisie's birthday. I can't afford to shop in Smiggle or similar places.' She spoke calmly but in such a tone that the headteacher was left in no doubt she was irritated by the current school rule. 'I try telling Masie to leave it at home, but she gets upset and says everyone brings such things to school, so I can hardly refuse her, can I?'

The headteacher said nothing as she digested Jess's words before letting out a sigh. 'Yes, well, I confess I hadn't really thought about the cost of such items. Maybe that's something we ought to have considered,' she conceded. 'Miss Jenson, have these items caused you any other problems in the classroom?'

'I won't lie, they can be a distraction at times,' said Maisie's teacher. 'And, in truth, I could have done without the incident today when Maisie thought Lottie had taken her pencil case. We have a lot to get through in the curriculum, without having to deal with this kind of thing. But there isn't a lot I can do if they are not actually banned from school,' she said pointedly.

Jess looked from the teacher to the headteacher, as she waited for them to come up with a solution.

The headteacher held up her hands. 'Okay, I think I have heard enough. As of today, anything from home must not be brought into school. I'll get the secretary to send out a text to parents and include it in Friday's newsletter.'

'Brilliant,' said Jess gratefully. 'And I will make sure Maisie apologises tomorrow morning to Lottie and her mother.'

'That would be good. Hopefully that is the matter resolved, then.' The headteacher opened her laptop once more, telling them the conversation was over.

It would probably make Jess late for work tomorrow, as Lottie's mother was always the last to arrive on the playground in the morning, but she was also the type to bad-mouth her and Maisie if it wasn't sorted. Besides, she really didn't want Maisie resorting to anything physical when she lost her temper.

'Thank you,' whispered Maisie's class teacher as they reached the end of the corridor. 'This is going to make teaching a lot easier without the distractions of things brought in from home.'

She told Jess that she had lost count of the times children

had cried when they had lost their personal possessions, or if they had got broken. Staff had brought it up in meetings, but the head adopted a more liberal attitude. Until today. The last thing she needed was parents getting on her back.

It occurred to Jess that she would always be the one to sort out any problems that Maisie might encounter. Her ex was never around enough, although he had appeared last weekend from working away and taken Maisie for a weekend to Blackpool. They had stayed at a child-friendly hotel that had candy dispensing machines in the bedroom. Maisie returned home with a fluffy toy, a giant sugar dummy, and no idea when she would see her father again.

Jess felt good that the matter had been dealt with regarding the pencil case, although there was still the small matter of speaking to the other child's parent.

She decided not to dwell on it as she and Maisie walked home, Maisie humming a tune from the latest pop band.

Jess knew the words to the song too, along with all the songs from the Disney movies they watched together in the evening. It was after Maisie was tucked in bed that Jess would have liked a grown-up conversation with someone, maybe watching a movie together that didn't feature animated singing animals.

They were just heading up the path to their apartment when they passed an old lady carrying some recycling to the outside bins.

'Hello there.' The lady smiled at them both, before introducing herself as Alice.

'Oh, hi. I'm Jess and this here is Maisie.'

The little girl, her hair in plaits, smiled a gappy-toothed smile. 'Pleased to meet you,' she said politely.

'Oh, such perfect manners from one so young,' exclaimed Alice, a broad smile on her face. She was wearing a white dress, with a pink cardigan over the top that matched her lipstick.

'I do my best,' said Jess proudly. 'I'm glad I caught you as I wanted to thank you for your dinner invite on Friday. Actually,' said Jess, frowning slightly, 'I think we have met before. Didn't you sit next to me on the train a while back?'

'Indeed, I did.' Alice smiled and Jess felt comforted by having such a lovely neighbour. She remembered telling Alice that day they met on the train that she was a single parent, heading to after-school club, and the difficulty of childcare. Alice had told her that what she enjoyed most about public transport was the chance to chat to someone. If they were open to it. Many people wore earphones these days, signalling they wanted no interaction. Or maybe they would be reading a book. It was a shame really, but she supposed that was the way of the world now.

'So are you coming?' asked Alice, placing some plastic bottles into a nearby recycling bin.

'I'd love to, I don't really get out that much,' Jess admitted. 'But I have Maisie here.'

'Who is perfectly welcome,' said Alice, turning to Jess's daughter. 'I'm not sure if you will have a taste for coq au vin, but I'm sure I can rustle up something else. What do you like, Maisie?'

'Everything,' said Maisie brightly. 'Katsu chicken curry is my favourite.'

'Well, well, katsu chicken. Did you know katsu came from Japan originally as a pork dish?' Alice informed her.

'No,' said Maisie, shaking her head. 'But I do know that Japan is known as the Land of the Rising Sun. And that Tokyo is the capital.'

'Indeed, it is. Clever girl.' Alice smiled affectionately.

'Katsu chicken is her *current* favourite,' said Jess, smiling. 'Although she isn't a fussy eater, thank goodness.'

Alice thought about her nephews then, and how she would cook for them, encouraging them to try different dishes. She could still recall the expression on her eldest nephew's face when he first tried a spicy Indian dish. Maybe he had been too young and she remembered feeling a little guilty when he glugged down some ice-cold water, his face flushed.

'I can imagine that being tiresome,' agreed Alice. 'Well, I look forward to seeing you both on Friday. Oh, and any allergies?' she asked.

'No, thankfully,' replied Jess.

'Good. I'm so glad you can make it.'

'I will look forward to it,' said Jess as Alice headed inside, leaving a lingering perfume which Jess recognised as Chanel Coco in her wake.

# FIVE

## DECLAN

'How was your day?' asked Alice as she stepped outside the block of apartments with Declan.

It was a mild evening and Alice was looking forward to the walk to the office building.

'Good,' said Declan, even though he had been a little distracted by the possibility of being self-employed and having his own office.

'Don't you want to go in the car?' asked Declan, car keys in hand, as Alice turned left outside the building.

'As it is such a nice evening I thought we could walk. If that's okay with you?'

Alice had been indoors all day, and was looking forward to a little fresh air and exercise.

'Fine by me.' He smiled.

They strolled along companionably, even though they barely knew each other, and Alice commented on some of the pretty front gardens as they walked past. Declan felt completely at ease in her company and wondered whether he would ever have knocked to say hello, had she not arranged the dinner party. Probably not.

As they turned onto the main road that was busy with traffic, Declan instinctively walked close to Alice as they crossed the road. There were some lunatic drivers around these days. Everyone seemed to be in such a hurry.

When they arrived at the office they accessed the single staircase and Declan was grateful that Alice was still physically fit for her age as there was no lift.

It smelt slightly musty inside as it had been unoccupied for a while, so Alice thrust the window open and let the early evening air drift into the room.

Declan glanced around the space that was carpeted with expensive-looking grey carpet. There was a wooden desk in one corner, and an archway that led to a tiny kitchen area. The room had a vaulted ceiling and with a little sprucing up, including a fresh coat of paint on the walls, it would be a smart place to meet with clients.

'So, what do you think, then?' asked Alice, as Declan took in his surroundings.

'I think it's brilliant,' he said, visualising himself sitting behind the desk and it felt good.

'I'm afraid there's no chair, but you can pick them up reasonably enough, especially second-hand,' suggested Alice. She didn't tell Declan but she had taken the battered green-leather chair home with her. Sometimes she would glance at it and imagine her husband sitting there reading.

'That won't be a problem.' Declan beamed. He had an office chair at home that he bought when he had toyed with the idea of setting up the second bedroom as an office which never quite came to fruition.

'I still can't believe you don't want any rent, though.' He glanced around the room. 'And how come you don't sell the place?' he asked. 'You do own it, don't you?'

'No. I'm just some crackpot old woman who managed to

obtain some keys and show you around an empty office.' She raised a perfectly pencilled eyebrow.

'Sorry. I just can't get my head around it. In my experience, no one does anything for free without an ulterior motive,' said Declan as he walked into the small kitchen. He would install a decent coffee machine to offer his clients a drink, he thought to himself.

'Including yourself?' she asked candidly.

'What? Um, no, I will always lend someone a hand if I can. I guess I just mean generally in this world we live in.' He shrugged.

Alice studied the young man standing in front of her. He was tall and muscular and may have been described as having an almost perfect face, had it not been for a nose that looked as though it had once been broken. The overall effect was a handsome-looking young man who had dark-brown eyes that crinkled at the corner when he smiled.

'What a sad state of affairs that is.' She sighed. 'As I said, if we all helped each other out a little more, the world would be a better place. And, actually, this was my husband's old office.' She walked over to the heavy wooden desk and ran her hand along it. 'He died two years ago, and I haven't been able to bring myself to sell it,' she admitted.

Alice still missed George every single day, especially his easy smile and sense of humour.

He had built up quite a reputation as a hot-shot lawyer in the city when he had been young and hungry for success, shrewdly investing money in stocks and shares, that over time had paid generous dividends.

It felt like yesterday when they had held parties that Alice loved to dress up for, or gone out for dinner in the city. Life was full of excitement and possibilities for the future, especially following the war years. As a young woman, she had enjoyed watching the regeneration of the city, particularly the ongoing building of Liverpool Cathedral that was finally completed in the nineteen seventies. It was still one of her favourite places.

Declan reckoned Alice must have been a right cracker when she was young. She was fine featured, with a slightly full mouth even at her age and piercing green eyes. She wore her silver-grey hair in soft curls, and he imagined it dark when she was younger, giving her the look of a Hollywood movie star. It would have amused Alice if she had known that Declan was studying her just as closely as she was him.

'So, what do you think?' she asked him.

'I think it's brilliant. Perfect. It's just that...' Declan hesitated for a moment. 'I don't have any clients, and I would need to work my notice with the council. I can't see it being something I could take advantage of right now.' He sighed.

Declan wondered if he was mad in considering a job move. He had a steady position with a decent pension, but he could not build up a successful business working for the council, which was what he dreamt of. He would need to do that himself, try and land some big accounts. Not something he could really do around his full-time job. It felt good to know that this space was available, though.

'Well, it's here if you need it.' Alice smiled, as if reading his thoughts. 'And it gives you time to advertise your services and take on some clients, should you decide to use the office.'

Despite Alice's optimism, something Declan usually possessed bags of himself, he gave himself a reality check. How could he just walk away from a well-paid job, even with some rent-free office space? Maybe he would stay put. For now, at least. A decent pension pot was everything these days, and everyone knew how good the council ones were. He told Alice this.

'I understand,' she reassured him. 'I have no intention of selling for a while yet, so if it can be put to good use, all the better. And if I am honest,' she continued, 'I still enjoy coming up here occasionally. My memories of George always come flooding back when I am here.'

'That must be nice.' He smiled.

'Bittersweet.' She sighed. 'But I would rather he remained strong in my memory than my thoughts of him fade away.'

Declan understood what she meant only too well. There were days when he worried that he might forget what his sister looked like.

'Anyway, thanks,' said Declan. 'And you never know, I might take it sooner rather than later.'

He would do everything within his power to secure some clients; there was no way he was going to pass up an opportunity for rent-free space like this in such a prime location.

'That's the spirit. Think positive.' She winked.

Outside, Alice offered to buy Declan a coffee from a local restaurant that had sprung up in town just recently. He glanced at his watch and as he had nothing to rush home for, he agreed.

He would have gone to the pub, but one of his mates was on holiday; the other, a single parent was unexpectedly having his son overnight. He was comfortable enough going on his own to his local pub as he knew plenty of people, but didn't really feel like it this evening. He supposed it was one of the benefits of being single, answering to no one and doing as you pleased.


The Forest, a vegan deli, looked inviting. The red-brick exterior had a black metal butcher's bike propped against the window, its basket filled with purple and yellow flowers. Inside, pale-blue painted walls contrasted perfectly with stripped, dark-wooden tables and benches; a string of bulb lights ran across the counter area, giving it a modern, cosy feel.

'So what made you become an accountant?' asked Alice as she sipped her coffee at a table for two as they waited for their food.

'Dunno. I was just good at it. I like having things in order I suppose.' He shrugged. 'And having a stint working in a meat factory made me realise I didn't want to do that for the rest of my life,' he told her as he stirred his coffee. 'I went to night school.'

He told Alice all about his high school and how most of the kids there had underachieved. There was no need to tell her anything else about his past life.

'That is such a shame. I think it unfair that you should only get a good education if you are in the right social class.' She shook her head.

'Too right.' He had lost count of the number of people from school who had to return to education to make something of themselves.

'Where did you go to school?' asked Declan.

'A private school not far from here; that was when I was a young child,' she explained. 'My father was a British diplomat.'

'Wow. Did you move around a lot?'

'A few times,' she told Declan. 'Although, my father often went off alone preferring not to uproot the family, which would have been almost impossible anyway during the war years.'

Just then their food arrived. Alice's thick, steaming bowl of soup looked amazing and Declan marvelled at the sight of his pizza loaded with vegetables and topped with huge basil leaves.

They were quiet as they ate their food, and Declan was surprised at just how easy he felt in the company of this older lady.

'That was tasty,' said Declan later, wiping his mouth with a napkin. 'I thought I might have missed a bit of spicy chicken or pepperoni, but it was spot on.'

'Glad you liked it,' said the blonde-haired woman in the black apron who had just arrived to take their plates away.

'I did. To be honest, I didn't realise the deli was even here. It was a sandwich takeaway last time I looked,' said Declan.

'We've only been open a week,' the woman explained. 'It's been absolutely mad busy, more than we dared to hope for and the online reviews have been fantastic.' She piled their blue bowls and plates that matched the colour of the walls onto a tray.

'I suppose more people are going vegan. You might even have converted me,' he said, although he could not imagine giving up his bacon sandwiches at the weekend or meat pies at the football match. 'Good luck anyway, and I'll definitely be leaving a review online.'

'Thanks for that.' She smiled warmly. 'And if this is the shape of things to come, I think I'm going to have to employ an accountant. I've done my own books in the past, but that was only for a kiosk serving drinks and snacks at a bus station.'

'An accountant?' Declan's ears pricked up.

'Yeah, but I'm not sure where I will find one, although saying that I haven't actually had the time to look, I have been so busy.' She blew a strand of her blonde hair that had escaped her bun away from her face.

'It might be your lucky day,' said Declan. 'I'm an accountant, and I live locally.'

'Really? Can you write your number down?' The café owner pulled a piece of paper from a pad and handed it to him as she juggled the tray of plates.

'Give me a call. Maybe I can help you out,' he said, handing her the paper with his number.

'That's brilliant. Can I call you tomorrow?'

'Sure. Lunchtime might be best, or after five.'

'No problem. Thanks for this.' She waved the piece of paper in the air, before putting it into her pocket.

Declan insisted on settling the bill. Alice had been really kind to him with the offer of the office premises if he needed it, so it was the least he could do.

He felt an excitement in the pit of his stomach. He thought

of names for his company. Johnson Accounting Services maybe. No, that sounded dull. He would think of something dynamic and modern.

A group of four people walked into the deli then asking for a table, and a waitress hurriedly cleared one that had just become vacant, before inviting them to sit down. Declan saw the blonde woman retrieve the paper from her pocket and glance at the number before she waved him and Alice off. His first potential client.

# SIX

## JESS

Jess hared down the stairs from the upstairs flat with Maisie just as Alice was taking delivery of a parcel. Thankfully there had been no tears this morning, with Maisie reluctantly accepting the new school rules about not bringing things from home into school. As she reached the main doors of the building, Alice called after her.

'Morning, Jess. Is everything okay?' she asked. 'You seem in rather a hurry.'

Jess stopped in her tracks.

'Of all the mornings, my alarm never went off,' she explained. 'I'll probably be late for work. Plus, I need to speak to a parent on the school playground. Sorry, but I must dash. Speak later.'

'Go.' Alice shooed her away. 'But I am taking a taxi into town in fifteen minutes. You can travel with me if I collect you outside the school? It's on the way.'

Jess was almost certain she would miss her bus to work.

'Oh my goodness, yes please, you are a lifesaver. Thank you.' She blew Alice a kiss and then she was gone.

As they walked to school, a little hurriedly that morning,

Jess thought about Alice and how grateful she was that she had taken the ground-floor flat.

She had never known her own maternal grandmother, as she had tragically died before she was born, and her father's mother moved abroad when she was around ten years old. She remembered feeling envious when her school friends would tell stories of their grans, after popping around to see them after school. Jess could already feel the positive impact of Alice living downstairs.

She was relieved that personal things were no longer allowed into school. It was hard to keep up with trends sometimes, although she had tried to explain to Maisie that owning the latest toy or fashion accessory did not make someone a better person. Besides, she was hardly in a position to be able to afford all the latest things for her daughter. She was already dreading the teenage years, when Maisie would probably insist on the latest designer trainers or whatever to fit in with her peers. It was a balancing act providing nice things for her, yet not wanting her to be spoilt.

'Am I going to be late for school?' asked Maisie as Jess pressed the button at a crossing on the busy road.

'No,' said Jess. 'You will be perfectly on time; I may have been late for work, though, had Alice not offered me a lift.'

She had spoken to Maisie about the school incident, and she had insisted the child on the playground had pushed her first. Even so, Jess wanted the matter cleared up.

# SEVEN

## ALICE

### Flat 1

Alice had already been up for over an hour and was pondering how she might spend the day.

She had considered taking a bus to Sefton Park and having a gentle stroll. She loved that park, with its soothing lake and Palm House reminiscent of Victorian days gone by. As a child, she had walked there regularly with her parents, especially on a Sunday after church.

It wasn't the closest park to their house, but her mother loved it so much her father would drive them there. There was a huge house overlooking the park that her mother dreamt of living in, and her father would smile and say, 'Maybe one day.' But they never did live on the leafy street.

The park visits held such lovely memories for Alice that she would occasionally catch a bus or train, and enjoy a trip down memory lane. There was a tree there that looked old and gnarly to her young eyes, but her father told her of an even older tree at Calderstones Park called the Allerton Oak and had taken her there to see it. She read recently that the tree was now around a thousand years old.

Alice often pondered why a tree could live for hundreds, even a thousand years, but humans, if they were lucky, had seven or eight decades. At ninety-one years old, Alice felt extremely grateful to be alive and in such good health. The problem with living as old as an oak tree, though, was that most of her friends had departed this earth, including her beloved husband, George. She looked forward to seeing them in the next life and hoped that the Bible stories she remembered from Sunday school were true, when they spoke of Jesus resurrecting people and giving them eternal life. She had so much to tell George.

She had heard the clattering of footsteps on the stairwell as Jess flew down with her daughter, and after hearing her plight, decided she would take a trip into the city centre instead of going to the park. That way she could treat herself to a new dress for Friday evening's dinner, as well as helping her neighbour out.

Exactly fifteen minutes later, after Alice had finished listening to a discussion about animal welfare on the radio and whether horse racing ought to be banned, she pulled up outside the school gates in a white taxi, to find Jess already waiting.

She had considered the horse debate but was unable to take a side, which was unusual for Alice, who was never one to sit on the fence. As a child, she had been taken to the horse racing with her parents and had viewed the Grand National from a private box. Watching the horses gallop through her binoculars and shouting the name of the horse her father had allowed her to have a little flutter on was exhilarating.

There had been no indication during those joyous days that horse racing would have such an impact on their future lives.

'Is everything okay now?' asked Alice as Jess took a seat beside her in the back of the white cab.

'Yeah, all sorted.' Jess told Alice all about the incident with the pencil case.

'And the girl's mother was okay really, after Maisie apologised. I told her about what Maisie said about being pushed first, so she made her daughter apologise too. Lottie did look a little shamefaced, so I am inclined to believe Maisie was telling the truth.'

'I'm glad it has been sorted,' said Alice.

'Me too. And at least I know there won't be any more problems regarding personal possessions.'

'I must say, it sounds as though some schools are far too liberal these days. No wonder there are so many issues with behaviour,' mused Alice. 'At least that's what I gather from reading the news. We had to work in silence when I was a child, although admittedly that is probably going a bit too far. Children like to chat.' She smiled.

'Tell me about it.' Jess laughed thinking of Maisie's constant chatter and questions about the world, but she wouldn't have her any other way.

Alice was appalled that teenagers were carrying knives these days, and the news of a teenager recently being stabbed outside a high school had led her to no longer tune in to the local evening news.

'I feel sorry for the teachers sometimes,' said Jess. 'Half the time the parents take the side of their little darlings, even when they are in the wrong.' She shook her head.

'Well, they are making a rod for their own back, believe me. Spare the rod, spoil the child,' said Alice sagely.

'Too right, love,' said the taxi driver, eyeing them in his rear-view mirror. 'The behaviour of some of the kids I have had in this taxi would make your hair curl.' He shook his head.

'Such a sad state of affairs, although I like to think that most young people have good hearts,' said Alice. She had to believe that, or the next generation did not bear thinking about.

Ten minutes later, after generally putting the world to rights, Alice and Jess stepped out of the taxi and Alice settled the taxi bill. She unknowingly dropped her purse onto the pavement then, and a passing teenager in a school uniform picked it up and handed it to her.

'Oh my goodness, thank you,' said Alice, peeling a five-pound note from her purse and handing it to the boy. She always carried some cash, and today she was glad that she did.

'I guess you are right about not all teenagers being bad, hey?' said Jess. 'I think maybe we only hear about the disruptive ones.'

'I suppose that's true. They are the ones that make the news, after all. And I do feel sorry for those that have no guidance.'

'I can't thank you enough for the lift,' said Jess as they walked. She glanced at her watch. 'And I am actually fifteen minutes early. I think I'll go and grab a takeaway coffee.' She gestured to the coffee shop they were standing outside. 'Fancy one? It's the least I can do.'

'That's very kind, but no thank you. I will get a pot of tea somewhere later, when I have finished my shopping.'

'Okay. See you later, then. Enjoy your shopping, and thanks again.'

'You're most welcome. Have a good day at work.'

Heading towards Ranelagh Street, Alice looked up at the old Lewis's Building and the memories came flooding back, as they always did. There was a statue of a naked man on a ledge, called the Liverpool Resurgent, but known locally as Dickie Lewis. Couples used to meet beneath it for a date and Alice wondered if they still did.

Thinking about it, the statue was probably considered quite risqué back in the day, yet it was a popular meeting place for couples. Alice had even met George there in the early days of their relationship.

The building had been destroyed in the blitz, and when it

was rebuilt the statue, a constant talking point, had been added. Sadly, Lewis's Department Store was no more and was probably earmarked for development into city dwellings.

Alice strolled along, taking in the new restaurants and bars and was thrilled at how the city seemed to be thriving despite an economic crisis. There was a freshness to the city, a feeling of hope for the future that was almost palpable. When she was fifty, Alice wished she were many years younger, but now she enjoyed her age, grateful to still be here. She was happy when people held doors open for her and offered her seats on trains, accepting of her age without the vanity she would have displayed twenty years ago when she thought people deemed her old enough to need assistance.

Walking through an art deco style arcade towards Liverpool One that housed some designer stores and an art gallery, a dress in the window of Mint Velvet caught her eye. It was a mock wrap-over and had the colours of the sea in a swirling pattern. She stepped inside and was greeted warmly by a young shop assistant.

'Ooh that looks gorgeous,' said the girl when Alice emerged from the dressing room. 'It really brings out the colour of your eyes.'

It might have been a sales pitch, had Alice not thought the same thing when she glanced in the mirror.

'Well, that was easy,' she said to the chatty assistant who placed her dress in a bag and took her payment at the till. 'The first dress I laid my eyes on, and I bought it.' She smiled. 'I hope I don't see another one and regret it.'

'Buy two, treat yourself,' the assistant replied with a wink.

'Do you know, I might just do that,' said Alice. 'Or at least buy a new pair of shoes.'

That was what Alice enjoyed about shopping in the city. She loved the interaction with people. The chats with the store assistants, the servers at the coffee shops, the demonstrators in the town squares. She had learnt a lot from a Syrian woman who had educated her about women's rights in her homeland on her last visit, handing leaflets out at a demonstration.

She had chatted to a young busker with the voice of an angel, after dropping some coins in her violin case, when she took a break. The young woman was at the Liverpool Institute for Performing Arts and hoped to have a singing career one day. Alice had no doubt that she would.

At home, especially in her large house near the sea, she had no such social interaction. The only sound of another human's voice came from the radio or television.

After an hour window shopping, feeling lucky she had bought the dress as she had not seen another she liked, she headed to a café and ordered a pot of tea and a bowl of vegetable soup, that came with some delicious home-made bread.

The restaurant window table gave a view of the Anglican Cathedral, a sight she marvelled at every time she headed into the Georgian quarter, the imposing Gothic-style building a sight to behold.

In her younger days, Alice had climbed a staircase in the cathedral that led to a viewing platform giving a view over the majestic city. It was something she could not quite manage now, at her advanced years, but thankfully there was a lift should she have the desire to view the city in all its glory once more.

The walk to the café had been a little tiring as it was slightly uphill, but Alice thought it important to keep moving and as she walked she looked forward to sitting down with a pot of tea.

The young server at the café had been perfectly pleasant and asked if everything was alright with her food. She reminded her a little of Jess from the apartment block. Not for the first time in her long life, Alice felt the regret of never having been a mother. She considered herself blessed in so many other ways, though. You could not have everything in life.

As she headed back towards the centre, the walk downhill easier, she passed an unkempt man sitting on the pavement, a paper cup in front of him hoping for some coins. She reached into her handbag and tossed three pound coins into the cup.

She knew some people discouraged this, arguing the money would only be spent on drink or drugs, but who was she to say how he should live his life? If she could bring some small comfort to his miserable day, then she would. Perhaps one day the man would be in a position to pay her kindness forward. Alice had learnt from an early age the importance of doing just that, after someone in her life had helped her immeasurably.

The man thanked her and smiled, an almost toothless smile, and she could not help wondering what his story was and how he had ended up on the street. Another time, she would have stopped and chatted with him, but having decided to take the train home, she needed to keep going if she was to be at the station on time.

The train platform was busy, and Alice stood back cautiously not wanting to be caught up in a scramble to get on the train. Luckily, a young man offered her his seat when she eventually boarded the crowded train, for which she was grateful.

As the train pulled out of the station, she thought of the homeless young man and all the other lost souls out there and once more counted her blessings.

She was excited for her dinner party and was grateful that the residents had had the good grace to accept her invitation. People were so busy these days, she hadn't been sure that they would.

As she gazed out of the train window she reflected that she really did have a lot to be thankful for. It was important to stay positive.

# EIGHT

## MARK

Mark was enjoying the snooker match on the television, but suddenly realised that the final would be televised the following evening and was tempted to decline his invitation to Alice's dinner.

It felt ridiculous to feel this unsettled about attending a dinner party, but it had been years since he had sat around a table chatting to strangers. In fact, he was not sure he ever had. Nights out or casual dinner invites had only ever included close friends or neighbours.

Diane would organise the whole thing, whether it be drinks and nibbles or a sit-down meal. Even then, it would be an informal affair, with something like a huge lasagne in the middle of the table and some nice wine.

He supposed there would be a lot of small talk; after all none of the guests knew each other. Maybe they would talk about hobbies or travel. He wasn't sure what would be the topic of conversation, but they would almost certainly talk about their families.

Then he would tell them about losing Diane and they would awkwardly offer their platitudes. He would be asked if he was okay, and how was he managing? Of course they would mean well, but all the same he would be marked out as different. Someone people pitied. He had no desire to be pitied.

He sighed deeply as he watched a snooker player clear the table with a score of one hundred and twenty. The party was still a day away, yet he could already feel his stomach churning over at the thought of it.

He worried that refusing the invitation at this late date would be rude, maybe even selfish. Perhaps Alice was lonely too. Was he lonely? Or did he simply enjoy being alone? He still had his friends at the marina whenever he felt the desire to socialise. But he had to admit that it was less frequent these days.

He tidied away his plate, the microwave curry a little better than he had expected. Maybe it would be nice to enjoy a home-cooked meal.

Perhaps he was worrying over nothing, and it would be just fine. He could just listen more than chat as he had always been a good listener. He would compliment Alice on her food, maybe even leave early, on the pretence of an early start in the morning. A few hours and it would all be over.

It would be the first party he would be going to without Diane, and he knew he ought to embrace it. Did he really want to spend the rest of his life in solitude, despite the feeling of nerves that refused to go away?

When Diane had been by his side she would carry the conversation, and put him at his ease. Tomorrow it would just be him. He could imagine his wife telling him to enjoy his evening, and that it would do him good to get to know his neighbours. And, of course, she would be right.

Mark hated how being alone made him overthink everything. When Diane was here, he would breeze through his days, and if he ever did have a slight worry about something, she would always reassure him.

'One day at a time,' she would tell him if he worried about something in the future.

He decided he would take her advice. Let tomorrow come, with its own challenges. For now, he would just enjoy this evening. He smiled to himself as he headed to the kitchen to grab a beer from the fridge and carry on watching the snooker match.

# NINE

## DECLAN

'Hi.'

Declan nodded as he was heading into the apartment block, just as Jess was returning with Maisie, a little after five o'clock. She had collected Maisie from after-school club, then lingered at the duck pond up the road, where Maisie was delighted to see a mother with a quartet of fluffy ducks gliding across the water.

'Hi.' Jess took in Declan's smart suit and handsome face, his dark hair that was always stylishly groomed, and his deep-brown eyes that gave him an almost Mediterranean look. She was surprised that she had never seen him with a partner or bumped into anyone leaving his place.

'Have you had a good day?' Declan asked amiably.

'Not bad, thanks. You?'

'Yeah, good thanks. It's nice to be out of the office, though, especially as the weather has warmed up.'

So he worked in an office? Jess kind of knew that already, as he always left in the mornings suited and booted just before she left with Maisie. She had observed him out of the bedroom window, heading to his car. Not that she was really looking, of course.

'I wish I could say the same. Half the city must have been out food shopping today,' said Jess. She had barely stopped for a second. Burgers and salad had been particularly popular, and she imagined people having get-togethers on a perfect summer evening.

They chatted about their respective workplaces and when they had finished, Maisie showed Declan a painting of a whale that she pulled from her school bag.

'They live in Antarctica and Norway mainly, but sometimes in other places around the world,' she told him knowledgeably. 'We are learning about them at school.'

'Wow, that's really good,' said Declan, appraising the picture of the huge orca leaping out of the water. He meant it. She had real talent for such a young girl. 'Do you like painting?' he asked her.

'Yes. I have got an art set this big.' She stretched out her arms as wide as they would go. 'Do you want to see it?'

'Maisie, I'm sure Declan has more important things to do,' said Jess, her face flushing slightly as she thought of her underwear draped over the radiator in the hall that she never had time to put away this morning.

'I'm off out shortly, but maybe another time?' Declan smiled at Maisie.

As Declan put his key in the door of his apartment on their shared landing, he turned to Jess and asked if she was going to dinner at Alice's place the following evening. When she said that she was, he surprised himself by feeling excited at the prospect of getting to know her a little better during the evening. Then again, would it be wise to get involved with someone living so close and who had a child? What if things didn't work out? There was also the small matter of his past to consider. All the same, an evening in the company of an attractive young woman might be nice.

'Good.' He smiled before he headed inside.

# TEN

## JESS

Jess felt a fluttering of nerves as she headed home from her Friday shift at work. She decided to take the train home for a change, and had passed the mix of people who were out in force, already in weekend mode. Groups of lads in smart shirts and girls in full make-up and wearing pretty dresses strolled alongside tourists on weekend breaks trundling their suitcases away from Lime Street train station chatting excitedly.

As she sat on the train watching the old warehouses of the docks whizz by and give way to the rows of back-to-back houses, Jess wondered what she was worried about. Alice was a lovely woman, and Declan seemed like a nice guy. She hadn't really met the older bloke from the other ground-floor flat, but they had exchanged friendly greetings on the odd occasion their paths had crossed.

A young girl boarded the train at the next stop and sat opposite her, plugging in her earbuds and avoiding eye contact. Jess wondered why people were so reluctant to even smile at you on trains but often chatted away on buses. Although thinking about it, maybe that was just the older generation that did that, the regular bus commuters often commenting on the weather, or their aches and pains good-naturedly in the morning.

What on earth would they talk about at this dinner party? thought Jess as she stared out of the window. It was kind of Alice to invite them for dinner, but she could not help wondering what people spoke about at these gatherings. Did they discuss politics and current affairs? Not that Jess was ignorant on those matters, she read the news online most mornings on the bus or the *Metro* newspaper, keeping herself up to date with what was going on in the world, but she never discussed such things on an evening out. On the odd occasion she did go out, she liked to let loose and have fun, dancing in a club and finishing the evening with a cocktail.

Her mum had called her this morning and said she would come and visit her next weekend and stay over, offering to babysit Maisie so she could go out if she liked. Her partner was going to travel with her and take the opportunity to visit his daughter and stay over at her place. She had told her how much she missed her and Maisie, and Jess told her mum that they missed her too.

They had taken the train to Windermere a couple of weeks ago, staying overnight, her mum kindly paying the train fare for them. They had had the best time, taking a boat trip on the lake and visiting Beatrix Potter's old house at Hill Top, the inspiration for her Peter Rabbit stories. Maisie had talked about the weekend all the way home on the train, telling Jess she couldn't wait to tell her teacher all about it. With Jess's mum offering to babysit Maisie, maybe she would join some of the gang from work heading into town on Saturday evening to celebrate someone's birthday.

Grabbing Maisie from school, they hurried along without lingering at the duck pond, until they were back home. Thankfully, after-school club provided a snack, which would keep

Maisie going until dinner. She thought of Alice then, preparing the meal, and wondered if she ought to offer to help. Then again, she needed to shower and decide on what she wanted to wear. Alice had suggested an arrival time of six thirty to have a pre-dinner drink.

'What do you think, Maisie?'

Jess held up a pretty knee-length dress with a floral pattern, and a red blouse.

'I'll wear my jeans with the blouse,' said Jess, thinking she would wear a pair of black jeans, her one staple for her occasional nights out, paired with the smart top.

'The dress. It is Friday night after all,' said Maisie, which made Jess laugh. When did she become so old-fashioned?

'You're probably right,' she said, putting away the jeans and blouse. Thinking about it, the dress would probably be a lot more forgiving if she overindulged in food.

Sitting at the small kitchen table, Maisie was colouring a picture of Merida, the brave Scottish princess with the cascading red hair from Disney Pixar's *Brave*, which was one of her favourite films. Maisie already looked tired, her cheeks flushed pink and strands of hair escaping its ponytail and falling around her face. Jess wondered how long the evening would last and debated taking Maisie's pyjamas with her to change into. She was used to being awake until about eight, maybe eight thirty at the weekend, but no later. This was going to be unusual for both of them.

Half an hour later, Maisie had changed into a floral cotton dress and Jess slid on her own dress. She brushed Maisie's hair into a neat ponytail, her own hair let loose this evening, before grabbing the red pot plant she would take for Alice as a thank you gift. She knew nothing about wine, other than her favourite white was Pinot Grigio, so thought a plant would be a better bet.

Popping Maisie's pyjamas into her large shoulder bag, just in case, she picked up her keys and headed downstairs. She breathed away a slight feeling of nervousness as she rang the bell of Alice's apartment.

# ELEVEN

## ALICE

'Jess, Maisie, do come in.'

Following her inside, Jess detected the smell of something delicious drifting through the air.

'This is for you.' Jess handed the red-flowering plant to Alice.

'You really shouldn't have, but thank you, it's beautiful,' Alice said with a smile as she placed it on the round wooden table in the hall that held nothing but a framed photograph of Alice and a man Jess assumed to be her husband.

'You see, it has a perfect home already, next to my late husband, George,' said Alice, confirming Jess's suspicions. 'Please, go through. You are the first to arrive.'

Jess took in the tastefully decorated lounge as Alice offered her a glass of champagne.

'Oh yes, please. I don't often drink champagne; it's usually Prosecco.' She smiled.

'And for you, Maisie? I have apple juice or lemonade?'

'Apple juice, please,' said Maisie politely and was delighted when Alice returned with it in a plastic princess-style goblet.

'Can I give you a hand with anything?' offered Jess. She

glanced at the beautifully laid table, that looked stylish but not stuffy, an almost perfect metaphor for Alice herself.

'No, everything is under control.' Alice went to a drawer then and pulled out a pad of paper and some pencils.

'Maisie, I wonder if you might like to draw a picture until dinner is ready. Or perhaps do a jigsaw?'

'Jigsaw, please,' said Maisie, her eyes widening when Alice handed her the jigsaw with a picture of some cute kittens on the front.

Alice had slipped into Waterstones on her shopping trip the other day and picked up a couple of things to entertain Maisie in case she got bored. Alice loved children and had been blessed with two nephews, who she had spent a lot of time with when they were growing up.

The boys were like chalk and cheese, one bookish and reserved, the other chatty and outgoing. She rarely saw them when they became adults, although the outgoing one called her regularly for a catch-up, which always delighted Alice. He had also turned up out of the blue the year after George's death and taken her to lunch.

She had treasured that day, eating delicious food and reminiscing about when they had spent time together when they were children. She hadn't wanted the day to end and felt the familiar sadness when her nephew boarded the train and headed off home. She had toyed with the idea of moving closer to her sister and nephews at one time, but the thought of it overwhelmed her now. Besides, all her memories were here. And there were still some things she wanted to achieve.

The realisation that her nephews were middle-aged men themselves was a shock to Alice, as she still imagined them as children, when she and George would take them for walks through Formby Woods, or buy them an ice cream at the beach. Sometimes they would visit the local library where she would sit and read them stories. It was ironic that now that she had all the time in the world to see her nephews, they were at their busiest, working hard to provide for their own families.

She had spent time with her great-niece and great-nephew when they were younger, of course, but they were now also leading busy lives at university or in full-time employment. She supposed not many people spent time with their great-aunts really. Gosh, great-aunt. The title made her feel ancient.

Her sister, now in her late eighties, struggled with arthritis and was looked after by her husband, who was thankfully in good health, along with a part-time carer. Alice kept in touch by phone these days as the long train journey to visit them down south had become a little arduous.

Maisie settled down with her chunky jigsaw, just as the doorbell rang.

Alice opened it to Declan, who walked into the lounge and said hi to Jess, who, Alice could not help noticing, had blushed slightly. Declan handed Alice a box of fancy-looking chocolates, and she handed him a glass of champagne in return.

Standing in the lounge making small talk, Jess felt like she was in an episode of *Come Dine With Me*. She had never done anything like this before and it felt a little odd to be about to have dinner with a bunch of people she knew nothing about and probably had nothing in common with.

Jess thought Declan looked really good tonight dressed in a smart white shirt and dark jeans. And he smelt gorgeous too. She was pleased he wouldn't be a stranger to her after this evening.

'You look nice.' Declan turned to Jess as Alice went into the kitchen to check on the food.

'Thanks. So do you,' she said honestly. She was glad she had chosen the dress that sat just above her knees and showed off her slender legs.

Mark was the last to arrive, clutching a hessian bag containing three bottles of wine.

'Sorry I'm a bit late, I was watching the snooker and lost track of time a little,' he explained, apologetically.

The collar on his shirt already felt too stiff, his smart shoes a little uncomfortable as he hadn't worn them in a while, but he wasn't sure if trainers and sweatpants would be appropriate.

As Alice welcomed him inside, he experienced a feeling of warmth as the sound of laughter rang from the lounge and the smell of delicious cooking reached his nostrils. Maybe everything would be okay after all.

'You're not late, and if you were this would more than make up for it. Thank you,' said Alice, gratefully accepting the wine and glancing at the labels.

'I hope they are okay. My wife and I did a vineyard tour in the Napa Valley, and the wine was pretty decent as I recall,' said Mark, remembering how they had felt a little drunk at the end of the tour, and giggled all the way home on the coach like a couple of teenagers.

'I'm sure they will be just fine,' Alice reassured him.

Ten minutes later Alice asked her guests to take a seat at the table as dinner was about to be served. Alice was delighted that all of her shopping had arrived early this morning from Waitrose. Online shopping really was a godsend, saving her a trip all the way across town. The nice delivery driver had even brought the food inside and unpacked it for her.

'You must let me help.' Jess placed her glass down and followed Alice into the kitchen, which looked surprisingly neat.

A huge cauldron of a casserole was carried to the table, alongside a mountain of buttery-looking mashed potato in a dish. Another bowl had green beans and julienne carrots.

'That smells amazing.' Declan rubbed his hands together. 'I'm starved.'

'Good,' said Alice as she ladled bowls of coq au vin out, at her guests' request, plus a small portion for Maisie.

'Help yourself to vegetables.'

Mark opened the wine and filled glasses, everyone opting for a glass of the Cabernet Sauvignon apart from Jess, who went for white, pleased Mark had brought her favourite Pinot Grigio.

'Now, I would firstly like to thank you all for coming. You have made an old lady very happy,' said Alice, feeling thrilled that they had accepted her invitation. She wasn't sure that they would, wondering if people of their age could be bothered with a woman of her age.

'There's no way I was missing out on a home-cooked meal,' said Declan and Mark agreed.

'Oh, I see, you are only here for the food,' said Alice in a serious tone. Declan looked a little embarrassed, as did Mark, before Alice burst out laughing. 'Your face was a picture,' she teased, and Declan breathed a sigh of relief, before taking a glug of his wine.

'You had me there.' He laughed.

'How can a face be a picture?' asked Maisie, puzzled by Alice's remark.

'I suppose it does sound funny, doesn't it? It simply means when someone shows their emotions in their face,' explained Alice.

'What are emotions? Are they like emojis?'

'Yes, they are,' said Jess, laughing. 'Emojis are cartoon emotions. They show our feelings.'

Maisie nodded and went back to her drawing.

'And now, I would like to propose a toast to Alice and thank her for inviting us. Here's to getting to know our new neighbours,' said Jess.

'To Alice and new friends,' said Mark, suppressing a knot in his stomach when he thought of how much Diane would have loved this. Why hadn't he reached out to his neighbours before now? Being here, getting to know these people was far more enjoyable than the feeling of being rushed in a restaurant, knowing you had a maximum two-hour window for the table.

'To new friends.' Everyone raised their glasses and Declan made eye contact with Jess. She could feel her face flush, as Alice gave a knowing look.

The coq au vin was a winner, the chicken melt in the mouth, the sauce rich and delicious. Maisie ate a piece of chicken and made an appreciative noise.

'Is that okay for you?' asked Alice.

'It's yummy,' declared Maisie.

'That sauce is spot on. What kind of red wine did you use?' asked Declan.

'A good Burgundy, although Beaujolais works just as well,' said Alice, before taking another mouthful of food.

She certainly had a good appetite for someone her age, thought Jess.

'Mummy, am I allowed wine?' asked Maisie, looking a little doubtful. Jess hadn't even thought about that.

'Don't worry, there is no alcohol in it now. It cooks away, so you are only left with the flavour,' explained Alice.

'Alcohol is the bit that makes you drunk,' whispered Declan, who was sitting next to Maisie, on the opposite side of Jess. He went cross-eyed, and she giggled.

For dessert Alice placed a banoffee pie and an Eton mess in the middle of the table that people helped themselves to. During dessert, Declan mentioned the picture hanging on the wall of the lounge that showed a brunette young woman with a group of girls, all smiling.

'Is that you in the middle?' asked Declan, thinking he was right about her being a stunner when she was young.

'It is, how very observant,' said Alice as she poured everyone more wine.

She remembered that photo well; it was taken in London on a rare night off with some of the girls from the dance troupe.

'Was that in London?' asked Mark, the telltale sign of the London Palladium in the background.

'It was. I worked there,' said Alice as she sipped her wine. 'I was twenty-one years old in that photo. I was a dancer.'

'I want to be a dancer,' piped up Maisie. 'I go to ballet.' She slid off her chair then and did a perfect pirouette.

'How wonderful. Well, you must follow your dreams. I'm sure you will make a wonderful dancer if you work hard at it,' said Alice wisely. 'You can achieve almost anything in life with hard work and dedication.'

Hard work and ambition had been the path to success for Alice. She remembered the evenings her feet almost bled, but the show would go on as there was always another young hopeful waiting in the wings for their big chance if you gave up.

'What type of dancing did you do?' asked Jess, who wasn't surprised to learn that Alice had once been a dancer. She stood tall with a straight back, with no sign of a stoop even at her advanced years.

'I was in a theatre dance troupe at the London Palladium. You may not have heard of them, but we were called the Tiller Girls.'

Mark almost spat his wine out.

'You were a Tiller Girl?' he asked open-mouthed. He'd sat watching them as a child, as they opened a variety show called *Sunday Night at the London Palladium*. They wore tall feather headdresses and linked arms as they high kicked their legs in unison.

'Yes, do you remember them?' asked Alice.

'Oh, I do. My dad was a big fan too, as I recall.' He smiled. 'I was just a little boy and every Sunday night after the usual bath, I would sit in my pyjamas and watch the show with my parents. They usually sent me to bed before it had finished, though, and I remember I was never very happy about that.' He laughed.

'What a lovely memory,' said Alice. 'Watching TV together I mean, not being sent to bed early.'

'I can't get my head around it.' Mark shook his head. 'Just think, I might have actually watched you dance.'

'Probably not. I did my dancing in the nineteen fifties; I'm guessing you weren't even born then.' She smiled.

'A couple of years later. Even so, you were a Tiller Girl, that's amazing.'

Alice found it amusing that Mark seemed a little star-struck.

'It was a good life, but we worked very hard. I met some wonderful stars,' she said casually. 'Frank Sinatra was particularly polite.'

This time everyone almost spat out their drinks.

'You met Sinatra?' asked Declan, open-mouthed.

'Yes. Amongst others. But that really is a story for another evening, I think,' Alice casually declared.

'Who was he with?' pressed Mark.

'Ava Gardner at the time. She was a head turner, although I personally thought she had a hardness about her. I much preferred Audrey Hepburn. She was just as nice as she was in the films.'

'You have to be kidding me!' said Jess.

'No really. She was lovely to everyone as I recall. I was never really star-struck. They were just people after all, like you and I.' Alice helped herself to a portion of banoffee pie.

'Apart from being rich and famous.' Mark smiled.

'It's not all it's made out to be,' said Alice, thinking of how one or two big names had succumbed to the temptations that went with fame, and ended up ruining their marriages.

Maisie began to yawn then and asked Jess if she could change into her pyjamas.

'Good thinking,' said Alice. 'Then would you like to sit on the sofa and watch a bedtime cartoon? If that's alright?' She turned to Jess.

'Yes, of course. Just for half an hour maybe, then we should probably get going.'

It was a shame really as the conversation was just getting interesting. Audrey Hepburn! Imagine meeting her in real life! Jess could hardly take it in. She had met a well-known reality star when they promoted a branch of their clothing at the shop, and thought that was exciting. What a life Alice must have lived.

'I will put them on in the dressing room.'

Maisie took the pyjamas from her mother and went behind the couch to change.

'That's what she does at home if we have visitors,' Jess told the others with a grin. 'Behind the couch is her dressing room.'

'What do you do, Mark? I know a little about Declan and Jess,' said Alice as Maisie settled down on the couch to watch a cartoon with her toy zebra.

'I'm retired now, but I was a firefighter,' he explained. 'I took early retirement with a good pension, so my wife and I could go travelling.' He took a sip of his wine before going on to tell them that his wife had passed away. 'I'm so glad we never waited to visit the places we wanted to. I miss her every day, though,' he said, and Alice reached over and patted his hand.

'Keeping busy is the key,' Alice advised. 'Isolating oneself just allows thoughts to develop. You must always go out, even if it is just for a walk. Maybe even join a club of some sort.'

'Don't worry, I've done that,' Mark replied. 'I'm a member of the boating club at the marina. I bought myself a boat on a bit of a whim with Di's life insurance and joined the club. They are a nice bunch down there. They saved me from myself when I was in a bit of a dark place,' he revealed.

Jess wondered if he had any other family but as he hadn't mentioned any, she didn't think that now was the time to ask.

Talk turned to movies and television shows then, and Alice's guests were surprised to hear that she enjoyed a little bit of reality TV.

'Travel programmes mainly, although I did enjoy one

programme recently about surviving in the wilds. Which I found quite ridiculous.' She laughed. 'Especially as the participants had a whole camera crew filming them. They were hardly going to starve to death, were they?' she said, rolling her eyes.

'You wouldn't catch me sleeping out in the forest without a camera crew.' Jess shuddered. 'There could be psychopaths out there.'

'We need more of those,' said Maisie, as she yawned sleepily.

'What?' Jess asked, startled. 'Why would you say that?'

'Because when we were walking home from school, I heard you say to Darcy's mum that we need more psychopaths around here.'

Jess racked her brains wondering why on earth Maisie would say such a thing.

'It was when that man on the bike nearly knocked into us.' Maisie snuggled into her blanket and cuddled her toy zebra.

Jess put two and two together then and almost fell off her chair laughing.

'I said "cycle paths",' she explained, and Alice, Declan and Mark joined in, roaring with laughter too.

# TWELVE

## ALICE

'There's nothing quite like laughter to bring people together. Children really are a joy, aren't they?' Alice laughed as she stood and began to clear the table.

'They are. Maisie is always coming out with things like that.' Jess wiped her eyes. 'Here, let me do that,' she said, taking some glasses from Alice.

'We'll do it together,' said Declan, getting to his feet and piling the dessert bowls on top of one another on a tray.

'If you insist, then thank you. I'm afraid I don't have a dishwasher but leave them on the side. I will leave them in to soak until the morning,' advised Alice.

'You will do no such thing,' said Jess. 'I'm quite happy to wash the dishes; it's the least I can do to thank you for a delicious meal.'

'I'll dry,' said Declan.

Alice caught Jess colouring slightly at the idea of being in the small kitchen with him. She smiled to herself.

Alice was still getting used to just how different Wisteria House now was to how it used to be. The close quarters of the flats contrasted so much to how large the rooms used to be. The original kitchen of Wisteria House had sprawled across much of the downstairs.

Her father had employed a cook and a cleaner, but never a nanny at the insistence of her mother. She and her sister went on long walks with their mother, an author, to local parks and museums, sparking her love of outside spaces and culture. Her father's role as a diplomat would often take him off around the world, especially during the war years, which she realised, when she was older, must have been difficult as well as dangerous.

'Shall I make some coffee while I'm in the kitchen?' asked Declan, but Alice declined, as did Mark.

She offered them a nightcap that only Mark accepted. 'But help yourself to coffee.'

Jess thought coffee would keep her awake half the night so poured herself a glass of water from a large bottle of Evian in the fridge.

'Anything I can do?' Mark asked Alice.

'There is. You can go to that cupboard and get the bottle of single malt and two glasses,' Alice instructed him, indicating a nearby cupboard.

Mark returned with the whisky and two glasses, and Alice poured them both a generous measure.

'I might regret this in the morning,' said Mark as he swirled the whisky in his glass, chuckling.

'Don't feel obliged to drink it all,' said Alice, but Mark tasted the whisky and smiled. It seemed the quality of the single malt might mean he would make short work of it.

When Jess and Declan came back in to collect some plates, Alice saw the possibility of something more than neighbours between them. As she finished dealing out some cards for herself and Mark, she was struck again with memories of living here before.

'I can't remember the last time this house was filled with so many people,' she found herself saying.

'This house?' asked Declan, confused.

'Yes indeed. It was once a grand house that has been converted into apartments, as I am sure you know.'

She hadn't really intended to mention it, as she rather hoped it would be a discussion for another day.

'So you came here when it was a house?'

'Yes.' Alice smiled. 'I spent my childhood here. It's one of the reasons I rented this flat.'

'Are you saying you lived here once before?' asked Jess, open-mouthed.

'I did indeed. But I think that is a story for another time.'

# THIRTEEN

## JESS

Back in the kitchen, Jess filled the sink with hot soapy water and dropped the plates in.

'That was some meal,' she said, grabbing a nearby dish brush. 'I wonder where Alice learnt to cook?'

'I know, it was fantastic. I bet she went to a cookery school or something. Cordon bleu, I reckon,' Declan said with a broad smile.

'Probably. And, I must admit, I haven't heard of the Tiller Girls but I am going to google them later,' said Jess. 'But, wow, dancing at the London Palladium. It sounds like Alice has led a really fabulous life.' She sighed, as she placed a clean plate onto a drying rack.

*Not like me*, she thought to herself. Married and pregnant at twenty-two, the extent of her travelling had been a couple of holidays on the Spanish Costas. Not that she was complaining. She enjoyed her life and knew she was very lucky compared to some people. You only had to look around parts of the city to realise that. It was just that her life was a bit short of adventure, she realised, maybe even a little fun.

They both went to place some cutlery in a drawer at the

same time, and when their hands collided, she felt something pass between them, but was not sure if it was purely the effects of the wine. Or if Declan had felt it too. She did know that she enjoyed being in his company, though.

When they returned to the lounge, Mark and Alice were laughing about something, as Alice nodded towards the couch, where Maisie was snoozing gently, her toy zebra clutched to her chest. It was just after nine fifteen.

'She did well to stay awake for this long,' said Jess. 'I had hoped she might stay awake until we had finished in the kitchen but never mind. Once she's asleep, there is no waking her. I'll head off soon, though.'

'I'll carry her up for you, if you like. If you think she won't wake,' offered Declan.

'Thanks, that's really kind of you,' Jess replied. 'I've had a lovely evening, Alice. I can't remember when I last spoke to adults for this long. And your food was delicious, thank you.'

'I'll second that,' agreed Declan. 'I especially liked your meringue.' He winked.

'You are most welcome.' Alice glanced at the sleeping child now slung over Declan's shoulder.

'Goodnight, then,' said Jess. 'Thanks again.'

'Goodnight. And thank you for coming.'

She and Declan headed upstairs in companionable silence.

'Come in,' she said to him when she unlocked her door.

The flat was spotless, as Jess had been certain to make sure everything was tidy before she went out for the evening. She led Declan to Maisie's room, where he gently laid her down, before Jess covered her over and switched on a string of pink night lights above her headboard.

'Thanks for that.' She walked him to the door and felt awkward for a second. Did he expect her to suggest staying for a nightcap? She was not keen on inviting someone she barely knew inside at this time of night, despite her attraction towards him. She had Maisie to think about.

'I can't believe Alice once lived in this house,' she said, diverting the subject away from themselves.

'Me neither. I had a feeling she was from a wealthy background, though. I believe her father was a British diplomat,' he told Jess.

'I bet these walls hold so many memories,' she said, idly wondering if her bedroom had been a library or some such thing. 'Are you going back down there?' she asked.

'No, I've already said goodnight. Besides, I'm rubbish at cards.' He grinned, thinking briefly about the times he had played with some blokes who were masters of the game. 'Anyway, the football highlights are about to begin on the telly,' he said, glancing at his watch. 'I might just get changed and lounge around in a food coma.'

'I know what you mean. Same here probably,' said Jess.

'You're going to watch the football?'

'No.' She smiled. 'I'll probably get into bed and watch a movie.'

'That sounds nice.'

For a second, he imagined Jess in her bedroom, that was probably every bit as neat and stylish as the rest of the apartment he had glimpsed, her long dark hair splayed across the pillow when she slept, before giving a little cough and pulling himself together.

'Right, I'll be off. Night, then.'

'Goodnight, Declan. And thanks again for carrying Maisie up.'

'No problem.' He smiled.

When Declan left, Jess thought about the fact she had been here for almost two years and never exchanged more than a quick hello with her neighbours. She had been lucky to get the place near the train station, as it was handy for taking her and Maisie into the city centre at the weekend.

Maisie loved a train journey. Sometimes, they would visit the museum or art gallery with friends, after browsing the shops. Occasionally they would go for a pizza at their favourite place on Bold Street.

The house across town that she had shared with her ex had become damp and when they separated she had looked around for somewhere nicer and with better transport links. When she discovered this place, she wondered how on earth she could afford the rental deposit and was grateful when her ex helped out with some new furniture when he was in one of his high-earning phases. He had his daughter to think about after all. When Mum had paid the first month's rent on the flat, Jess vowed to pay her back.

Jess was a natural homemaker, and scoured discount stores to accessorise the apartment, until it was a warm and cosy home. It was a shame the garden flat had not been available at the time, but she was happy with the home she had created for her and Maisie.

Jess felt her eyes growing heavy when she climbed into her bed just after ten thirty. She had really enjoyed this evening and felt blessed that Alice had suddenly appeared in her life. She hadn't realised just how much she missed having her mum on the doorstep these days, so it was nice to chat to Alice, who was like a grandmother, albeit one who had led a pretty cool life by the sound of things. She couldn't help wondering what would happen next in her life, although for now, a lie-in might be nice.

# FOURTEEN

## MARK

The sun streamed through the bedroom window just after seven, and Mark held a hand to his throbbing head. He was too old to be knocking back the whiskies and wondered how the hell Alice had managed to keep up and stay awake until almost midnight.

In a break between card games, he had asked Alice more about her life here. But she just told him she had been a teenager when the family moved elsewhere. He had learnt no more, as she thrashed him in the next game. She'd won a total of thirty quid from him over the poker games.

But Alice had pushed her winnings into his hand at the front door, saying she only ever played for fun, and he remembered that she had only upped the stakes at his insistence. He wouldn't make the same mistake next time. He hoped there would be a next time.

After a cold shower, Mark wandered outside to the garden he shared with Alice and as he assessed the lawn, a feeling of shame washed over him. He took in the overgrown grass with clusters of dandelions poking through. Glazed pots stood forlornly against the fence and withered flowers that once bloomed with colour stared back at him. A stone bird bath that he and Di had chosen together at a garden centre was covered in moss. Diane had been the gardener. She would be mad at him if she could see it now.

'Sorry, Di.' He looked heavenward as he let out a deep sigh, vowing to sort it out.

Heading inside, he swallowed down a large glass of water and two paracetamols, before flicking the kettle on.

Cupping his tea in his hands, he thought about last night's dinner party. The people in the block really were a nice bunch of people. Different in many ways, but they had chatted easily enough, which he was relieved about. Diane would have breezed through it regardless – she was the extrovert in their partnership. She would have doted on Maisie and would have loved chatting to Jess and Declan. And she would have been fascinated by Alice.

Why had it taken a woman of such advanced years to bring the residents of the apartments together? he wondered. Was that the world they now lived in? Sure, the people in the block would say a quick hello in greeting, but usually on the way in or out, as they got on with their busy lives. People minded their own business, too busy to stop and chat so as not to disrupt their carefully planned routine. And he had been caught up in his own grief.

As a young boy he remembered his mother chatting to the other women in the street at the weekend, even pulling out chairs to the front and watching their kids playing in the street whilst they had a cup of tea and a natter in the fine weather.

Last time he had walked down the road there had not been a child in sight. There were no groups of children playing on scooters or bikes, every leisure pursuit organised by their parents. Even trips to the park had to be supervised by an adult.

He thought of how he would run to the park to see his friends when he was young and wondered when and why the world had become so terrifying.

Two of his friends had escorted him home one day, when he fell straight onto concrete from some metal climbing bars, the blood pouring from his head. No soft wood chippings to land on back then. Not that he thought that was a good thing, but somehow it had gone too far the other way. Kids were wrapped in cotton wool, destined to fall apart at the first problem they would encounter in their later years.

Di would tease him when he forgot something, telling him that the bang on the head as a kid probably had something to do with it. Maybe it did. Things were never investigated when he was a kid, unless you were knocked out cold. He did not think he would have survived thirty years as an active firefighter had there been anything wrong, though, despite his wife's teasing.

An hour later, after his painkillers had kicked in, along with a bacon sandwich and another cup of strong tea – his go-to hang-over cure – he felt ready to face the day.

It was another pleasant morning, and he briefly considered taking his boat out. It was always mad busy on a Saturday at the marina, though, and he wasn't sure if he was quite up to all the social activity.

He went inside and rifled through a drawer in the kitchen that was full of odds and ends. Nuts and bolts mainly, a couple of buttons, some silver coins, and a few keys. One of them was the key to the garden shed that contained the gardening tools, so he picked it up and strolled outside.

He found himself wondering if the garden might be a good place for a get-together. That was if anyone would be inter-ested. He had enjoyed himself at Alice's dinner far more than he imagined he would, although maybe hosting something would be a bit much. He would have a think about it.

Either way, it was high time he got the garden sorted. And there was no time like the present.

# FIFTEEN
## DECLAN

Declan had woken early and was surprised at how fresh he felt. Then again, he hadn't really overdone it with the booze last night. He had enjoyed himself and hoped Jess might have invited him in for a drink, but she had escorted him straight to the door after he had put Maisie to bed. Not that it mattered; she barely knew him, after all. He sincerely hoped that would change, though, if he could pluck up the courage to ask her out.

He was changed and ready to go for an early morning run, cutting through the park and heading down to the beach for a run along a section of the coastal path. He hated gyms. He always felt claustrophobic building up a sweat indoors and much preferred being outside with nature, earphones plugged in erasing all thoughts of his working week. He had spent enough time indoors to last him a lifetime.

'Morning, Declan.' Alice was heading out of her front door.

'Hi, Alice. How are you this morning?' Declan asked cheerfully.

'Wonderful. I so enjoyed having company over; it was lovely having people to cook for. I've missed it since George passed.'

'I'd be very happy to do it again. I'm not volunteering you

for cooking, of course. Though I haven't had a meal like that in ages.' He smiled.

'You're most welcome. Are you off running?' she asked, and Declan told her about his plan to run along the coastal path near the beach.

'Well, enjoy yourself. I'm off out for a walk towards the beach later,' she told him.

'That's a long walk. I thought you would be putting your feet up today,' Declan commented.

'It's important to keep active at my age,' she replied, not answering his implied question about the location. 'I don't want these old muscles to seize up.'

Once outside, Declan plugged his earbuds in, and crossed the road towards a small park, favoured by dog walkers, that had several benches dotted around and a war memorial looking out across a main road. He took a left turn then, onto Mersey Road, passing the old church opposite the Co-op and listening to his music as he jogged. This slow jog was the warming up part. At the beach, he would grab a bottle of water from the ice-cream van and head off, pushing himself as he ran.

Despite the music in his ears, he found himself thinking about Jess. Had he imagined it, or had there been a spark of attraction between them? He could not be sure, but he thought she felt something when their hands reached for the cutlery drawer together. He had certainly felt something, and although he enjoyed his single life, out with his friends at the weekend going to the pub and the football, perhaps it was time for him to start dating again. He was only twenty-nine years old, but he was out of practice. His last relationship was, shockingly, over five years ago. Before everything in his life had changed.

Declan placed his hands on his knees after his run and breathed deeply. He was happy with his time of six miles in around an hour. He scrunched up the water bottle and placed it in a nearby recycling bin before moving on.

Taking a shortcut home, on a path behind some sand dunes, he was approaching a junction ready to head back towards the apartments. Unplugging his earphones, he pulled his phone from his pocket and glanced at it. He had received a couple of texts, one from his mate asking if he fancied a pint later, and one from his mum. He realised guiltily that he hadn't been to visit for a couple of weeks, although he did message her regularly.

'Mum, hi. How are things?' he asked, deciding to give her a call.

He was sitting on a bench admiring the view of the rolling sea beyond.

'Hello, Declan.' His mum sounded happy to hear from him. 'Oh, you know, not too bad, love. How are you?'

'I'm fine, Mum. I was calling to see if it was okay to pop over tomorrow actually,' he told her.

He supposed the call was prompted by a stab of guilt, although he was thinking of visiting his mum sometime soon.

Not that he had a problem with his mum. They were in regular contact, but what with work, and the weekends going so quickly, the time seemed to fly by. But he ought to try harder. She had become good friends with the bloke next door, and maybe in some way it subconsciously absolved him from calling round as often as he should do, which was shocking really when he thought about it.

'That would be nice, love. Will you be having Sunday lunch?' she asked.

'Are you making a roast?' He smiled, her lunches conjuring up happy memories of times gone by when the family would sit around the table. Things had changed so much since then.

'I could do, although Norman next door suggested a carvery at the pub. Come with us if you like?' she offered.

'No, you go for it, I'm only joking. A cup of tea will be fine. I'll bring some of that lemon cake from Satterthwaites Bakehouse that I know you like.'

'Lovely. I will have to share that, though; the doctor told me to watch my sugar after my last blood test, remember?'

Did he? Had she told him that?

'A little of what you fancy should be okay, though, hey. See you tomorrow, Mum.'

He decided he would go and see her straight after Sunday morning football. They chatted for a few more minutes before he stood up to head off.

He had been thinking about his mum's comments, trying to recall the conversation about her blood sugar, so he hadn't paid much attention to the two blokes who walked past, both wearing black hoodies.

He was blindsided by the searing pain in his head as the punch landed. The younger bloke had tried to grab his phone, the latest iPhone model, but he gripped it tightly to his chest. His whole life was in that phone. He landed a strong punch on one of the pair, who fell backwards onto a patch of grass. He squared up to the second bloke then, who ran away, quickly followed by his friend.

He realised they were just kids as he watched them running off, and pulled a tissue from his pocket and dabbed at the blood running down his cheek. The bloke must have been wearing a ring. The cut below his eyebrow was a few centimetres away from his eye and it could have caused some real damage. What was wrong with the world today? he thought to himself as he walked on, his heart still beating wildly.

Walking up the path to his flat a while later, he saw Jess and Maisie were just heading out, both dressed in summer dresses.

'Oh my gosh, what's happened to you?' Jess's hand flew to her mouth.

'You should see the other bloke,' joked Declan. 'I fell over whilst running.' He smiled brightly at Maisie before whispering to Jess that he had been mugged.

'I held on to my phone, though.' He raised it and managed a smile.

Maisie frowned as she studied Declan's face.

'That looks sore. Our teacher tells us to get a wet paper towel if we have an accident,' she told him innocently.

'That's what I will do, then. Well, kitchen roll will have to do.' He smiled. 'Are you off out somewhere nice, then?' he asked Jess.

'Just a bit of shopping in town. Maisie has a friend's birthday party next weekend, so we are going to buy her a present; I'm also meeting a friend who has a daughter the same age as Maisie. We're going to the museum,' she told him.

'I'm going to see the mummies,' said Maisie. 'We are learning about Egyptians at school.'

'Cool.' Declan smiled at Maisie, who reminded him of Dorothy from *The Wizard of Oz* in her gingham dress and plaited hair. 'Have a nice time.'

'And you. I hope the rest of it goes well, after your fall.' Jess raised her eyebrow at him.

'Cheers. Catch you later.'

Once inside, Declan looked in the mirror and could already see the purple hue emerging below his cheek. He would have a right shiner in the morning. He inspected the slit above his eye, that wasn't long but seemed quite deep. He considered going to the walk-in centre; perhaps it needed some glue or a stitch or two. In the end, though, he pinched it together and covered it tightly with a fabric plaster. The lovely evening at Alice's dinner party had restored his faith in human nature before those young chancers had made him think again. He wondered whether he deserved nice things to happen to him, given his past history. Even though he hadn't been entirely to blame.

Sitting down with a coffee, his thoughts went into overdrive. Did one of those blokes look familiar? No, they were far too young; he was just being paranoid. Surely, he would not have been targeted, not after all this time? Besides, they would have done him with a knife, rather than just attempted to steal his phone. They were opportunists, that was all. Maybe next time he would keep his phone firmly in his pocket when he was on that side of the path, where it was almost always quiet. Keep temptation away.

After showering and changing, he decided to stay home for the evening and watch a film, the attack having shaken him up more than he realised.

Pulling a beer from the fridge, he sat on the couch and scrolled through his phone. Some photos of his sister popped up, and he caught his breath. He treasured the last photograph of them together, taken at Blackpool Pleasure Beach on a roller-coaster when she was twelve, and he was fourteen. They had gone on a school trip as a reward for good attendance. Their mum was not one to indulge them in a day off school when all they had was something as simple as a cold.

Declan gripped the phone tightly as he sank back into the deep, black leather sofa. He would back up his photos and anything else of importance onto a computer hard drive, in case he ever lost his phone. Today had made him realise that. He glanced at the picture once more and managed a smile. At least he and his sister had enjoyed some good times together.

He flicked on the TV, then searched for a movie to watch later. Then he would head out to buy that lemon cake for his mum.

# SIXTEEN

## JESS

Jess had a lovely day in town, meeting up with her friend, a mum she had met on the school playground two years ago and befriended. Buoyed by the dinner invitation, she realised that she really ought to arrange things with her friends a little more and concentrate on her social life too, rather than just dropping her daughter off at yet another party.

Her friend's daughter was the same age as Maisie, and sometimes they would go to each other's house after school for tea. Today, they were sitting on benches in a small park close to the art gallery, eating a picnic lunch after a play in the kids' craft room in the gallery, and a trip to the museum.

'That's scary.' Maisie had frowned, as she stared into a glass case at a mummy, and Jess had to agree. The princess swathed in faded brown bandages had an almost tortured look on her face. They visited the planetarium upstairs after that and spent a while looking through telescopes at the solar system, before visiting the aquarium downstairs. You could spend the whole day at the museum, and it was free, if you were unable to make a small donation. A rush of memories came flooding back every time she brought Maisie here, as her own mum had done the same with her when she was a child.

After the museum visit, Jess's friend led her to a discount shop down a side street that Jess did not know existed.

'You can pretty much get anything for kids here, and at great prices,' said Jess's friend as she pushed open the door of the shop, that was Tardis-like, filled with row after row of discounted toys.

'Oh my goodness.' Jess stood open-mouthed as she glanced around. 'How come I don't know about this place?'

'I stumbled on it too. I have never really seen it advertised, but maybe they don't need to. It's been a godsend with all the parties Lily gets invited to. She has a better social life than me,' laughed her friend.

Her friend's comment had really resonated with Jess as Maisie had already been to half a dozen parties this year. She was surprised at just how much she had enjoyed the dinner party the other evening, despite her initial reservations. Perhaps it was time to get out there a little more and experience new things. As long as it fitted in with her daughter, of course.

After selecting a toy pony set, complete with brushes and mirrors for grooming, she said goodbye to her friend and headed towards Central station for the train home.

On the journey home, Jess found herself wondering if Declan was okay. That gash above his eye looked pretty nasty, and must have shaken him up a bit, but he never let on. Maybe she would knock and see if he was alright. Then again, what was she thinking? It was Saturday; he would probably be getting ready for a night out with his friends. Not everyone spent their Saturday evenings with popcorn watching *Minions* on Netflix.

As they walked towards the apartment, Jess and Maisie bumped into a red-faced Mark coming out of a local shop, carrying a case of Diet Coke.

'Hi, Mark. Are you okay?' asked Jess cheerfully, before Maisie launched into details of their day out, and mimicking the haunted look on the face of the princess.

'Yes. Just a bit exhausted.' He grinned. 'I've spent the day tidying the garden. I'm ashamed to say it had become a bit of a jungle.'

'Well, you have certainly had the weather for it. You have caught a bit of a tan,' Jess commented, although Mark thought the redness in his face was more down to his lack of fitness these days. Then again, he had spent hours pulling up weeds, digging and strimming borders before mowing the lawn. They fell into step as they approached the flats.

'Actually, would you like to come and see what I've done?' he asked.

Jess knew that his ground-floor flat garden was a bit on the wild side. She could see it from Maisie's bedroom window.

'Sure.' She followed him into his flat, through his tidy lounge and into the outside space.

'Oh wow, you have been busy,' she said, viewing the freshly mown lawn. The once redundant pots were filled with pretty flowers and shrubs and a water feature with stone fairies tipping water from buckets trickled peacefully.

Jess would love a garden like this for Maisie to run around in.

'You've seen the garden before?' asked Mark.

'I can see it from Maisie's bedroom window.' She smiled.

'Oh right, yes, of course. Sorry about that, I bet it's been a bit of an eyesore.' He pulled a face.

'Don't be silly.' She smiled again. 'Maybe you weren't up to doing anything about it.' She touched his arm gently. 'There's a time for everything.'

'You did say it was a bit of a jungle,' said Maisie and Jess felt her cheeks colour.

'Out of the mouth of babes.' Mark shrugged.

'Sorry.' Jess grimaced.

'Don't worry about it.' He smiled as Maisie ran over to the water feature. 'I know I have left it far too long before tackling it,' he admitted. 'Di was the gardener and somehow, I am ashamed to say, I let things slide. I kept imagining us both sitting out here, which is a poor excuse, but the thought of us enjoying the garden together, knowing that it could never happen, well, it got to me, you know?' He took a deep breath. 'Anyway, I nipped to the garden centre for the plants after I had given myself a good talking-to and decided to get stuck in.'

'Well, you have done a really good job,' said Jess. 'Especially as you don't consider yourself to be a gardener. Really, it looks lovely,' she told him sincerely.

She wondered what it had been like when Alice had lived here, picturing stone fountains and maybe raised beds for growing vegetables. Perhaps they had a gardener. She would love to know more about Alice's life at Wisteria House.

'Thanks.' Mark smiled. 'And actually, now that it looks presentable, maybe I will have a BBQ to repay Alice for dinner the other evening. I know Di would want me to enjoy the garden as well as the work.'

'That sounds lovely,' said Jess.

'Great. I will see when everyone in the block is free.'

Even though the thought of hosting a party scared him a little, he found himself looking forward to being in the company of his neighbours again.

'Do you have any family nearby?' Jess found herself asking. She had never noticed anyone visiting, but then she was usually too busy dashing off somewhere.

'No.' Mark shook his head. 'I was thinking about getting some of that bamboo fencing, or some fake foliage with flowers,' he said, quickly changing the subject. 'Some of it can look quite natural.'

'Clematis is a good climber if you want real plants. So is honeysuckle,' Jess advised.

Her mum's garden had the loveliest scent of honeysuckle in the summer evenings, when they would sit out and have a coffee or a glass of wine in the small but pretty garden. She missed her mum, and could hardly wait for the following weekend when she was coming to stay from Friday to Sunday.

Inside her apartment that evening, Jess made beans on toast for her and Maisie, as they had eaten a huge picnic earlier. It had been such a lovely day. Maisie was tucked up and fast asleep just before eight o'clock and Jess headed to bed a couple of hours later. She switched the TV on and idly flicked channels. She never did knock and see how Declan was doing. Maybe she would do that in the morning.

<h1 style="text-align:center">SEVENTEEN</h1>

## Alice's House Near the Sea

The sun began to fade far quicker than Alice had expected it to, although she had read for almost three hours, enjoying the pot of tea in the library room. It had always been her favourite room in the house with its sash windows and heavy drapes. Looking upwards at the tall ceiling with a beautiful rose at its centre, she recalled her joy when she first noticed it when viewing the house.

She was spending one last evening in the house that she once lived in with her husband as it would soon be someone else's home.

Alice's stomach had rumbled an hour ago, and grateful to have mastered the art of ordering food online, she had enjoyed a tasty curry that had arrived from her favourite place on South Road. She ate her meal at a small table that overlooked the distant sand dunes, a strip of the wild Irish Sea beyond just visible. She thought about herself and George then, as she often did, taking windswept walks when they were younger.

One particularly windy day they had laughed when a gust

of wind made George's trousers billow out like a windsock and lifted her hat from her head, sending it rolling towards the water. George had run after it, and managed to rescue it, not before falling flat on his backside in the wet sand, to roars of laughter from Alice.

They had warmed up at home in front of a blazing fire, drinking hot chocolate with a slug of brandy added. The house, long neglected, had been a project, but they saw the potential and over time had transformed it into a stunning home.

It had been fortunate that George's brother was a carpenter and at weekends they all rolled their sleeves up and got stuck in together. There were so many memories made in this house but, in some ways, it was like a mausoleum now.

She had rattled around the empty rooms of the four-bedroomed Georgian house for long enough when she decided to sell up and rent the small apartment. The fact that it had once been a part of her childhood home felt like fate stepping in.

With the light fading, Alice decided to stay for the evening and take a taxi back to the flat in the morning, so after a whisky nightcap she settled into her bedroom with the primrose-coloured walls and dark-wooden furniture. Her fingers ran over the framed photograph of George that sat on the bedside table in a silver frame.

'Hello, George,' she said as she settled down into the bed with the white Egyptian cotton sheets. 'I have met some lovely people in an apartment I am renting, and I know you would like them,' she told him. 'I did consider buying, as I know you think renting is no investment, but at my age I'm not sure there is a lot to invest in,' she told him. 'I like to think I can help them in some way, and I know you would agree. Especially Jess and her daughter, Maisie. A more adorable child you could never meet.' She smiled to herself.

She chatted away to George as if he was in the room.

'Declan is a fine young man too. I get the feeling it won't be too long before he is working in the office. Oh, George, can you imagine how wonderful it would be for someone to bring the old office back to life, having meetings with clients, just like the old days?'

She closed her eyes and recalled the busy days in the office when she would call in and insist George took a lunch break and would drag him to a café nearby, where they would drink coffee and eat chicken Caesar salad.

It was the nineteen sixties and they would sit at a window seat in the café, and observe the mini-skirted ladies, some in striking black and white clothes and wearing black winged eyeliner. Workers in suits would walk alongside the hippie types with their psychedelic colours and long hair. It had been the most exhilarating time, yet it all felt like yesterday.

'Mark is a lovely man too,' she continued. 'A little shy, and clearly still missing his wife, but he is coming out of his shell a little each day I think.'

'Anyway, my darling, this is the last time I will be staying here as the new family will be moving in in the very near future. I hope the house brings them as many treasured memories as it did us,' she said, her voice breaking. 'Oh, and they loved the period furniture here, so most of it is staying. I agreed a good price with them, you will be pleased to hear.' She smiled. 'I don't really know if you can hear me.' She glanced heavenward. 'But I like to think that you can. Goodnight, my love, until we meet again.' She kissed her finger and pressed it against the glass of the picture.

Every day was a blessing at her age, she knew that. She looked forward to spending the day doing something wonderful and unexpected tomorrow. But for now, she would enjoy one last evening in the home that held such wonderful memories.

# EIGHTEEN

## MARK

Mark woke with aching legs the next morning. The gardening had given him a workout he had not had in ages, reaching muscles he had forgotten all about.

Years ago, he had been at peak fitness, which he needed to be, as you never knew when you would have to carry someone over your shoulder from a blazing house, navigating smoke-filled rooms. Thankfully, towards the end of his career, he had witnessed less of the heart-wrenching things he had come across early in his firefighter role. Most people had ditched the chip fans, the number one cause of fires back in the day. Then candles became popular, and things were briefly busy again, when people would forget to extinguish them before bed and they might fall and catch something flammable, like a curtain.

He had spent the last few years before his retirement visiting schools and educating children about fire safety, as well as fitting homes with fire alarms. He had learnt that kids were pretty good at nagging their parents into being fire safe, even encouraging them to quit smoking.

After a shower and a coffee, he thought about asking the neighbours to a BBQ on Friday evening. But would they want to come?

Perhaps they only accepted Alice's dinner invitation because it came from a lonely, elderly woman? Would he be able to cope without Diane fixing drinks and holding court so naturally?

Before he could talk himself out of it, he got dressed and knocked at Alice's front door. For a second, he thought it might have been a little early when there was no response, even though it was almost nine o'clock. He was certain she had mentioned being an early riser and felt a flicker of concern. Just then he heard voices on the upstairs landing and headed up there to find Declan standing outside Jess's door chatting.

'You're going to make a cake?' Jess asked Declan, obviously finding it amusing. Declan had forgotten that the bakery closed at 2 p.m. on a Saturday and had missed them after he had watched a film yesterday. He had found a recipe online for a lemon drizzle cake and had nipped to the Co-op for the ingredients, but he had no cake tin. He decided to call at Jess's flat to see if she had one that he could borrow.

'Morning, guys.' Mark smiled at them both. 'I'm probably worrying over nothing but have either of you seen Alice this morning?' he asked them.

'No. Maybe she went out early?' suggested Jess.

'Yes, of course, you're probably right,' he said, although he could not help wondering where she would go so early on a Sunday morning. Unless she had nipped out for a newspaper. He could imagine her poring over *The Observer* with its Sunday supplement.

'What's this about baking a cake?' asked Mark, and Declan told him all about his promise to his mum, before realising the bakery was closed.

'Sounds good. Anyway, I'm glad I've caught you both. Do you fancy a BBQ early Friday evening? I have checked the weather; it's going to be good apparently,' said Mark confidently.

'That sounds lovely, but my mum is arriving for the weekend on Friday,' explained Jess. She was planning to go out on Saturday as her mum had offered to babysit, happy to spend time with her granddaughter. On Friday they would all go to the pub together for a meal.

'She is most welcome to join us. Unless you have other plans, of course,' Mark quickly added.

Jess could think of nothing nicer than having a BBQ in the sunshine.

'Not especially. We would probably end up going out for food, but I think it would be lovely to spend time outside if the weather forecast is good. Thanks, Mark.'

'And you?' He turned to Declan.

'Nice one, yeah.' He smiled, glad of a chance to be spending some time with Jess again. He had not quite plucked up the courage to ask her out as he thought it might be a bit awkward if she refused, what with living in such close proximity. Probably better to get to know her a bit first.

'Do you think maybe I ought to knock again at Alice's?' suggested Mark.

Jess picked up her front door key from a hook in the hall, and closing the door headed downstairs with Mark and Maisie in tow. Declan followed them, clutching the cake tin.

Finding no response after knocking again, Jess made her way outside to see if the curtains of Alice's apartment were open, and when she saw that they were firmly closed, her heart sank.

With increasing concern, the trio were pondering their next move, when a taxi pulled up outside the block and out stepped Alice.

'Alice. You're okay!' Jess breathed a sigh of relief.

'Gosh, this is quite the welcoming committee. Why wouldn't I be?' asked Alice as she walked up the path. As she spoke, she noticed the drawn curtains on the lounge window. She hadn't thought about that.

'I knocked to invite you to a BBQ. I know you are an early riser; you told me so. I guess I became a little concerned when there was no answer,' Mark explained.

'And what with the curtains being drawn,' added Jess.

'Well, I feel blessed to have such wonderful neighbours looking out for me.' Alice smiled, truly touched. She could lie dead for goodness knows how long in the big house, and it reinforced to her that it had been the right decision moving here.

Jess and Declan headed back upstairs then and Mark, struck by sudden inspiration after the relief of finding Alice was okay, asked if she had any plans for the day.

'Not especially,' she replied.

'In that case, do you fancy a day out on the boat?'

'Your boat at the marina?'

'Yes. Maybe a spot of lunch later,' suggested Mark.

'That sounds simply perfect. When are you thinking of leaving?'

'Say in an hour?' Mark glanced at his watch.

'Wonderful. I'll be ready.' She smiled.

# NINETEEN

## ALICE

Alice loved spontaneous invitations, when a day turned out completely differently from the way you might have imagined. She especially enjoyed this invitation from Mark, as it seemed to be inspired by her wish to bring everyone together here. Life was definitely returning to Wisteria House.

She opened the windows and curtains and let some fresh air into the lounge, before going to her bedroom to decide what to wear. As Alice headed off to shower and change, she thought, not for the first time, how fortunate she was that the residents of the block had taken her up on her offer of dinner that Friday evening. She had observed their comings and goings during that first week, not in an intrusive way, but at the end of the week she had deduced that the residents didn't have partners. That was probably why they were open to the dinner invite in the first place.

She never saw her neighbours much at the house near the sea. A family occupied the house on one side, with two teenagers who nodded politely on the rare occasion she encountered them. They had gatherings that she was never invited to.

She would observe guests making their way up the path,

laughing and clutching bottles of wine, and push down a tinge of envy. But then, why would they want a woman of her age at their parties? Or maybe they simply never thought to ask? That was the problem with putting people into pigeonholes according to their age, thought Alice. She would have loved to have chatted to the young people, hearing all about their hopes and ambitions for the future. Growing old seemed an almost impossible notion when you were young, she realised that, but it would arrive before they knew it.

The residents of the house on the other side were business owners and rarely at home. Alice and George had socialised with the previous neighbours when he had been alive, but when they both moved on to nursing homes, the new neighbours never engaged with them. Her and George's offer of drinks and nibbles had been politely declined by the new, younger families and that was that.

Exactly an hour later, Mark knocked at Alice's door. She was wearing white trousers and a navy and white striped T-shirt.

'You look very nautical,' Mark said with a wry smile.

'I suppose I do, don't I?' she replied. 'I have a headscarf too. I know how windy it can be out on the water.'

A memory came rushing back to Alice of when she and some friends had taken a boat trip along the River Thames in between shows at the Palladium and attracted the attention of some handsome men at a bachelor party. The men had bought them drinks, probably hoping for something in return, but the girls had giggled and ran off to their lodgings when the boat returned from its sail as the men headed off to a bar. Life had been so good then, the possibilities endless for all of the girls, and Alice had enjoyed every minute of her life, especially after she met George.

They took the short drive to the marina and, after parking up, walked along the waterfront, where sailing boats rubbed shoulders with small speedboats and single-engine vessels. As they walked along the wooden path, several people said hello. One guy, a friend of Mark's, stopped for a chat and Mark introduced him to Alice.

'Pleasure to meet you,' said the grey-haired man, who was perhaps in his seventies.

'Alice here used to be a Tiller Girl, you know,' Mark told his friend proudly.

'You never did!' The man stood open-mouthed, and recounted a similar tale to Mark, of watching *Sunday Night at the London Palladium*.

'It was a lifetime ago,' she told him when he had finished speaking, amused how it always elicited an excited response, particularly from someone of the older generation, even though the Tiller Girls still performed today.

'Well, it was a pleasure to meet you,' said the guy when they had finished chatting. 'A Tiller Girl, hey.' He shook his head as he walked off, as if he had just met royalty.

'Here she is,' Mark announced presently. His sailboat was moored at the end of a row of a dozen or so vessels.

'Oh, it's perfectly lovely.' Alice eyed the smart boat, white with a green stripe and the name *The Oyster* painted on the side.

'Unusual choice of name,' she commented as he took her hand and guided her into the boat.

'It was inspired by my grandmother, who was called Pearl and was the happiest woman I knew,' explained Mark. 'And would you believe, Diane's gran was also called Pearl. She was a cheerful woman too apparently, so it was a no-brainer.' He smiled. 'We did think about calling it simply *Pearl*, but *The Oyster* sounded more special somehow.'

'I take it your mother was not so happy?' Alice could not help asking, wondering why the boat was named after his grandmother rather than his mother. Mark was silent for a few seconds as he stared out across the water.

'No,' he said, keeping his eyes fixed on the water. Finally, looking at Alice, he continued. 'At least not when she was around me.'

For the first time Alice saw a pain behind his eyes. She would talk to him about it. But not right now.

Taking a seat on the boat, Alice listened with interest as Mark proudly told her of his previous sail, including a boat race last year. He started the engine up then, and they were soon gliding across the water.

'Would you like to take the wheel?' asked Mark a while later, when they were a little further out, the wind whipping up a little around them.

'I'd love to.' Alice took the wheel of the boat, glancing at the distant Welsh hills in one direction, the cranes from the docks and the wind farms to the right, overlooking the beach. It was a little cool and she was glad she had brought a cardigan that she slipped on after a while, before fastening her scarf tightly around her neck. It was exhilarating being out on the water.

Alice recalled a day when the tutor of the drama group she attended as a teenager took them across the Mersey for a day out to New Brighton Pavilion to see a show. Watching the glamorous dancers in the chorus line had fired in Alice her desire to be a professional dancer more than ever.

A boy serving them ice cream at a kiosk took a fancy to Alice, and her friend reminded her that her dad would kill her if she got off with someone from the funfair. It was true, of course, but Alice felt flattered all the same. Her friends teased her all the way home about how her ice cream had been bigger than everyone else's.

The following year when the dance troupe she was in had gained quite a reputation, they performed in St Tropez at a private party. After the show, a rich businessman had wowed the girls with a sail on his yacht in the blazing sunshine. Halcyon days indeed.

After an hour had slipped by, Mark suggested mooring up and visiting his favourite beach restaurant. The squawking of gulls above greeted them as they stepped out of the boat and headed to the café that had stainless steel tables and chairs outside.

'We will eat inside, if that's okay,' suggested Mark. 'Unless you fancy sharing your food with the seagulls.'

Right on cue, a gull swooped down and grabbed a chip from a polystyrene tray in a bin. 'I booked us a nice table, as it can get really busy at the weekend.'

She followed him inside the restaurant that was larger than it appeared from the outside and had cream painted walls and some cheerful vintage bunting stretched across a wall behind the counter.

'What can I get you?' asked a pretty young woman in a black apron, the word 'Lucy's' embroidered across it in white stitching.

'A pot of tea, please. And it has to be fish and chips I think,' said Alice.

'On a Sunday?' Mark frowned.

'I don't see why not. Fish and chips seem perfect after a bracing sail.' She smiled.

'No roast lunch on a Sunday.' Mark tutted then laughed, before ordering roast beef and Yorkshire pudding with all the trimmings.

'This is the best you will get around here,' he told her and the girl behind the counter smiled.

They were shown to their table then, a window table that overlooked the sand dunes with a strip of sparkling sea beyond.

A pot of tea for two arrived, and in no time at all, so had their food.

'How did you know I would accept your invitation for

lunch?' asked Alice as she cut into the crispy batter, revealing white flakes of fish.

'I would have dined here alone. I do sometimes.' He shrugged. 'But I much prefer company, especially yours,' he told her and Alice smiled.

Talk turned to family and Alice told him all about George, and he spoke fondly of Diane.

'You must miss her dreadfully. I know I do George. Are your parents still alive?' asked Alice and she saw Mark's jaw tighten.

'My mother is.' He took a sip of tea.

'And in good health?' She estimated she was maybe somewhere in her eighties.

'I wouldn't know.' He forked the last of his lunch into his mouth, before picking up a dessert menu.

'That's a shame,' ventured Alice.

Alice would have been utterly heartbroken to have had a child and then become estranged from them. Although, of course, she never knew the circumstances for the estrangement.

Mark quietly perused the menu.

'Do you have any siblings?' Alice asked, breaking the silence.

Mark put the menu down and let out a deep sigh.

'I have a younger sister, yes, and a nephew. He must be coming up for twenty-one now. I don't see them much. We lost touch,' he said, answering what he was certain would be Alice's next question.

Alice finished her meal and placed her knife and fork in the centre of the plate before she spoke again.

'Why did you lose touch? I would have thought family would be important to you, especially after you lost your wife,' she asked gently.

Mark drummed his fingers on the laminate table and Alice wondered if she had gone too far with her questioning.

'Honestly? I don't know.' He glanced out of the window, and Alice noticed his eyes moisten a little. 'Lynn is three years younger than me, yet she looked after me when I was little.' He allowed a smile to play around his mouth. 'As teenagers we would sometimes sit together in my room, listening to music, her teasing me over my Debbie Harry posters on the wall, and me teasing her over her Donny Osmond pictures.' He laughed. 'She would make us tea and bring it up on a tray with a plate of chocolate digestives. My mother hated her fussing over me, though.'

Alice could see the pain in his eyes.

'Why?' she asked gently.

'Because she couldn't stand me,' he said without a trace of emotion. 'I tried to figure out why over the years but could never understand why a mother would act that way. It was eating me up.' He sighed. 'So, after a lot of soul searching, I cut her out of my life.' He took a moment, then continued. 'As an adult the coldness and criticism had continued whenever I visited her. She was never like that with my sister. I decided enough was enough,' he said, as he fiddled with a cardboard drink coaster.

Alice remained silent as he talked, seemingly happy to get it all off his chest.

'Anyway, the last straw was when she didn't even bother to turn up for Diane's funeral. I just thought, what's the point? Who needs that kind of toxicity in their life?'

He asked a passing waitress for another pot of tea.

'Oh, Mark, how dreadful. I am so sorry to hear that,' said Alice sincerely. 'Did you ever ask her why she treated you the way she did?'

'Ask her?' He frowned.

'Yes. Why not? I'm not trying to excuse her behaviour, but there might at least be a reason why she behaved that way. There usually is,' she suggested.

Alice could not really imagine why any mother could

behave in that way, but then human nature was very complicated. She had lived long enough to realise that.

'In answer to your first question, she would have denied it. Said it was all in my imagination,' Mark told her. 'I remember Diane being furious with her once for belittling me at a family gathering. She cornered her in the kitchen out of earshot of others and gave her a bit of a dressing-down. Mum clutched at her chest, feigning stress and denying everything. She never spoke to Di again after that.'

'Oh, Mark, that's truly awful. But why don't you speak to your sister?'

'I can't lie, I do feel a bit ashamed about that. She came to the funeral, and we went out a couple of times later, but things just drifted,' he admitted. 'We haven't fallen out exactly; we just aren't close anymore.' He shrugged. 'She's busy, still working as she can't afford to retire just yet. Weeks turn into months, and suddenly you are not a part of each other's life anymore.'

A waitress appeared then and set down the second pot of tea.

'Do you miss her?' asked Alice as she poured tea for them both.

'Sometimes, yes. But I guess adult siblings often lose touch, don't they?' He sipped his tea.

'Not usually without good reason,' Alice told him honestly.

'Maybe you're right.' Mark sighed. 'I think it started when I called her a couple of times to arrange a visit, but Mum was staying with her at the time after a fall so I never went, and somehow we never rearranged.' He gazed out of the window once more.

Alice felt for Mark. He had a sister who he was once so close to, yet she was becoming a stranger to him.

'You should contact her,' said Alice firmly. 'Your relationship with your sister should not be a casualty of the relationship with your mum.' She leant over and placed her hand over Mark's and heard him take a deep intake of breath.

'I know, of course you're right. You usually are.' He smiled.

'Well, it's easier to see things as an outsider. And maybe I have reached an age where I have seen it all before.' She raised an eyebrow.

They resisted a dessert and headed outside where the sun was shining brightly and everything felt a little warmer. They would head back to the boat soon. Alice had had a wonderful time and hoped Mark had too, despite her questions. And she really hoped that he would make that call to his sister.

# TWENTY
## DECLAN

Declan was worried his mother would give him the third degree about the impressive black eye he was now sporting. He considered cancelling today as she would probably only worry if she saw it, but then again, he hadn't visited her in a while. But the connections he'd made with his neighbours gave him a good feeling about this visit going better than some of them had.

His mum was feeling a little better these days, although of course you never truly got over the death of a child. But at least she was able to manage a smile from time to time and find some happiness in her day. He had Norman, who had moved into the bungalow next door, to partly thank for that.

Norman had been a real tonic to his mum when, in all honesty, Declan was at the point where he had no idea how to deal with her. Norman, a smiling, grey haired seventy-five-year-old had befriended her and Declan thanked God that he did.

It took a while, but the drinking gradually stopped, and a glimpse of his old mother was revealed. The house would appear a little tidier and fresher whenever he called over, as previously Declan would visit every Friday after work and give the house a good going over, as well as placing the empty bottles in the recycling bin. He had tried to talk to her, soothe her, even suggesting days out to give her a change of scenery, but to no avail.

He remembered the argument they had a few years after his sister's death when he had called over. The house had smelt stale, and he'd flung the windows open as his mum sat at the kitchen table in her dressing gown drinking gin and singing loudly to a song on the radio, the sink piled high with dishes.

They had rowed then, him telling her that if she wanted to kill herself then there were quicker ways to go about it. He couldn't imagine what she must have gone through, especially when he had to go away for a while too, but she couldn't spend the rest of her life stuck in this soul-destroying hell. She had thrown him out then, the shattering sound of the glass she was drinking from hitting the kitchen door as he left. Declan wondered how long his mum could go on, but there had been no reasoning with her.

And then along came Norman, like a gift from above. Kind, patient Norman, who invited his mum to sit in his pristine garden on sunny days, drinking tea and talking about his plants. He was a good listener and over time it would appear she had something to live for once more.

Looking back, Declan realised she had been locked in grief, despite him selfishly wondering why he had not been enough of a reason for her to want to carry on. It had taken a stranger without any emotional attachment to restore the balance a little. Norman had encouraged his mum to talk about her daughter, Kelly, and over time she was able to once again display the photographs that she had ripped from the walls, unable to look at her daughter's face.

Norman was a great guy, steadfast and reliable, and with a cheeky sense of humour. Declan was pleased his mum was recovering, although he knew it was still one day at a time. She would never be truly happy, he knew that, but she was managing to at least find some joy in her life, and he was grateful for that.

He still felt angry when he thought about the boys who went after his phone, and it frustrated him that his reactions were not as sharp as they used to be. A couple of years ago he would have anticipated the situation, every nerve of his body tuned in ready for fight or flight.

That morning, having never baked a cake in his life, Declan carefully followed the recipe and was shocked when it appeared to turn out okay. At least it looked that way. Half an hour later, having drizzled the lemon icing over the top, he took a tentative bite of a thin slice to sample it. He nodded to himself, savouring the lemony tang. It tasted surprisingly good.

He cut off two more slices – he didn't need to take the whole cake, after his mum telling him she was watching her sugar – so popping the slices of cake onto a plate, he headed across the landing.

'Thought you might like to try my effort, since you lent me the cake tin.' He presented the cake to Jess.

'Oh, so we are the guinea pigs, to make sure you don't poison your mum?' she teased.

'I've eaten some, and I'm okay. Although, actually, aargh.' Declan put his hands around his throat and staggered just as Maisie appeared.

'Are you alright?' She frowned at him.

'Yes, just having a joke.' He recovered himself as Jess shook her head and laughed.

'Declan has brought us some cake.'

'Yummy,' said Maisie, eyeing the sponge.

'What are you up to today, then?' Declan asked cheerfully.

'Not a lot. I have a bit of shopping to do, then we are going to the park later; we usually run into some of Maisie's friends from school.'

'Sounds nice.'

'Is it today you are going to see your mum?' asked Jess.

'Yeah, but I'm not sure what she will say about this,' said Declan, pointing to the purple bruising around his eye. 'I don't want her worrying.'

'Well, it's a nice enough day to wear sunglasses, although it might seem a bit odd wearing them indoors. I could help you disguise it if you like,' she offered.

'Really? That would be great, if it's no trouble.'

'Not at all. Come in.' Jess invited him inside, thankful she had just tidied up.

Declan followed her into the white painted hall, the walls adorned with black and white photos of her and Maisie, before entering the lounge that was neat and stylish, with grey painted walls, a large burnt-orange sofa and plants dotted about. The room felt minimalist but made cosy with cushions and throws. Overlooking the window was a small light-wood dining table with two chairs, where Jess invited him to sit down.

'I'll be back in a tick,' she said, before returning with her make-up bag.

'This should do it.' She shook a bottle of concealer and searched in her bag for a make-up brush.

As Jess leant in close, dabbing at his eye, he could smell her perfume and feel the warmth of her body. He closed his eyes as she dabbed with a sponge, losing himself in a daydream where she was in his arms and he was about to kiss her. She took her time, with small strokes and finally a dab with a make-up sponge. He was disappointed when she had finished, and he opened his eyes.

'That should do it.' She handed him a small mirror, and to Declan's astonishment, the bruising was invisible.

'Wow, that's impressive. You should be a make-up artist,' he commented, examining his reflection in the mirror.

'I did actually do a course,' Jess told him as she put away her things. 'But things don't always work out the way we expect them to, do they?'

'You can say that again,' agreed Declan, thinking of his life and the unexpected direction it had taken. 'But it's never too late. Surely there are part-time courses?' he asked.

'Maybe when Maisie is a little older.' She put her make-up things away, before offering him a drink.

'No, thanks, I'd better be off. And thanks for this.' He pointed to his cheek before taking a deep breath. 'Maybe we could grab a coffee another time, though?'

'I'd like that.' Jess smiled and Declan felt like punching the air. He thought of how he almost took a tenancy on a building a few streets away, and how he might never have met Jess. Maybe everything really did happen for a reason.

# TWENTY-ONE

## JESS

Jess felt sick to her stomach when she read the letter that had just arrived by recorded delivery. No one ever sent her mail this way, and she felt an unexplained feeling of dread in her stomach. She briefly wondered if it was something official from a solicitor, informing her that Maisie's dad could no longer afford child maintenance. She hoped not. Things were just about ticking over as they were.

As she ripped the envelope open and read the words inside, she felt her heart sink.

She had barely had time to digest the words when there was a knock at her front door.

'Have you had one of these?' asked Mark, waving the official-looking envelope. He was quickly joined by Declan.

'I have. I assume Alice will have received one too,' he said with a sigh.

Normally post was deposited into the communal box downstairs, although any important mail was posted directly to the tenants through their front door.

'Can you believe this?' said Declan, shaking his head. 'The building is up for sale.'

'And we have been given two months' notice to get out once a sale has been agreed,' said Mark, feeling suddenly stressed.

'It isn't long, is it?' said Jess, fear gripping her. Especially as her mum no longer had her house. She thought of her and Maisie staying in some temporary accommodation somewhere, although hopefully it would not come to that. 'I simply don't know where Maisie and I will go.'

'I know what you mean,' said Declan.

'But I imagine you could move back in with your mum,' said Jess.

'Maybe in an emergency.' He shrugged. 'But I can't see that happening. It's Alice I am really worried about, though.' He sighed. 'She is too old and frail to be making another house move so soon. We need to speak to her.'


'It isn't uncommon for landlords to sell a property, especially one of this quality,' Alice told her friends calmly as she poured them tea from a china pot. 'They make very desirable purchases, especially one that has been divided up into apartments.'

'But don't we have rights as tenants?' asked Mark anxiously.

He cursed his foolishness in not buying an apartment when he and Diane had downsized. Instead, they chose to rent and spend the proceeds of the house travelling the world. And then he bought a bloody boat. Maybe he could live on it, short-term at least, but he feared for his friends.

'Unfortunately, as we don't have fixed-term contracts, but rather periodic ones, I am rather afraid the owner can do as he likes,' Alice told them. 'But I will have a solicitor friend of mine look over the contract. At least the two months' notice will only start after the agreed sale, which should give us longer here. Especially as the housing market is a little uncertain at the moment.'

'Let's hope it doesn't sell for ages, then,' said Jess hopefully. She thought of Maisie's bedroom and how beautiful it looked and tried to quell a feeling of rising panic. The rent was reasonable too. Even if they were allowed to stay, the new owners could double the rent.

'Let's not worry for now,' said Declan, his calmness belying the uncertainty he felt inside. 'It hasn't actually gone on the market yet. I'm sure everything will work out fine.' He smiled. 'And it might simply be that we get a new landlord.'

'Yes, let's not panic for now,' said Mark, sounding far more assured than he felt.

'You're right,' said Jess, managing a smile. 'And as my mum likes to say, something always turns up in the end.'

She would spend every spare minute she had looking for a place for her and Maisie. There was no way they were going to be homeless. She would fight for her daughter as she always had.

# TWENTY-TWO
## DECLAN

Declan tried to shake thoughts of the impending sale of Wisteria House from his head as he drove through the estate where he once lived. As he drove the memories of growing up there came flooding back as they always did. There was no way he could stay here with his mum, even for a short time.

One thing was for certain, he needed to up his search for accommodation. The reality was that Wisteria House could be sold anytime soon.

Driving past the park, he noticed a couple of adults pushing kids on swings or guiding the younger ones down the slide. A young woman sat on a bench glued to her phone, before finally answering her daughter's pleas to push her on the swing.

In the evening the park would become a hang-out for the local youths. He had been one of those teenagers himself once, flirting with the local girls and drinking cheap cider.

He drove on past the parade of shops, which consisted of a chemist, a supermarket, fish and chip shop and a betting shop.

Two of the shops, a clothing store and a cake shop, were long gone. As a child he remembered his mum calling into the fashion shop and buying something to wear for the occasional evening out with his dad at the weekend. She had taken a pride in her appearance then, but after his sister had gone, she gave up on almost everything including her marriage to his dad.

He remembered the rows, his dad raising his voice and reminding his mother that he was grieving too, when she had shut him out. It was too much for them, and when Declan was twenty years old, they went their separate ways. He was still in touch with his father, enjoying a pint with him on his birthday, and that sort of thing, but he wasn't a big part of his life these days, something he regretted.

Driving past the primary school he once attended, he noticed that the bright-green railings and newly painted frontage were the only thing that had really changed over the years. The memory of running along the playground, half watching out for his sister as she played with her friends, had him swallow down a lump in his throat.

He had tried to dissuade his sister from hanging around the park with the friends she had made in high school, even though he had once done the same. There wasn't much else for the kids to do around here, so they would gather in the park, and the kids on bikes peddling drugs had tempted them with cannabis. A lot of teenagers smoked a bit of weed but thankfully grew out of it. Others carried on, a few progressing to harder drugs. His sister had been one of those people. Driving around these parts got to him every single time.

Pulling up outside his mum's bungalow, one of six dwellings, Declan was cheered to see that the front lawn looked neat and tidy, and a fresh hanging basket bursting with colourful blooms was displayed near the front door.

Clutching the lemon cake, he knocked on the door and his mum answered. Her dark, bobbed hair was streaked with grey, something she would have once kept at bay with trips to the hairdresser, he was sure of that. She was wearing a blue floral dress and even though the events of life had wearied her, she looked better than she did the last time he saw her.

'Hiya, Mum,' said Declan as he planted a kiss on her cheek, before heading into the kitchen with the cake where his mum put the kettle on.

'So how have you been?' asked Declan. He had removed his sunglasses and placed them on top of his head; he would have only drawn attention to himself had he kept them on.

'Oh, you know, not bad. Pretty good most days actually.' She turned and smiled as she retrieved two mugs from a cupboard.

'That's good to hear, Mum. Here, look what I brought you. I won't lie, the bakery was closed, so I baked you a lemon cake,' he said proudly. 'I have brought most of it, after I sampled it first.'

His mum opened the cake tin and inhaled the scent of lemon.

'You made it?' His mum looked shocked.

'With my own fair hands. Shall I grab a couple of plates?' He grinned.

'Ooh yes, love, that looks really good. I'm impressed. Just a small piece for me, though. In fact, you go on through; I'll bring the tea and cake in a minute,' she said, shooing him into the other room.

Declan walked into the lounge and glanced around. The red leather sofa had seen better days, but his mum looked after it and spruced it up with nice cushions.

'Is that a new rug?' he asked, pointing to the large rug on the laminate wooden floor when his mum entered the room.

'Yes, it looks nice, doesn't it? Norman took me to Great Homer Street Market last Saturday, and it was a real bargain. I got the cushions too.'

'The room looks lovely.'

'Thanks, love.' She smiled proudly.

His mum set the tea and cake down on a coffee table and sat

opposite him. Her gaze seemed to linger on him for a minute, and Declan wondered whether she had spotted the bruising on his face.

'Are you sure you can't join us later for a carvery?' she asked Declan as he sipped his tea. 'You look as though you have lost a bit of weight. Are you eating properly?'

'Of course, Mum. I had a huge meal last night,' he told her, thinking of the takeaway he had ordered. 'I go running to keep the pounds at bay.' He laughed, patting his stomach.

They chatted about this and that, and his mum asked him, as she often did, whether he had a girlfriend.

'Not at the moment, but there is someone living in the apartment block.' He told her all about Jess and how they had met up at a dinner party.

'She sounds nice.' His mum smiled. 'And a dinner party, hey, sounds lovely. Maybe you could ask her around here. I could make my shepherd's pie.' She winked.

'Now that does sound good. But I haven't actually asked her out yet,' he told his mum.

He idly wondered whether Jess would agree to a proper date with him, rather than just going for a coffee, as he took a bite of cake. It really was quite good. He also wondered if there was any point, if they were soon to be going their separate ways.

'Well, I hope things go well,' his mum told him. 'I would like to see you settled before I depart this world,' she said, glancing upwards.

'I know you would, although hopefully you will be around for many years yet, Mum,' he said. 'I would quite like to settle down myself, but the opportunity hasn't really presented itself.' He shrugged, although truthfully he had not really been looking.

A couple of hours later, Declan stood to leave as Norman tapped on the back door.

'Hello there, young Declan.' Norman shook Declan's hand with the grip of a much younger man. 'How are things?'

'Can't complain. How's yourself, Norman?'

'Good, good. I can't complain either. I'm still here, waking up every day. We have to count our blessings, don't we?' Norman, a bear of a man, grinned broadly. 'Fancy joining us at the pub?' he asked amiably.

'No, thanks, Mum has already asked. Another time, though?' suggested Declan.

'Whenever you like,' Norman said, shaking his hand once more.

Declan kissed his mum on the cheek goodbye.

'Tell me how it goes with Jess,' she said as he stepped outside, where the sun had suddenly put in an appearance. He thought he saw her gazing at the cut above his eye, although she never said anything.

'Will do, Mum. Speak soon.'

He felt good when he left and watched his mum and Norman wave until his car disappeared around the corner. His mum seemed to be doing okay these days, but even so he resolved to not leave it so long next time. *Life is precious. None of us know how long we have got. Carpe diem,* he thought to himself as he headed out of the estate, wishing he could close his eyes tightly when he drove past that damn park.

# TWENTY-THREE

## MARK

The following morning Mark made himself a coffee and took it outside to the newly refurbished garden. As he admired the surroundings, Alice's words went round and round in his head and although he always felt better after spending time with Alice, her words weighed heavy on his mind. 'Call your sister.'

As he stood watching a sparrow on the fence, he knew Alice was right. After Diane's death, he realised how life could change at any moment. The sale of the apartments was another stark reminder of that. Perhaps he ought to seize the moment a little more. Besides, what kind of an older brother didn't check up on his sister just because she was a big part of his mother's life? How hard could it be to pick up the phone? But what would he say to her after all this time?

He tried to justify it slightly by reasoning that she had his number too and could have called him. Especially knowing he had lost Diane. She had been kind in the months following Diane's death, though, there was no doubt about that. Maybe they had simply grown apart, or she was happy to have no contact, taking the easier road of keeping their mother happy.

Who knew? One thing was for sure, he would never get those answers without speaking to her.

He had really enjoyed himself yesterday. Alice was such good company and although he hadn't known her long, he felt completely at ease in her company. Life was strange, he pondered as he listened to the soothing sound of the water feature. He would have loved a mum like Alice, who was unable to have children, and yet was the son of a mother who might have preferred it if he had never been born.

Alice had divulged the information about not being able to have children without any emotion the evening he had stayed after the dinner party, and they were playing cards. He remembered thinking at the time that there was no justice in the world. She had told him all about George too, who sounded like a great guy. She had empathised when he told her how much he missed his wife and had asked him all about her.

He had been blessed to meet a loving woman in Diane, who had showered him with affection, which he had hardly known what to do with when they first met. But over time, he had opened up, and her love had poured through him like a river until he became a loving husband in return.

He took a deep breath and resolved to contact his sister. But right now there were more pressing matters at hand. Someone from the marina had called to inform him of an act of vandalism where some of the boats, including his, had been daubed with paint. He downed his coffee before heading down there to find out what the hell had happened.

# TWENTY-FOUR

## DECLAN

On Monday payment from the lady at the café had dropped into Declan's bank account. He'd met with her one day after work and looked over her books. He'd been impressed that she had logged all of her incomings and outgoings, and saved every single receipt of purchases, all held together with a bulldog clip. She had apologised to him and said she really ought to have it all organised in a folder on the computer, but Declan didn't mind. In some ways he found it easier to manually look at receipts and do the calculations. He presented her with a bill, which she had now paid. His first customer.

With the extra cash he thought he might take Jess out somewhere extra special, if she would agree to that. In the meantime, there was the BBQ at Mark's place to look forward to this coming Friday. This morning when he had showered, all the make-up Jess had carefully applied to his face slid down the plughole. At least his mum had not noticed the bruising, though; at least he hoped so. He hated the thought of her worrying about him.

He dressed for work and as he glanced in the mirror, his

impressive-looking black eye stared back at him. He was bound to take some ribbing from his colleagues, but he could handle it. He had handled far worse.

As he crossed the landing, Jess's front door opened.

'Morning.' He smiled.

'Morning. Oh, and thanks for the cake. I have to say, I was very impressed. It was lovely,' said Jess.

'Thanks, and you're welcome.'

'Yes, it was yummy.'

Maisie pushed in front of her mother at the front door. 'Do you know how to make chocolate brownies?' she enquired.

'Oh, putting in orders now, are we?' He laughed. 'No, actually I don't, but it's easy enough to find out I suppose.'

'Maybe Nanny will make some with you on Saturday when she babysits,' suggested Jess.

'Off anywhere nice?' Declan found himself asking.

'No solid plans.' Jess tucked a piece of hair that escaped her ponytail behind her ear. 'But as Mum's watching Maisie, I might join the work gang for a night out.'

Declan hesitated and found his heart beating a bit faster than usual. *Sod it.*

'Do you fancy going out somewhere? Unless you would rather go out with your friends from work, that is.' He held his hands up.

'That sounds nice.' She smiled and he felt his heart soar. 'The work crowd are always going somewhere or other; I can go out with them another time.'

'Great. Right, I'd better go.' He glanced at his watch. 'Catch you later.'

He stopped and turned around then. 'Actually. Do you want a lift?'

'No, thanks, honestly. We have our routine in the morning.'

Jess had worked hard to make sure the mornings went like clockwork, without relying on anyone else. She and Maisie were a team, their morning routine well practised. Especially now that Maisie didn't spend time poring over things she might take into school.

'No problem. See you later,' said Declan, before he bounded down the stairs.

# TWENTY-FIVE

## JESS

As the weekend approached, Jess thought how much she was looking forward to it. Her mum was coming to stay, Mark was hosting a BBQ and Declan had just asked her out. She was grateful that all of these things were pushing thoughts of the sale of Wisteria House to the back of her mind.

As they walked along, Jess with a spring in her step, a gust of wind blew the painting Maisie was carrying for her teacher into the road. She stepped off the pavement to retrieve it, when Jess grabbed her by the wrist. She pulled her daughter to safety just as a speeding car whizzed past, missing her by inches. For a second Jess wondered whether it might not have happened, had Maisie been walking to school with two parents, one on either side.

'Oh my goodness, Maisie. What have I told you about going into the road?' she said, her heart hammering wildly as Maisie burst into tears.

'Sorry, Mummy,' sobbed Maisie.

Jess hugged her daughter then. She closed her eyes and pushed away any thoughts of what might have happened.

'You must never go into the road suddenly, even to chase

after something. You must always stop at the kerb, look both ways and listen, remember?'

'Okay, Mummy,' sniffed Maisie, nodding her head.

Jess remembered learning all about road safety when she was at school and wondered if schools still taught that sort of thing. She doubted it, with everything else they were under pressure to fit into the curriculum. She would mention it to Maisie's teacher, though. Living in a city, Jess was certain it would be something the other parents would welcome.

When Maisie's teacher had ushered the children into the classroom, Maisie none the worse and chatting to her friend, Jess quickly explained what had happened on the road.

'So you see, I was wondering whether you ought to do a lesson about road safety, especially with all the cars on the road in a city. Maybe even an assembly for the whole school?'

'You're probably right,' agreed Miss Jenson. 'And, yes, of course, I will talk about it at carpet time at the end of the day. I've seen a few near misses in supermarket car parks myself, with children and moving vehicles.' She shook her head. 'It's definitely something we should talk about. Perhaps an assembly for the whole school is a good idea. Right, I'd better go.' Miss Jenson smiled as the children's chatter became louder with their teacher distracted.

'Of course, yes, and thank you.'

Jess felt better when she made her journey to work and was thankful that Maisie had such a great teacher. Maybe the school that was closer to her had better facilities, but she reminded herself that a good teacher was worth its weight in gold.

On the bus journey Jess allowed herself to think about Declan, and going out on a date with him. She hadn't felt an attraction towards anyone for a while, she realised as the bus stopped and started, the hiss of the doors opening and closing as it made its way to the city centre. Men had been firmly on the back-burner, and she would never dream of introducing

Maisie to a boyfriend unless she thought they had a future together.

She recalled how her heart had beat that little bit faster when she had stood close to Declan, applying the concealer to his face after the attempted mugging. She liked how he kept the truth from Maisie, explaining away the cut above his eye as being from a fall. She liked how he baked his mother a cake, after realising the bakery had closed. It occurred to her that she liked rather a lot about Declan and found herself really looking forward to spending time with him again.

She also wondered what would happen if they no longer lived in the same building. Maybe they would all head off in different directions and lose touch with each other? The thought of it gave her a sinking feeling in her stomach.

After alighting the bus, she found herself staring into the window of an estate agent's. Maybe in her lunch hour she would pop inside and see if there was anything available to rent.

# TWENTY-SIX

## MARK

'You think it was kids?'

Mark scratched his head as he studied his boat. It looked like he had suffered the least, a green streak of paint along the hull of the boat just missing the name, probably the tail end of what looked like a tin of paint being thrown along a row of vessels. The poor bloke three boats along had copped most of it.

'I'd say so. Wanton vandalism. Either that or someone has a grudge against the club, but why they would target individual boats is beyond me,' said the caretaker. 'I would have thought the clubhouse would be more of a target, if that was the case.'

'Maybe it's someone who was refused a membership,' suggested Mark.

'That rarely happens.' The caretaker shook his head. 'Probably just kids with nothing better to do,' he decided.

Mark set about removing the paint, along with the other boat owners, who were furious. One couple were in tears, the wife asking why you could not have anything these days and it was probably just an act of jealousy.

The security cameras near the entrance would be checked, but there wasn't much chance of catching anyone, especially if it was teenagers who all seemed to dress the same and would probably have their faces covered.

Two hours later, having successfully removed the paint from his boat, and given another bloke a hand with his, he was in the clubhouse enjoying a drink, the vandalism the topic of conversation.

'Maybe we ought to have a couple more CCTV cameras near the boats, and not just at the entrance,' suggested one of the boat owners, and Mark reminded him that such things would increase the annual fees for the boat owners.

'Well, we need something,' the man grumbled, although the cost of a twenty-four-hour security guard would also impact on the site fees.

'It's not my day, second bit of bad news this week. I hope nothing else happens, as they do say things come in threes,' said the guy called Ken, a local business owner. He might consider footing the cost of extra security cameras himself, if it meant the boats stayed intact.

'What was the second thing?' asked Mark.

'My bloody accountant has been fiddling the books,' Ken, owner of a string of bathroom showrooms and a successful warehouse, told him. 'He never bloody passed any money my way, and I had nothing to do with it,' he quickly added.

'No, I can't imagine you would,' said Mark. Despite being rich and successful, Ken Watson was the nicest, straight down the middle guy you could wish to meet.

'He's been arrested. I'm not sure I trust anyone in that building now.' He shook his head.

'So, you need an accountant, then?' asked Mark, the cogs in his brain working.

'Pretty much as soon as possible, yes. Why do you ask?'

Mark recalled his discussions with Declan and how he dreamt of setting himself up.

'Let me just have a chat with someone,' said Mark. 'I know

an accountant who works for the council. Ambitious, and a cracking young man who is looking to go self-employed.'

'Interesting,' said Ken, stroking his chin. 'Okay, let me know what he says, and I will set up a meeting.'

Mark had enjoyed a second pint, glad that he had walked down to the marina, especially as it was such a pleasant day. He wondered what on earth he would do with his days if he wasn't a member of the club. No doubt he would waste his days away, watching too much television or going to the pub. But then, he did enjoy the company of Alice, who was quickly becoming the confidante he never knew he needed.

Some might say he viewed her as the mother he never really had, but it was more than that. She was a friend. She had a gift of being someone you could talk to about anything, and you would always head home feeling so much better about life. Not many people could do that.

He couldn't bear the thought of not seeing her around anymore. But there were some things that even the wonderful Alice had no control over.

# TWENTY-SEVEN

## JESS

'Mum!' Jess crushed her mum in an embrace as she dropped her floral overnight bag in the hall.

'Hello, love.' Her mum's partner, Pete, said a quick hello, before telling her mum he would see her on Sunday.

'Nanny!' Maisie came running out from the bathroom then, and wrapped her arms around her grandmother's waist, resting her head on her hip.

'How's my gorgeous girl.' Jess's mum picked Maisie up and swirled her around, before kissing her on the cheek.

'It's so good to see you both. It's just not the same on Face-Time,' said Jess's mum and Jess agreed.

Carol, an attractive redhead who looked younger than her sixty-two years, pulled a packet of fudge and a small dolly for Maisie from her bag, much to the little girl's delight.

'Is it too early?' she asked Jess hopefully, producing a bottle of white wine. It was just after two o'clock in the afternoon.

'Not really, but I think I'll wait for the BBQ later. I'll be asleep by six otherwise. You go ahead, though,' said Jess.

'You probably have a point. Shall we have one before we leave instead, whilst we get ready?' suggested Carol.

Jess thought of the days preparing for a night out with her friends as a teenager then, music blaring and a glass of wine in her hand. She had lost touch with her best friend from school, who had moved to Scotland a year before Jess became pregnant.

They had been back and forth visiting each other for a while, but their friendship came to a natural end as the years rolled by.

It occurred to Jess that even though she had made friends at work and at the school gates, she didn't really have what you might call a best friend. Perhaps she ought to get herself a hobby or join a club of some sort, but it was difficult being a single parent.

'I'll pop the kettle on,' Jess said, taking the bottle of white wine and placing it in the fridge to chill.

She left her mum in the lounge with Maisie, who her mum squeezed for the umpteenth time, before popping a square of fudge into her mouth that Maisie had given to her. She was a lovely child. Jess had done such a good job with her and she could not imagine life without her.

Not for the first time, Carol felt bad about not being involved in her daughter's life more, having moved out of the area. She missed collecting her granddaughter from school and collecting shells from the beach on fine days. Thank goodness for her tablet and all the FaceTime calls after school, although sometimes they left her feeling a little down afterwards.

On one such occasion, she took the ninety-minute drive back to Liverpool, to tuck her granddaughter into bed and read her a bedtime story and ended up staying the night. She admonished herself all the way home the following morning and told herself to get a life. Pete had been a little surprised too, as he had planned to cook a steak for them and open a bottle of wine the previous evening.

After Jess's dad had left, Carol never imagined herself being with anyone else. She remembered Jess being concerned that her mum had sold up and moved to the Lake District a bit too quickly with someone she met at a school reunion, although she was happy for her.

Maybe she had been right all along. Jess's dad had handed over the house to Carol, no doubt riddled with guilt when he upped sticks and moved in with a work colleague ten years his junior.

'There you go.' Jess placed a mug of tea down onto a coffee table in front of her mum. 'Do you want a biscuit?'

'No, thanks, love. I'll wait for later. Do we need to take anything?' Carol asked.

'Mark said not to, but I'll walk down to the Co-op and buy some beers in a bit. Maybe a cheesecake or something for dessert,' she said.

'I'll go, after I've had my cup of tea,' said Carol. 'It will give me a chance to say hi to everyone. Do you want to come with me, Maisie?'

Maisie nodded as she sucked on the piece of fudge.

Although she hadn't really needed the money – Carol had always been a saver and was mortgage free – she had worked part-time at the Co-op to keep her occupied. Along with her yoga classes at the church hall and with collecting Maisie from school a couple of days a week, her days were full.

On Sundays, Jess, Maisie and Carol would walk down to the beach for a picnic in the fine weather or have a Sunday roast at Carol's house.

Jess thought that her mum's life had been ticking over nicely, before her head had been turned by the handsome Pete Riley at that damn school reunion. He made it clear to her mum he would not return to Liverpool, so after being smitten by his charm she relocated to the Lake District. It seemed you were never too old to make mistakes.

Jess lifted the bag of fudge from Maisie, as she was about to take another piece.

'That's enough for now. Save one or two for later,' she told Maisie, who protested mildly.

Jess had taken the day off work today, as the teachers at Maisie's school were taking industrial action. Jess was worried that the country was grinding to a halt. It had been junior doctors the week before, and the train drivers before that. She would be in a right fix if the bus drivers went on strike. When Maisie skipped off to her room to play with her new dolly, Jess sat down opposite her mum.

'So how are you, then, Mum?' she asked as she sipped her tea.

'I'm fine.' Carol smiled. 'I've already told you.'

'I mean *really*.' She looked her mum in the eye, who had been averting her gaze.

'I'm okay.' Carol paused for a moment. 'Most of the time anyway, but the truth is I'm finding things a bit difficult.' She took a compact from her bag and reapplied some peach lipstick that complemented her chestnut-coloured hair.

'Difficult? In what way?' Jess frowned.

'Oh, I don't know. It's just not the same in Pete's house. It's so quiet.' Carol closed her compact and managed a smile. 'You can hear the sheep in the morning, instead of the rumbling of trains. I suppose it will just take a bit of getting used to, for a city girl like me, that's all.' She smiled, but it didn't quite reach her eyes.

'Is that the only thing that is bothering you?' Jess asked, hoping her mum would open up to her.

'I'm not sure, is the honest answer,' Carol replied, finally looking into her daughter's eyes. 'Everything is so different living with another man. Me and your dad were together for so long, I'm finding it hard to live with someone else.' She sighed. 'You just sort of rub along together in a long marriage. Although maybe that was the problem. We got too comfortable, which is why he sodded off with Lisa from accounts.'

'Oh, Mum.' Jess's heart broke for her mother.

'Oh, don't worry, I'm well and truly over things, but it's made me realise how much I miss everything around here, especially you and Maisie.' Carol sighed. 'I was very flattered by Pete, and he was good for my self-esteem, that's for sure, but moving in with him? Perhaps it was a bad idea.' She shook her head.

Jess swallowed down a lump of regret, her heart breaking for her mum, who after over thirty years together never dreamt her husband would leave her for another woman. Jess was still having trouble believing it too.

She still carried the guilt of seeing her dad one day in a café with another woman, but not saying anything to her mum. He told her mum that he barely left the office, such was his workload, yet there he was smiling and drinking coffee with the woman in the café tucked down a side street. She had walked over to say hi, and his reaction was so cool as he introduced the staff member that Jess thought nothing of it. It had been the woman he ended up with.

'Oh, Mum. Do you really think you have made a mistake?' asked Jess, dreading the answer.

It had only been a few months since the school reunion, and, if Jess was honest, she did think things had moved a little quickly, but she was happy her mum had found someone else.

'He's still so good-looking,' Carol had told Jess dreamily after she had run into Pete Riley in their old school hall. 'A real silver fox if ever there was one.' She had sighed, a besotted look on her face.

Jess recalled the red roses that would arrive at her mum's door, and reservations for dinner at romantic restaurants. Her mum had sent her a selfie one evening from a skyscraper restaurant that gave a panoramic view of the city.

Now it would seem that Pete Riley was not all that he

appeared to be. No doubt her mum would tell her everything when the time was right.

'Yes, Jess,' she said to her daughter eventually. 'I think I have been far too hasty. But we can talk about that another time,' she finished, as Maisie reappeared in the lounge.

'We will definitely talk later. Are you sure you are okay?' asked Jess once more.

'I'm fine, love, really. Being here is exactly what I need,' Carol reassured her.

'Oh, and I hope you don't mind, but Maisie is having a friend for a sleepover this evening. I thought they might keep each other entertained at the BBQ,' said Jess.

'Of course I don't mind. In fact, that is probably a good idea as she might get bored otherwise,' agreed Carol.

'I can't wait for you to meet Alice. She's quite remarkable, especially for her age,' said Jess, keen to take her mum's mind off things, and really hoping she would enjoy herself.

'She sounds it. I'm looking forward to meeting her too. And the others,' Carol replied with a genuine smile.

'Can we go to the shop now, Nanny?' asked Maisie, clutching her little Minnie Mouse handbag.

'Of course we can,' said Carol, standing up. 'We'll talk later, I promise,' she said to her daughter, before kissing her on the cheek.

Jess hated the thought of her mum regretting her move with Pete. She still loved her dad but was alarmed by how selfishly he had behaved. One thing was for sure, though, her mum deserved to be happy. And if there was anything Jess could do to help her she would do it in a heartbeat. Even if it meant putting her own hopes for dating on hold for a while.

# TWENTY-EIGHT

## MARK

With a sinking feeling Mark wondered how many more meetings with his friends there would be at Wisteria House, even though there had been no viewings of the building. At least not yet. He supposed he still had enough money for a deposit on something else, but property was snapped up really quickly around these parts. Still, he would enjoy today and the opportunity to further foster his new friendships that had taken him completely by surprise.

'Welcome. It's lovely to meet you.'

Mark, dressed in jeans and a pale-green polo shirt, shook hands with Carol, as Maisie and her friend raced to the corner of the garden to look at the fairy water feature.

'Thanks, and it's nice to meet you too.' Carol smiled and blushed a little.

Jess introduced her mum to Declan, but Alice was nowhere to be found.

'Is Alice making a late entrance?' asked Jess as Mark passed bottles of beers to his guests. He was pleased the weather had turned out well as predicted, the afternoon sunny and bright.

'Yes, I called her. She said she will be here in ten minutes.

She was running a bit late today; she said something about having an appointment somewhere,' said Mark, just as the sound of the doorbell drifted through to the garden and he went to answer it.

'There you are.' Mark beamed as he answered the door and led Alice outside. She looked smart in a stylish cream linen shirt dress, accessorised with a necklace of coloured glass beads.

When introductions were made, Mark saw Carol's mouth fall open.

'You can't be Alice. Is it true you're ninety years old?' She was unable to help herself as the straight-backed woman standing in front of her looked at least a decade younger.

'I am. Ninety-one actually, and that's very kind of you to say.' Alice smiled. 'Although don't be fooled by the exterior. These old bones are feeling it a bit these days.' She rubbed her back.

'Nonsense,' said Mark, gratefully accepting a bottle of whisky from her and whispering, 'Maybe just the one later.' He didn't want the repeat of a hangover after the last time he had overindulged. 'Alice here was steering the boat out on the river last week,' he informed his guests, and they all marvelled at her spirit.

'Ah, but you don't see how long it takes me to get out of bed in the morning,' said Alice. 'Or how I have to grip onto the handrail whilst walking down the steps outside. That does make me feel old. Anyway, I am not here to talk about my aging problems.' She laughed. 'This is meant to be a party.'

'Alice.' Maisie came running over and gave Alice a hug, as her friend stood watching.

'Maisie, who is your little friend?' Alice smiled warmly at the little girls.

'I'm Libby,' said the little blonde girl with the face of an angel.

'Well, I am pleased to meet you, Libby,' said Alice.

'I have something for you,' said Maisie, running into the kitchen to retrieve her little pink handbag. She opened it up and pulled out a square of fudge wrapped in cellophane. 'I saved one for you,' she said, handing it to Alice, whose eyes were welling up.

The kindness of children never failed to astonish.

'Thank you so much. Do you mind if I save it for later after some food? And I have something for you and your friend too.' She handed them the gingerbread men she had bought. 'Although maybe you should eat a little food first too.' She winked.

'Thank you,' said Maisie, before racing off with her friend once more.

Alice glanced at them across the garden, sitting on the grass playing a game that involved patting their hands together and singing. The sound of their laughter dancing across the garden was music to her ears.

A table alongside the BBQ was soon piled with spicy chicken wings, burgers, and good quality sausages. A huge salad and buns sat alongside them, and Carol had bought a potato salad and a cheesecake.

'Sorry they are not home-made, although it is from Co-op's finest range,' she told Mark as she set the food down on the table.

They were all sitting around on plastic garden chairs that Mark had found online and ordered half a dozen from Amazon. He had retrieved an old table from the shed and covered it with a nice tablecloth for the food, and thankfully it looked quite presentable.

Carol, chatty and entertaining, charmed everyone and had Mark in fits of laughter, as she recounted tales about this and that, including customers at the Co-op when she worked there.

'One lady used to call in and occasionally bring her parrot with her, tethered to her wrist like one of those birds of prey you see at displays.' She chuckled. 'She said it enjoyed the fresh air and hated being alone.'

'You're kidding!' said Mark.

'No, it's quite true. The manager didn't mind at first, as she was usually in and out for some milk or something, but he had to ban it when it told a customer in the queue to—' She looked at the girls and continued, 'Well, you can guess what it said!'

The group laughed loudly. Alice said it took all sorts, which was so true. A day in the city and you could just about observe a whole cross section of life right there.

Mark felt a sudden gratitude sitting here and laughing with these people. It occurred to him that we never really know what is going on in other people's lives. And without taking that first step to get to know those around us, we never will.

# TWENTY-NINE

## JESS

Jess was sitting next to Declan, and their legs brushed once or twice, giving her those butterflies once more. She was sure he must have felt it too, and the way she caught him glancing at her told her that it maybe was not just in her imagination.

All the same, she wasn't sure about letting another man into her life. Could she go through the heartache again if things didn't work out? It had taken all of her strength to get her life together, juggling work and being a parent to Maisie after she split with Maisie's dad. It would have to be someone very special if she was to open her heart again.

At least her mum looked happy and a little like her old self again, thought Jess, as she observed her and Mark laughing at something together. It struck her that she had not really looked like that in quite a while and realised that it was important for her to be around good people who shared her sense of humour.

The pain from her dad's betrayal seemed, thankfully, a little easier for her mum to bear these days, and maybe Pete had been a distraction when she needed it.

There was no doubting it now, though: her mum had made a mistake moving in with Pete. However pretty the Lake

District was, with its stone houses and river running through the village, she had told Jess it just didn't feel like home.

By all accounts the problem had been Pete himself, who had presented himself as fun and adventurous in the early stages of the relationship. Despite his good looks, it hadn't taken long for him to reveal his serious, and at times, dull nature. Ironically, when Jess was young, her mother had warned her about the exceptionally handsome guys, believing they didn't try as hard, and relied on their looks. Maybe there was a grain of truth in that.

The problem was that Carol had sold her old house that was snapped up in five minutes, such was the popularity of the area. She had bought a decent car to get her to and from the Lake District and settled a credit card debt.

She had revealed to Jess that she would never be able to afford to return here with the money she had left in the bank with the current house prices and would probably be forced to rent.

Jess was delighted that her mum was having such a good evening and hopefully not thinking about such matters. She was proud to have a mother who always found the solution to things in life, something Jess herself had inherited. It was comforting to know that if life knocked them down, they would always be there to lift each other up.

# THIRTY

## ALICE

Alice was happy to sit back this evening and enjoy watching those around her have a good time. She generally enjoyed holding court and contributing to the evening a lot more, but this evening she still felt a little tired. Maybe all that sea air the other day had taken it out of her, although there was no denying that something else was troubling her.

'Are you okay, Alice?' asked Mark as he placed some freshly cooked pork and red onion sausages on to the table.

'Yes, I'm perfectly fine.' Alice smiled. 'A little tired maybe, it's been rather a long day.' She didn't need to tell him that she had recently felt a little sleepier than usual and her breathing felt a little laboured. Not when they were having such a lovely time together. And when she could see the seeds of friendship, and more, growing in this group after she'd planted them at the dinner.

It was also bothering her somewhat that she had lost a gold necklace that George had bought her for their golden wedding anniversary. She tried to tell her herself that things like jewellery were unimportant and merely possessions. You could not take them with you when you departed this earth. Even so, her neck felt strangely bare when she touched it this morning, and it had upset her having to replace the gold jewellery with a glass necklace.

She had scoured the flat this morning, but it was nowhere to be seen. It puzzled her why it would become loose after all these years and slip from her neck. It had subdued her mood far more than she might have expected it to, but she would soon bounce back as she always did. There were terrible things happening in the world right now, so in the great scheme of things losing a necklace was not so tragic, was it? she told herself.

When Mark put some music on later, and Maisie and her little friend danced around the garden, Alice's mood was instantly lifted. They waved their arms in the air and danced with such unabandoned joy that she found herself clapping along to the music and tapping her feet.

Dear little Maisie pulled Alice to her feet then and Alice found her rhythm and began to dance. Soon enough she was laughing. Children were such a tonic, she reminded herself as Carol stood up and joined in the dancing too.

Soon enough everyone was on their feet, and the look of sheer delight on the children's faces was something to behold. The sound of their giggling rang around the garden, thrilled that the adults were joining in, especially when Mark did the 'Gangnam Style' dance, that had everyone in fits of laughter.

When the adults sat down, and Mark announced in a whisper to the adults that he was 'buggered' after all the dancing, Maisie did a perfect cartwheel and Jess clapped loudly.

'Well done, Maisie! She has been practising that for so long,' she revealed to the other guests.

'What an achievement,' said Alice. 'It is certainly true that practice makes perfect.'

'Did I keep my legs straight, Mummy?' asked Maisie.

'You did! Alice is right, all of that practice has paid off.' She smiled at her daughter.

Later, as the night began to close in, and the friends grazed on the last of the buffet, they sat with drinks listening to the sound of the pretty fountain gently trickling. A row of solar lights along the garden fence had begun to quietly glow in the semi-darkness.

Talk turned to dancing, and of course the fact that Alice had been a Tiller Girl became the topic of conversation.

'That must have been exciting,' said Carol as she sipped a glass of white wine. 'I would have loved to have been a dancer, but I don't think I have the build. My legs are too short.' She laughed. 'Not like Jess's, lucky thing.'

'And yet I had no desire to be a dancer.' Jess smiled. 'Such is life.'

'Oh, it was an exciting life,' agreed Alice. 'I have met some wonderful people. But you know, the most interesting people I have met have not been famous people, but ordinary folk. Like the man who owned a kiosk near the Palladium, where me and the girls would buy cigarettes,' she reflected. 'A habit I abandoned years ago, I hasten to add. He would tell us the most wonderful tales of his homeland.'

'Where was he from?' asked Jess with interest.

'He came from Morocco. I bombarded him with questions about his homeland and one evening he invited me and a friend to his family home. It was filled with such warmth and love, and of course the food was amazing. We marvelled at all the bright colours and spicy flavours which were completely new to us, but it was wonderful. The company is far more important than the food, though. I enjoyed that evening far more than the one with Tony Bennett at the Ivy in London.'

'You're kidding.' Carol looked stunned.

'No really. It wasn't uncommon for some of the performers to take a shine to some of us Tiller Girls and ask us out to dinner after the show. I never felt physically attracted to anyone, though, apart from one but I knew he was married.' She took a sip of her drink. She would never reveal his identity but remembered feeling sorry for his wife.

'I bet you could write a book,' said Jess.

'I imagine I could,' agreed Alice. 'Although maybe not write it myself, but I would certainly have the tales for a ghost writer to jot down my memoirs.'

Maybe she ought to have done that, thought Alice. Leave behind a legacy. Her younger years were pretty exciting, she supposed, but maybe she was not famous enough to write an autobiography that anyone would be interested in reading.

As darkness descended the group headed inside and made themselves comfortable in Mark's lounge, that had a huge corner sofa. She tried not to think of how many more gatherings there would be like this. And not just with the future of Wisteria House unclear. Better just to live for today.

When Maisie and Libby began to yawn, Jess decided it was time it call it a night.

'You stay,' she told her mum, who was chatting away to everyone. It was a glimpse of the old Carol that Jess was pleased to witness. Wisteria House was starting to have that effect on everyone who passed through its doors, it seemed.

'Are you sure?' Carol seemed uncertain.

'Course I am.' Jess smiled.

'Okay, but I won't be far behind you, love. I'll just finish my drink,' she told her.

'I'll walk you to the door,' said Declan, who was dying to get Jess alone and ask her if she fancied a game of indoor golf at an immersive experience, complete with a DJ spinning club tunes through the night. He thought a light, fun evening might be the right thing for a first date, rather than a candlelit meal somewhere.

Outside Jess's flat, Declan tentatively suggested the night out to Jess.

'That sounds perfect.' She smiled. 'I've been thinking I

could do with a bit more fun in my life these days,' she admitted.

'Brilliant. I'll get it booked,' said Declan, hoping they still had an available slot.

'Night, then.' He stood a little awkwardly for a second, before leaning in and kissing Jess on the cheek, whilst Maisie and Libby giggled.

'Goodnight, Declan.'

Inside, Jess touched her cheek, and thought about how it might have felt if Declan's lips had brushed hers. Tomorrow evening could not come quick enough.

As she put the girls to bed, Jess found herself thinking about Declan. She couldn't deny the chemistry between them any longer, yet a part of her was worried. Maisie was already fond of Declan and she couldn't bear the thought of her growing used to having him around if things didn't work out between them.

In her own head, she could hear her mum's voice telling her that sometimes you had to go with the flow, otherwise you would never do anything in life. She was right, of course. She certainly didn't want to live with a lifetime of regrets.

All the same, Jess thought it right to tread carefully for the sake of her daughter. Yet despite her reservations she was really looking forward to her date tomorrow.

## THIRTY-TWO

### DECLAN

This time he did return to the party, his face beaming like he had just won the lottery.

'Here, come and join us,' said Mark, waving the bottle of scotch in Declan's direction.

'Right. I think that's my cue to head upstairs,' said Carol. 'I might have a little nightcap with Jess.' She winked. 'Thank you so much, Mark, for the invite; I've had a lovely evening.' She got to her feet, and he walked her to the front door.

'My pleasure. It was good to meet you.' He shook Carol's hand warmly before she headed upstairs.

Declan accepted one for the road, but there was no way he was going to spend the day feeling rough tomorrow after overindulging. Mark, remembering his last hangover, enjoyed one final drink too.

'What a lovely lady,' commented Alice after Carol had left. 'Jess must miss her a lot since she moved away.'

'I bet she does,' agreed Mark, who had not felt so comfortable in a woman's company in a long time. And her sense of humour! Humour was so important, yet it surprised him how many people took life so seriously. Bad things happened in life, but he believed in not letting things consume you. Although he also acknowledged that sometimes, that was easier said than done.

Alice, who had enjoyed a wonderful evening, insisted on placing the paper plates and the debris from the BBQ into a black bin liner, despite Mark's protestations. She thought it important to show manners wherever you went, something her parents had instilled in her from a very young age.

Declan insisted on walking Alice to her front door and seeing her inside.

'Thank you, Declan. And I hope you don't mind me asking, but have you thought of asking Jess out on a date?' she asked.

'As a matter of fact, yes. I have asked her out tomorrow night.' He grinned.

'Well, I am pleased to hear it,' she said, thinking what a lovely couple they would make. 'Because someone like Jess won't stay single forever.'

She thought of the early days of her relationship with George then, and the fun they had together. Jess and Declan deserved to be happy.

They said their goodnights, and as Declan sprinted upstairs to his flat, he realised that Alice was right. Jess was a real looker as well as a good person. He had better not hang about. Or mess things up. Although that might depend on how she would react when he told her about his past. If he did. At all.

# THIRTY-THREE

## JESS

'I really enjoyed that.'

Carol flopped down onto the sofa of her daughter's flat half an hour later, the two little girls flat out in bed after all their dancing.

'I'm so glad, Mum. They are a nice bunch of people, aren't they?'

'Oh, they really are,' said Carol as she accepted a cup of tea from Jess. 'And to think it was Alice who brought you all together. What a woman she is. I still can't believe her age.' She shook her head. 'And I have to say, you look happier.'

'She's remarkable, isn't she?' Jess sat next to her mum on the large sofa, both having changed into their cosy pyjamas. Jess had made up the sofa bed for her mum in her spacious bedroom.

'But I would rather talk about you.' Jess gave her mum her full attention.

'What do you want to know?' asked Carol as she sipped her tea.

'I want to know what you are going to do. You admitted you

think you have been hasty, selling up and moving in with Pete. You are obviously not happy,' she ventured.

Carol took a deep breath as she fought back tears. 'No, I'm not happy, but I don't want you worrying about me.' She sighed. 'I well and truly had my head turned by Pete Riley, the heartthrob of my high school. Maybe I was a little lonely,' she confessed, as even though her days were full between her part-time job and looking after Maisie, the silence that fell over the house in the evening was almost unbearable. 'And definitely flattered.'

'I can understand that,' Jess empathised. 'I mean about the loneliness in the evening.'

'I should have spotted the signs with your dad.' Carol sighed. 'We hadn't exactly been intimate for months on end— Sorry, I'm sure you don't need to hear that,' she said, pulling a face.

'It's fine, Mum; I'm a big girl now.' Jess smiled.

'And when I think about it, he always had his bloody phone in his hand. Even when he went to the bathroom.' She shook her head. 'And he was always nipping out somewhere too, now I think about it. Hindsight is a wonderful thing, though. But really, I am fine now, so as I said, don't you worry about me.' She gripped her daughter's hand and squeezed it.

'Oh, Mum, why shouldn't I worry about you? You have always looked out for me.'

'Well, what can I do?' Carol sighed. 'I have well and truly burnt my bridges, haven't I? As you know, I settled a few debts and bought a car out of the money from the house sale. What I have left would never buy me another house, and I would never get a mortgage at my age. Maybe I could look at a one-bedroomed flat, though,' Carol mused as it was all she needed. She would never live with another man again as long as she lived.

Jess thought of how her mum had always been so generous,

paying for lunch if they went out, or bringing little treats for Maisie. Not to mention helping with the initial rent on the flat. She reminded her mum of this. 'So now it's my turn to help you. You can stay here, if you really want to come back to Liverpool, until you find a small place of your own.'

'But you don't have the room,' protested Carol.

'We will manage. You're my mum,' insisted Jess. 'If you can put up with the sofa bed, I actually quite like sharing a room,' she reassured her. 'Although I have to tell you, the building is up for sale.'

'It is? Then I ought to look for a rental quickly in case it is sold,' she told her daughter. 'You could stay with me, if need be. I have enough for a deposit on a rented place.'

'Thanks, Mum, but for now you can stay here. Let's just take one day at a time.'

'Okay,' said Carol. 'And thank you.'

Jess knew her mum wouldn't wait now she'd made a decision. She would be looking for her own place as soon as possible; that way she wouldn't worry too much about Jess and Maisie. Whatever the future held, though, she knew they would weather any storm together.

# THIRTY-FOUR

## ALICE

Alice was feeling her age today. That was the thing with being old. Her mind was as young as the young woman she once was, high kicking her legs on the stage at the Palladium, but some days her body reminded her of the reality. She still craved adventure, though, and was on a high for a couple of days after the boat trip last Sunday, and the lovely BBQ last evening.

She had vowed to rest during the week, but ended up going shopping into town, as well as giving the apartment a good clean. It had frustrated her that she had had to stop several times to catch her breath, but she was determined to press on.

She really ought to consider getting someone in to clean once a week, but while she was still able to, she would do it. Perhaps a deep clean once a month by someone younger who could pull out the sofa and freshen everywhere up would be something to consider. And change the duvet cover. That had become a rather tiresome task of late and taken forever the last time she did it.

She had sat reading for most of the morning, before her thoughts turned to Mark.

Alice liked Mark a lot, although she did worry about him a

little. She found it sad that he was estranged from his family, especially his sister, who it appeared he had once been close to. She wondered whether he would ever pick up the phone and call her. She could not help thinking of all the wasted years between some families who no longer had contact with each other, thinking things would magically sort themselves out one day. The reality being that it would never be the case without honest communication. Maybe even the chance to forgive each other. After all, the Lord himself said that to err is human, to forgive divine.

On her trip into town, Alice had bought a bottle of good whisky, and yesterday she had walked down to Satterthwaites Bakehouse and purchased gingerbread men for Maisie, along with a freshly baked brown loaf. Alice believed in a good breakfast, and most mornings she would eat a bowl of porridge, or a slice of wholemeal toast with scrambled eggs.

She was about to head into her bedroom, when her phone rang. She listened to the voice at the other end for a minute.

'I am owed a tax rebate, how interesting. Oh, I see, you need my bank details to deposit it.' She nodded.

She had moved over to the window now and was glancing at the road outside. It was quiet at this time in the afternoon, a brief respite from the sound of cars zipping by, the occasional toot of a horn from an impatient driver. The only sound outside now was the sound of birdsong in the wide, tree-lined street.

'Well, as I haven't actually been employed for over thirty years, I find that a little hard to believe,' Alice told the caller. 'Even so, if you send me a letter through the post with all the details that would be most satisfactory.'

The caller had tried to respond, but she had already ended the call. It made her blood boil that people could fall foul of scammers in this way and was thankful that she still had her wits about her. It was the downside of online shopping, she supposed, entering personal details that fraudsters might tap into. That was the last time she would add her phone number to anything online, although she supposed it was already out there now and there was little she could do about that.

Whilst she had the phone in her hand, she decided to do something she had been putting off. It was time to make an appointment with her doctor.

As she looked out of the window she thought about her first encounter with the residents. She had first observed Mark at the cemetery from a distance tending his wife's plot, as she placed flowers on her husband's grave. She could hardly believe he was the same man who had walked out from Wisteria House the day she stood watching it. It was as if the stars were aligning. She knew Jess lived at Wisteria House, as the day she encountered her on the train Jess had walked up the path of the building as Alice continued on to her dental appointment at a nearby surgery. She had enquired almost at once about renting the apartment, and was relieved that it had still been available. Now that she was here, she had decided to put her affairs in order. Before it was too late.

# THIRTY-FIVE

## JESS

'You don't have to leave, Mum. It'd be nice to have the company.'

'It will give you a chance to get ready for your date with us out of the way,' said Carol, standing by the door.

Jess's stomach had been turning over with nerves from the second she woke up, anticipating her evening with Declan. And she wanted company to stop her spiralling. What if things didn't work out between them? It was one thing being friends and stopping for a chat on the shared landing, but a proper date. It would be awkward if things did not go well, with living so close to each other. She reminded herself then of how she felt when he stood close to her.

Her mum was taking Maisie and Libby to the cinema on South Road to watch the latest Pixar movie, before dropping Libby off home. She had board games for her and Maisie to play this evening, including Hungry Hippos that Maisie adored playing. Carol couldn't wait to spend time alone with her grand-daughter, and was trying not to think of the journey home, and the inevitable conversation that would follow.

'Thanks, Mum. I'll probably spend the whole time stressing over what I should wear,' said Jess, desperate to look just right.

'You'll look gorgeous whatever you choose,' Carol replied with a wink. 'Right, let's go.' She ushered the excited girls out of the front door.

Jess could not remember the last time she had been on a date, even with Maisie's father. They had been part of a group of friends who hung around the local haunts, and things progressed quickly to cosy nights in, often just the two of them in his flat, eating takeaways and drinking beer.

Sunday mornings had involved her standing on the touchline and cheering him on when he played football. They never really went on romantic dates, and when she became pregnant with Maisie there was even less chance of that, especially with Jess's terrible morning sickness. She dreamt of being wined and dined somewhere nice and dared to hope that if the golf date went well with Declan, she might have the chance to get dressed up and go somewhere special with him.

'Actually, I will walk out with you. I need to nip to the Coop for some hairspray,' said Jess.

As they walked down the path of the apartment block, Maisie bent down and picked something up at the edge of the path near the grass.

'What do you have there?' asked Jess as Maisie held up the pretty gold necklace.

'This belongs to Alice,' said Maisie with certainty. 'She always wears it.'

'Really? Then we must return it,' said Jess as she led Maisie to her door.

When Alice was presented with the necklace she was overwhelmed.

'Oh, my dear girl.' Alice's hand flew to her mouth. 'Where did you find it?'

'Just outside, near the grass,' Maisie told her.

Alice had been deadheading roses yesterday when she returned home, and it must have slipped off somehow, although she was bewildered as to how.

'You don't know what this means to me.' Her eyes filled with tears of gratitude as she grasped the necklace to her chest. 'I thought I would never see it again.'

'Well, it's a beautiful necklace,' said Carol. 'I would hate to have lost it. Well done, Maisie. Thank goodness for children, and their eagle eyes, hey.' She smiled.

'Oh indeed. The necklace has rather a lot of sentimental value as my late husband bought it for our golden wedding anniversary,' she explained. 'I'm so thrilled. Thank you, Maisie.' She pulled the little girl to her and hugged her.

When Alice learnt they were heading to the cinema, she insisted on giving Carol a twenty-pound note to buy them all some popcorn, before clutching the necklace and saying a silent prayer of thanks. If Maisie had not found the necklace, goodness knows where it might have ended up. It seemed God really did work in mysterious ways.

After fastening her necklace on, she stroked it, and the tears she had been holding back from the children flowed freely. She hadn't realised how upset she had been about losing it, but having it around her neck once more brought her such peace.

'Have fun,' said Jess as she left Carol and the girls and headed into the shop. She would have a little glass of wine whilst she curled her hair, as despite any reservations she may have about entering into a new relationship, she could still feel those dancing butterflies in her stomach.

## THIRTY-SIX

### DECLAN

Two hours later Declan took a deep breath and knocked on Jess's front door. He hoped she could not sense how nervous he was feeling.

'Ready? We might just make the next train.' He glanced at his watch. 'Oh, and you look lovely,' he remarked, taking in her appearance. She was wearing jeans and a red top that matched her lipstick.

'Thanks,' she said, feeling suddenly self-conscious and tucking a strand of her softly curled hair behind her ear. As they took the short walk to the train station, the scent of Declan's cologne drifted towards her in the warm summer breeze. Jess never dreamt she would live on this wide, tree-lined avenue albeit in a rented apartment. Places like hers rarely came onto the market at a price she could afford.

'Your mum's nice,' said Declan, making conversation as they walked, and feeling inexplicably nervous. Maybe things would lighten up when they got to the golf venue and had a bit of fun. At least he hoped so.

'She's great,' agreed Jess. 'I miss her a lot,' she confided as they walked.

They strolled along wide, tree-lined streets, and Jess admired the splendid mix of Victorian and Georgian houses as they turned corners.

Some of the homes had beautifully manicured front gardens and expensive-looking cars in the driveway. Jess imagined living in such a house, with stained-glass windows filling the rooms with shafts of rainbow light. She had browsed such properties on websites, daydreaming about living in one, when she had been looking for a place to rent following her divorce.

'Imagine living in one of those,' commented Declan, nodding to a particularly handsome house on Eshe Road North and tapping into her thoughts.

'I know. Although I like to think the people that live in those houses can't be completely happy,' she said and he laughed. 'Otherwise, there really is no justice in the world.'

Before long, the familiar green painted hut outside the station that offered coffees and snacks during daytime hours came into view, and Declan insisted on purchasing the train tickets.

Boarding the train, they sat opposite each other and chatted easily as the train rumbled along the familiar route towards the city centre.

Declan remembered the days out he had enjoyed on the train with his mum and his sister during the school holidays. Sometimes they would head into Southport for a day at the funfair and the amusement arcades. His mum would save a tub full of coppers to feed the machines that would churn out tickets in exchange for a small prize. Pocket puzzles, or packets of crayons and jelly sweets, were like gold to him and his sister. He took comfort in the fact that his sibling had at least enjoyed a happy childhood.

Pulling into the station, Declan glanced at his watch. They were in good time for their slot at the indoor golf, and he hoped

Jess would agree to heading to a city bar before they caught the train home.

'Wow this is some place,' said Jess when they arrived at the venue, glancing around at the colourful, mind-blowing graffiti on the walls. Street artists from all over the world expressed themselves on the walls of the urban indoor golf course as club music pumped out, giving it all an exciting but chilled vibe.

'I thought it was something a bit different.' Declan smiled, feeling happy with his choice of venue.

Jess discovered a talent she did not realise she possessed, as she struck golf balls that negotiated humps and bends, and fell straight into the hole.

'You've done this before,' said Declan, trailing behind.

'I haven't. Well, apart from the pitch and putt at Southport, but even that only once or twice.' She laughed.

They were behind a group of blokes on a stag do at a further hole, who kindly ushered them ahead. Declan hit one of his balls so fiercely it hit the ceiling, missing the hole by miles and almost hitting him on the head when it descended, having Jess crease up with laughter.

'They should give you crash helmets at the entrance,' Declan said, laughing. 'Or maybe I'm just really bad at this.'

'No comment,' said Jess, who continued to play her shots with ease. By the end of the course, passing through landscapes created from old buses, and disused rail tracks, they sat in a café area having some food and Jess clutched her winning score card.

'That was a lot of fun,' said Jess as she sipped a beer. 'And I won, so bonus!'

'I'm glad the golf was a good choice. Not so glad that you beat me,' he said good-naturedly.

'It was perfect,' said Jess, unable to remember a time just recently when she had laughed so much. Declan was such engaging company, though, it would not have mattered where they had gone on their date. She thought of her ex, who was so competitive, he would have sulked at getting such a thrashing and ruined the whole evening.

Talk turned to their respective jobs then, and Jess asked Declan if he enjoyed his work.

'I do, but I would really like to work for myself one day.' He told her all about Alice's offer of the building in Liverpool Road. 'Working for the council is a safe enough job; I just think I would like to get my teeth into something bigger,' he confided.

'That's brilliant,' Jess said enthusiastically. 'Alice really is something, isn't she? Are you going to take her up on her offer?'

'I would if I had some clients,' he told her, desperately wishing that was the case. 'Although I am doing the books for a new café around my full-time job. It's something to consider for the future, though.'

There was also the possibility of doing the accounts for a small painting and decorating company in the near future.

'How about you?' Declan asked as he sipped his drink. 'Do you like working in a shop?'

'It's an honest way to earn a living and I enjoy chatting to customers who are often lonely, when time allows. I think it's one of the reasons it is so easy with Alice,' she told Declan. 'Although one day I would like to own a little beauty salon,' Jess admitted as she sipped her beer. 'I trained as a beauty therapist when I left school.'

'You mentioned that,' said Declan, recalling the day she stood close to him and disguised his black eye. 'Will you pick it up one day, do you think?'

'A job in a salon doesn't really work around school hours, and they are especially busy of a weekend,' she explained. 'But maybe, in the future, who knows?' She shrugged.

It made Jess wonder just how many people give up on their dreams, trading a real passion for something mundane in order to have job security. Having said that, she truly believed that things came to you at the right time in life, and that you must never give up.

'Talent cannot be suppressed; it will always rise to the surface given the right opportunity,' her old teacher once told her, and she had never forgotten it. In fact, her comment had inspired one of her old classmates, who she had run into recently, a bloke with an exceptional gift for painting who married young and had a family. His interest resurfaced years later, when his kids were a bit older, so he enrolled on an art course and was now selling his paintings.

'Well, here's to fulfilling our ambitions,' said Declan, raising his glass of beer, and Jess tapped hers against it.

'I'll drink to that,' she said, and blushed as he smiled.

An hour later, having strolled in the direction of the train station along the city streets, they were seated in a cool cocktail bar, with jazz music gently playing in the background, sipping espresso martinis.

'I've had a really lovely evening, Declan. Thank you,' said Jess, her shoulders relaxing more and more.

'It isn't over yet.' He looked into her eyes, and as he moved in closer his heart began to race. He leant over and kissed her on the lips that thrilled him even more than he expected it to, every nerve in his body tingling.

'I hope that was okay,' he said, as Jess looked around a little self-consciously.

'It was fine. Lovely, in fact. I am just not one for public displays of affection.' She tucked a strand of her softly curled hair behind her ear.

'Me neither,' said Declan, taking hold of her hand. 'But I couldn't help myself, I've been dying to do that all evening. If not longer.'

# THIRTY-SEVEN

## JESS

After finishing their cocktails, they strolled hand in hand to the train station and during the journey home, Jess found herself wondering if Declan might invite her into his apartment. And what would she do if he did? She didn't want to arrive home too late, despite her mum telling her not to rush back and that she should go and enjoy herself.

She found herself thinking about the last time she had been to bed with a man and realised it was over three years ago. It had been a disastrous encounter that Jess preferred not to think about, after she had spent the evening in Chester at a hen party. She had never been into casual encounters, especially as she always had Maisie to consider.

Departing the train, they walked along the familiar tree-lined road beneath a bright moon, with white stars studded against an indigo sky. Every now and then, Declan would squeeze her hand and smile at her, and her stomach would do a little somersault.

As they turned a corner close to the apartment, two blokes walked past, and Jess could not help noticing that Declan visibly jumped.

'You okay?' asked Jess as they walked on.

'What? Yeah, fine, I just wasn't expecting them to be there, that's all. The streets are usually so quiet at this time,' he explained, but she noticed him turn around and glance at the blokes, and that one of them had turned around too.

It was dark so maybe he'd just seen movement out of the corner of his eye. And he wasn't from around these parts. By the time they had arrived back at the apartments, Jess could not help noticing that Declan's earlier mood had shifted.

'Thanks for tonight, Declan; I had a really great time,' she told him.

'Me too.' He smiled, but he seemed distracted.

They were standing on the landing outside her apartment and if Jess was expecting a passionate kiss or an invitation into Declan's place, she was about to be disappointed on both counts. Instead, Declan kissed her lightly on the lips and said goodnight before heading to his own flat.

As Jess undressed for bed, her mum and Maisie fast asleep, she felt deflated. Was Declan regretting kissing her like that at the cocktail bar? Or maybe it was something she said? And why did he seem so jumpy when the two blokes emerged from around the corner earlier? One thing was for sure, for some reason, he had turned cold on her, and she had no idea why.

She tried not to dwell on things as she wanted to spend a nice morning with her mum tomorrow before she headed home. Sleep never came easily but eventually her tiredness gave way to a fitful slumber. Tomorrow was another day that she hoped would turn out well.

# THIRTY-EIGHT

## JESS

'Morning, love.'

Jess opened a bleary eye to her mum placing a cup of coffee on to the bedside table. She glanced at her phone, which showed a time of just after eight thirty.

'Thanks, Mum. Why didn't you wake me? I bet Maisie has been awake for ages.' She stretched out her arms before gratefully taking a sip of her drink.

'Oh, don't worry, she woke at seven and is currently watching a cartoon. I thought you deserved a bit of a lie-in. So, how did the date go?' her mum asked, plonking herself on the end of the bed, ready to hear all about it.

'It was great,' said Jess, painting on her best smile.

There was no need to tell her mum that she had felt confused at the end of what she thought had been a perfect evening. And that kiss at the bar still sent her into a spin every time she thought about it.

'Will you be going out together again?' asked her mum, excited for her daughter.

'Hopefully, yes, but we haven't arranged anything yet. I guess he is literally only across the landing, though.' She forced a smile.

Would Declan ask her out again? Jess wondered, hoping that he would. She went over the events of the evening in her head, the fun they had had at the golf, their loud laughter ringing out, and the easy way they seemed to connect with each other. She recalled the drinks in the cocktail bar, the kiss, and the feeling of floating on air she felt as they walked home beneath the stars. Had she imagined that he had enjoyed it all as much as she had? He seemed so tense on the walk home.

'So how was the cinema?' asked Jess, the rich coffee reviving her with every sip.

'Noisy.' Her mum laughed. 'Dozens of over-excited kids squealing every time the bad guy came onto the screen. Maisie and Libby loved it, though. Now, what would you like for breakfast? Unless you fancy a walk to a café? My treat.'

'I wouldn't mind a little walk. I'll take a quick shower, then we'll set off. And breakfast is on me,' she told her mum firmly.

When she was ready, she said to her mum, 'I will just knock and see how Alice is. I felt she seemed a little tired yesterday, although maybe that isn't so surprising at her age.'

'Of course.' Carol smiled. 'She can come with us if she fancies it.'

Jess was surprised to see Alice open the door in her dressing gown and looking a little weary.

'Are you okay?' she asked anxiously.

'Truthfully? I have felt better. I am afraid I have a chest infection,' she informed Jess.

'Alice! Why didn't you say something?' said Jess.

'Oh, don't worry about me.' Alice batted away any fuss. 'I have some antibiotics from the doctor and have been drinking plenty of water. I am sure I will be just fine in a few days.'

'So did you go to the doctor alone?' asked Jess, feeling bad for her friend.

'I took a taxi. The surgery is only up the road,' Alice explained.

'Can I get you anything?' offered Jess. 'Something to eat maybe, is there anything you fancy?'

'I don't have much of an appetite, but I do have some fresh soup in the fridge if I get hungry, so don't worry.' She gave a little cough into a tissue.

Jess couldn't bear the thought of her being all alone in her apartment. She quickly texted Mark, asking if he could call in sometime this morning and literally a minute later he came out of his door.

'We are going out now, but I will call in later,' a concerned Jess told Mark.

'I'll look after her,' said Mark, ushering Alice inside and ordering her to sit down while he made a pot of tea.


After breakfast in a café not far from the train station, Carol suggested a little train trip into Southport. 'I've been saving these.' She smiled as she pulled a bag of coins from her hand-bag, as Maisie's eyes lit up at the thought of going to the arcades and playing on the machines.

'That would be lovely.' Jess felt reassured knowing Mark was spending some time with Alice so felt able to enjoy these last few hours with her mum. 'What time is Pete collecting you, though?'

Jess's heart sank when she thought about her mum and how she was regretting her move. She had only been thinking of her mum's happiness at the time, but kind of wished she had made her think a little more before rushing in and could not help but feel guilty about that.

'Oh, not until around four. We can easily be back by then. It's only ten thirty,' said Carol, glancing at her watch.

'You don't have to go back with him if you don't want to,

you know that?' said Jess, as they stood in a small queue outside the ticket kiosk ready to purchase their train tickets.

'Thanks, love, but I think I do. Besides, all my clothes are there, and so is my car. We came down in Pete's car. I'll sort things, though, don't you worry,' she tried to reassure her daughter.

'You don't think he will be angry with you?' asked Jess, slightly concerned for her mum.

'I don't know.' Carol frowned. 'I shouldn't think so, but then I really don't know much about him at all, now I come to think of it.' She sighed. 'He doesn't seem to be an angry type, though.' At least she had seen no evidence of it.

'But you think things are definitely over between you?' asked Jess as they wandered over to the platform. She kept her voice down so Maisie could not hear.

Jess simply couldn't bear the thought of her mother staying in an unhappy relationship because she thought she might be a burden to her. She had been nothing but a brilliant mum, always there for Jess and Maisie, even when she was going through her own pain after Jess's dad had left.

'I do, love,' she told her daughter, before they boarded the train that was rumbling towards the station. 'And please, don't worry. I'm a big girl now.' She winked.

They had a wonderful time in Southport, Maisie excited by her haul of gifts from the streams of pink tickets pouring from the machine. She was thrilled with her new soft toy, a pink elephant to go with the dozens of soft toys she already had in her bedroom. They went to the ice-cream parlour afterwards and enjoyed ice-cream sundaes dripping with chocolate sauce.

It was almost three o'clock when they headed back towards the station, passing the throng of holidaymakers and shoppers out in force as the sun beamed down.

Turning a corner past some high street stores, Jess noticed a familiar face. Her heart sank when she saw the bloke hold the door of a restaurant open for a woman as they both headed inside.

'Is everything alright, love?' her mum asked. 'You look as though you have seen a ghost.'

'What? No, I'm okay, thanks.' She painted on a smile. 'Maybe I shouldn't have eaten all that ice cream.'

'It was a bit indulgent but lovely, though, hey,' said Carol as she stopped to admire a pair of dusky-pink kitten-heeled shoes in a shop window.

'Do you think I am too old for those shoes?' asked Carol, debating whether to buy them or not.

'Absolutely not,' said Jess. 'Anyone can wear a kitten heel.'

They headed inside the shop, and after trying the shoes on, Carol made a decision to buy them.

'You look pretty, Nanny,' said Maisie as Carol looked in the mirror, and viewed her feet at various angles.

'We should go somewhere nice for dinner some time so you can wear them,' Jess told her mum, even though her mind was suddenly elsewhere.

'Do you know, I think I will wear them now,' Carol said to the assistant as she popped her trusty trainers into a bag. 'Why do we need a special occasion? Being here with my two favourite girls is as good as it gets.' She winked.

'You should treat yourself more often, Nanny; you always treat us,' said Maisie as she slipped her hand into hers.

'Maybe I will.' Carol smiled. She was suddenly filled with the reassurance that whatever happened in the future, the three of them would be alright.


'Are you sure you're alright, love?'

They had returned home now, and Carol was filling the kettle to make a cup of tea before she left.

'I am. It's just that...' She waited for Maisie to leave the room before telling Carol what she had seen earlier in town.

'Don't go jumping to conclusions, love, there's probably a very simple explanation,' Carol reassured her daughter. 'Did he kiss her or something, is that why you're puzzled?'

Thinking about it, he hadn't even kissed her on the cheek; he had just smiled in greeting as he opened the restaurant door.

'No, but she was dressed really smart for a Sunday afternoon. It looked like she had made a real effort.'

'And Declan?'

'Not especially. Jeans, smart T-shirt.' She shrugged. Thinking about it, he wasn't really dressed up at all.

'There you go, then. Didn't you tell me he's an accountant? Could it have been a meeting with a client?' Carol suggested.

'I never actually thought about that,' said Jess, although maybe it was unlikely on a Sunday, and he definitely wasn't dressed for that, although she supposed he could conduct business any day of the week.

It was out of character for Jess to feel remotely jealous, but the events of last night would confuse anyone. One minute Declan was kissing her and saying he had been dying to do so all evening, the next he was giving her a perfunctory kiss goodnight outside her front door with no plans for any further dates. Maybe the woman was an ex, who Declan realised he missed after spending time with her. Whatever the reason, she was not about to play those games; she had been hurt before and now she had Maisie to think about. She would ask Declan what was going on when she next saw him.

Just over an hour later, Carol hugged Jess goodbye, and Maisie hugged her so hard it almost brought a tear to her eye. She was already desperate to return to her family permanently.

'I'll see you very soon.'

Pete had stepped inside briefly, refusing a drink and glancing at his watch, saying they had better get going if they were to miss the evening traffic. As they left, Jess almost ran after them, telling her mother to stay right now, but she stopped herself. Her mother would need to collect her car and her belongings as she had pointed out. Besides, it was only fair for her mum to have a proper conversation with Pete. However difficult that might be.

As the car pulled away, Jess brushed away a silent tear that had slid down her cheek. It had been lovely having her mum around for a few days. She hadn't realised quite how much she had missed her.

She tried not to dwell on things but dearly hoped her mum would be alright and that Pete wouldn't take things too badly when her mum told him she was leaving. Did she really know him well enough to know how he would react?

As she tidied around and put some washing on, she also wondered how long she would be doing such things here in the apartment. *Life throws curveballs sometimes,* she thought to herself as she sat with a cup of tea in the kitchen, watching her washing go around in the drum. *And other than try to be strong during difficult times, there really isn't much we can do about that.*

Mark was satisfied that Alice was on the mend. She had eaten all of the chicken stew he had made, and even a little bread.

Jess, Declan and Mark had a group chat now to make sure one of them popped in regularly to check on Alice. To the point of her having to shoo them away after complaining that she had no chance of recovering if her sleep was constantly disturbed, albeit with a grateful smile on her face. So he'd left her to it a little.

Despite her assurances that she never needed anything, Mark was just heading out to the newsagent to buy a magazine for Alice, when he noticed someone step out of a red car.

'Lynn, what are you doing here?' asked Mark, shocked, yet pleased to see his sister standing in front of him.

He hadn't recognised the car parked outside the block of apartments, as the last time they had spoken her car had been black. It was a reminder of how quickly time passes, and how quickly things can change.

They stood facing each other for a few seconds, before Mark threw his arms around his sister.

'Maybe we ought to go inside.' She smiled.

In his flat, Mark made coffee, and as they chatted she revealed the real reason for her visit.

'It's Mum,' she said, cupping her coffee cup.

'What about her?' was all Mark could think to say.

'She's in hospital,' Lynn told him.

Mark admonished himself for selfishly thinking that she had come to see him out of a genuine desire to do so. He had hardly done anything to rectify things between them, after all.

'What happened?' asked Mark, thinking that maybe his mother had suffered a fall.

'She has recently been diagnosed with dementia,' said Lynn, sighing deeply and placing her cup down onto a coffee table. 'She was staying with me, but things are a bit difficult. Social services are looking for a suitable home for her to settle into as she appears to be getting worse.'

Mark wasn't sure how he ought to react to the news. He felt a wave of regret as well as guilt that Lynn was shouldering the burden of caring for her.

'Dementia?' he said, quietly absorbing the news.

'Yes. I suspected as such to be honest,' said Lynn. 'She had become very confused. When she started asking me when we were going to the shops, not long after we had returned home, I knew I couldn't ignore things any longer,' she explained. 'Then a couple of days ago, she left the grill on that went up in flames, whilst I nipped out to pick Kyle up from college. Thank goodness for the smoke alarms you made sure we had fitted.' She smiled.

Mark quietly digested the news. He recalled fitting the smoke alarm in his sister's house, which all felt like such a long time ago.

'She has deteriorated so rapidly these last couple of weeks. Sometimes she does not even seem to recognise me.' Lynn stifled a sob.

'That must be hard,' said Mark softly.

'It's horrible. And I know you are not close, and this might sound wrong, but I just thought you might like to see her, before her memory disappears altogether, or before she—' She broke off, her voice cracked with emotion.

Mark placed his own coffee down and pulled his sister into a hug and her tears flowed freely.

'I'm sorry,' she said when they pulled apart, and she dabbed at her eyes with a tissue.

'Don't be sorry,' he comforted her. 'I'm the one who should be sorry for not helping with Mum more. Sorry for not being there for you and Kyle.'

'I'm guilty of that too. Not being there for you, I mean, especially after losing Di. We are a right pair, aren't we?' She wiped her mascara-streaked face with a fresh tissue from a box on the coffee table.

'You have a busy life,' he said kindly, thinking of his sister's punishing shifts working as a nurse, unable to afford to take early retirement. 'Me not so much, but maybe we all ought to try a bit harder,' he admitted. 'But it is no good apportioning blame. Life gets busy. Days turn into weeks, and the good intentions to make contact are suddenly months behind you.'

It was a strange situation, thought Mark. There had been no falling out as such, but they had slipped from each other's lives like a sun obscured by a cloud, waiting for the day the cloud would pass, and the sun would beam down once more and all would be well with the world. Of course, that kind of thing never happened in real life. Not without someone putting in the effort.

'You always were the voice of reason,' said Lynn, smiling at her big brother, who she had missed so much. Maybe he was right. Blaming one another never solved anything; moving forward was the key. She was pleased she had come here today.

She had no idea if Mark would visit their mother, but perhaps it was more important that *they* were back in contact with each other. She hoped that regardless of the situation with their mother, this would not be the last she would see of him for a while.

'I'm glad you came, Lynn, and you shouldn't be shouldering the burden of looking after Mum all by yourself. I will go and see her,' he said, curling his hand around his sister's and squeezing it.

'I won't lie, though, I'm not sure there is much point.' He sighed. 'She never seemed to like having me around, but I will help if I can.'

'She was troubled.' Lynn tucked a strand of hair behind her ear. 'I don't think she was aware of the impact her actions were having on you.'

'Don't make excuses for her.' Mark tried to keep any sharpness out of his voice, as he did not want tensions between them already.

'I'm not,' said Lynn gently. 'It was wrong how she treated you. I didn't notice it too much growing up, but as we got older...' She paused and sighed deeply. 'I could see that she was always a bit harsher with you.'

The confirmation that it had not been in his imagination left him feeling empty and angry all at the same time. Why the hell should he go and see this woman who was a stranger to him now? His memories of the way she had treated him would never be erased. He owed her nothing.

He could not help but think of Alice then. He owed her nothing either, but knew that he would be happy to help her in a heartbeat.

'Well, I thank my lucky stars I met Diane,' he said eventually. 'I was shown what true love really was then,' he admitted.

He had been almost on edge when they first met, just waiting for something bad to happen. A snide comment, a criticism, anything that would attempt to reduce his self-worth. But it didn't. Instead, he was showered with love and affection.

Even if he messed up in some way, Di would kiss him and laugh, telling him not to worry about it and reminding him that we all messed up occasionally.

He had barely known what to do with her warmth, and pushed back a little at first, but Di chipped away at his armour. Thank God. She showed him what true love really was.

'I know. Oh, Mark.' A tear rolled down Lynn's check. 'I always loved you, although, of course, a sister's love is not the same as a mother's.'

'And I loved you too,' said Mark.

'She told me once that you reminded her so much of our father,' said Lynn eventually. 'It was wrong, but I just think she found it difficult.'

'What, difficult to even look at me?'

'I don't know. God, was she really that bad?' Lynn asked tentatively.

'Most of the time, yes.' A rush of emotion threatened to spill over and turn Mark into a quivering mess. He'd known that his father, who had died when Mark was a young boy, had beaten his mother regularly in drunken rages. He knew that he looked just like him, so maybe his presence brought those memories to the surface for her, although it was hardly his fault.

'Do you know, I asked her once if she thought she treated you differently,' Lynn continued.

'And?'

'She said something about mothers usually being closer to their daughters,' said Lynn.

'That sounds about right.' He shook his head, unsurprised that she was not prepared to acknowledge her behaviour. 'Maybe I will never know. Anyway, I don't want it ruining today.' He mustered up a smile. 'It really is good to see you.'

'And you,' Lynn said, smiling in return. 'But maybe for your own peace of mind you might want to tell her how she made you feel?'

'I guess I could do, but what good would it do? Give her the chance for some sort of deathbed apology?' Mark remained unconvinced. 'But maybe I will think about it.'

Truthfully, Mark didn't think he needed any kind of closure. He had resigned himself to the way things were a long time ago. But maybe he would do it for Lynn, if that was what she wanted. He couldn't help wondering what Diane would say, if she were here.

'Anyway, as it is almost lunchtime, do you fancy something to eat?' offered Mark, smiling at his sister. 'I think I have perfected the perfect Spanish omelette, even if I say so myself.'

'Then how can I refuse,' Lynn replied as she sank back into the deep sofa.

After grabbing a magazine from the shop and quickly delivering it to a grateful Alice, Mark headed into the kitchen with a bunch of emotions swirling around in his head. He had been so surprised, yet happy, to see his sister, even though the news of their mother had thrown him into turmoil.

He still felt unsure about going to visit his mother, but if she died, as Lynn had all but pointed out, he would be denied the opportunity of having a conversation with her.

Not for the first time, Mark wished that he could have had a mother like Alice, who had been denied the opportunity to have a child of her own. Life really could be cruel sometimes.

Perhaps he would go and say a final goodbye to his mother after all. Maybe it would bring them both some peace of mind. And he knew that Alice would approve.

The day seemed to be dragging in the supermarket. Monday was always a little quiet in the shop, but it was going at a snail's pace today, the time on Jess's watch hardly moving every time she glanced at it.

The tills were quiet, so she was replenishing shelves with fresh sandwiches and snacks in the fridge section, part of meal deals ready for the lunchtime shoppers.

'Penny for your thoughts?'

A middle-aged colleague pulled Jess out of her daydream, after she had absent-mindedly placed a box of Scotch eggs in the drinks section.

'You've been miles away all morning,' said her co-worker as she took the food and placed it in the correct section of the fridge.

Try as she might, Jess had been unable to stop thinking about the kiss in the cocktail bar. Surely Declan must have thought about it too? She could not recall the last time a kiss had given her goosebumps like the ones she had felt. She had also been thinking about the house sale, and could feel the beginnings of a headache.

'Oh my goodness, what am I like? I am just tired I think,' replied Jess, who had tossed and turned in her bed last night going over the events of Saturday evening.

A part of her wished she had never agreed to go on a date with Declan. Her life was fine with Maisie, despite her occasional longing for some company in the evening. Things were uncomplicated and Jess liked it that way. Maybe there was something to be said for keeping yourself to yourself.

For the first time she wondered whether it might be a good thing if the house sale forced them to go their separate ways, despite the small matter of finding somewhere else to live.

'Then go and grab a coffee; I'll take my break later,' said her co-worker kindly.

'Thanks, I might just do that,' said Jess gratefully.

She had half expected to run into Declan this morning, but there had been no sign of him. He was clearly regretting Saturday night but didn't have the courage to tell her. She hoped he was not deliberately avoiding her. She would rather he came straight out and told her he didn't think there could be anything between them, for whatever reason, rather than have blurred lines.

As she sipped her coffee in the canteen she decided that when she eventually spoke to him she would not mention seeing him in Southport, as what would be the point? Better off to find out early that he was a player. There was no way she would let anyone into her and Maisie's life who was unreliable, no matter how handsome they were.

*This is why I have stayed single for so long,* Jess thought to herself as she sipped her strong coffee, hoping it might help her get through her shift. She had survived this long without a man in their lives and that was not about to change any time soon.

# FORTY-ONE
## DECLAN

Declan decided to call in sick this morning. He had barely slept a wink last night and ended up with a bad stomach, although perhaps he had worked himself up over nothing.

He hated the thought of that being the case. He was made from stronger stuff than that, but the guys he had walked past near the train station on his date with Jess had looked familiar, even in the dark. He could not bear the thought of having to look over his shoulder when he went out. His life was peaceful around here. He wanted it to stay that way.

More than anything, he was worried he had screwed things up with Jess. He had gone cold on her at the door when they had said goodnight, and he could sense her unease, but his head had been all over the place. And after that he'd avoided her, even when looking after Alice.

Although still in Merseyside, his old neighbourhood miles across the city felt like a world away from Blundellsands, with its wide, leafy streets. Here people sat on benches in local parks reading books rather than doing drug deals. If it was the bloke he thought it was, he had no right being in a place like this.

He would be lucky if Jess gave him the time of day after the abrupt end to their evening on Saturday, he thought to himself as he made himself a coffee, and sat staring into space.

At least popping in and checking on Alice had distracted him a little and thank God she was almost better now. She was certainly made of strong stuff, he thought to himself. And at least she would not have the upheaval of searching for accommodation just now, as the house was showing no sign of being sold quickly.

He idly flicked through TV channels to find something that might distract him, but his mind kept reliving the events of all those years ago.

He had decided to call a cousin from his old neighbourhood who he had lost contact with, and asked to meet her in Southport, which, despite her initial surprise, she had agreed to. Chatting to her over lunch ought to have put his mind at rest, yet he still felt spooked. He wondered if he always would.

As he sipped his coffee he told himself to get a grip. He'd paid his dues, and surely if the guy had recognised him he would have done something about it, rather than walking away? Years had passed, he reasoned, telling himself that he really ought to stop imagining things. His cousin had pretty much told him the same thing. She had last heard that the family in question had moved to Ireland.

Glancing at his watch, he realised it would be a few hours before Jess returned from work, when he would go and have a word with her. He had enjoyed every minute of their date, Jess was a lot of fun, and he had clocked the looks some blokes gave her when she walked into a room, which was hardly surprising. She was a stunner, and he prayed he hadn't screwed things up with her. And that kiss. He hadn't felt anything stir inside him like that for a long time.

He dropped some bread into the toaster, then found a documentary on Netflix about a one-time footballer who had beaten a gambling addiction and settled down to watch it. It made him realise that addiction came in all forms, as he thought about his sister.

Following her death he had wished he had a switch in his brain that could erase all memory of his sister. Then he might have avoided the gut-wrenching pain he felt. Especially after nightfall when the thoughts would creep in and prevent him from sleeping.

Running had helped him in the months following her passing. Plugging in his earphones and pounding the pavements to a good beat had preserved his sanity. Even during the small hours, he had occasionally gone for a run whilst the city slept. It soon became a habit.

He recalled a time when he had stopped at a bench in the early hours of the morning, and howled with grief, thankful that no one was around. Night running became his thing. His safe place until he felt ready to do it during daylight hours once more.

He fancied a bit of fresh air, though, so shrugged on his jacket and decided to head out for a walk, before grabbing some milk from the shop on the way home. And if he did encounter someone from his past, there would be no mistaking them away from the dark shadows of the night.

He thought about going to see Alice before he spoke to Jess, as she would know what to do, without a doubt, but decided against it. This was his mess, so he needed to be the one to fix it.

# FORTY-TWO

## ALICE

'Morning, Declan,' said Alice as she was leaving her apartment. 'How are you?'

'I didn't sleep much last night. I think I might be coming down with a bit of a virus,' he explained, not wanting to divulge the real reason for him feeling unsettled. 'I am just off out for a bit of fresh air.'

'Oh dear. Well, I hope you feel better soon,' she said kindly.

'So, where are you off to?' he asked Alice.

'The cinema. And don't worry, I am not overdoing things; my taxi will be arriving any minute now.'

Declan stood several feet away from her at the foot of the stairs.

'Oh, by the way, how did your date with Jess go?' She turned to him as she was about to open the front door.

'Good. Great actually, although I think I might have messed things up,' he found himself telling Alice.

'Really. How so?' She frowned.

'Bit of a long story. Maybe I will tell you when I feel a bit better,' he suggested.

*I am turning into a right wuss*, he thought to himself, *lying awake with a bad stomach over a woman.* Jess was really special to him, though, he realised that now. He had not met anyone like her in a long time.

'Hmm,' said Alice, finding it strange to be conducting a conversation across the hallway. 'Then maybe you ought to speak to Jess, sooner rather than later,' she advised.

'I will do.' He nodded.

'Or perhaps you could post a letter through her door? Especially as you are worried about passing on a virus,' she suggested. 'Disinfect your hands first.' She winked.

He felt a bit guilty feigning a virus, but he hadn't wanted to quite tell Alice the whole truth.

'A letter?' Declan could not remember the last time he wrote someone a short note, never mind a letter. He wasn't even sure what he would say. Did anyone write letters these days?

'Yes, why not? I have always believed in the power of the written word,' said Alice firmly. 'And I find it much nicer than a text, don't you think? It takes a lot more effort.'

'Thanks, Alice, maybe I will give it a go.' He smiled. 'Anyway, enjoy your cinema trip.'

'I'm sure I will. There is a special screening of *Brief Encounter* this morning. One of my absolute favourite films.' She smiled.

Alice had read about a pensioners' morning at The Plaza and decided to go along. She was beginning to suffer from cabin fever holed up in her apartment for two days but was grateful to have made a full recovery. She read that there would be free tea and biscuits and imagined herself being the oldest customer there, or at least one of them. She thought it important to embrace new experiences, otherwise you were simply waiting for God. She might even make a new friend, she told herself as she got ready that morning, choosing a smart black dress and her favourite red blazer.

'Bye, then, take care,' said Declan.

'Thank you. And do let me know how things go with Jess,' she said, ready to step outside.

'I will do.'

Alice walked carefully down the half a dozen steps, holding on to the handrail as she did so. Even though Alice's recent blood work at the doctor's had not revealed anything immediately life threatening, there was no doubting that she was becoming frailer.

Her doctor had asked her to blow into a tube on her recent visit, and the result had shown a slight problem with her breathing.

'Which is probably not that unusual,' the kindly GP had told her.

'At my age,' Alice added.

'And especially with a slight chest infection.'

He had told her then that she probably had the beginning of heart failure.

'Which I realise sounds dramatic,' said the doctor. 'But it just means the heart is working less efficiently, as it does not pump blood around the body as quickly as it once did,' he explained.

'I see,' Alice had said as she digested the news. 'So my dancing days are definitely over, then?' she joked.

'Maybe. Although moderate exercise is recommended. I would suggest carrying on with the walking that you seem to enjoy. Keep moving,' he had advised. 'You are obviously strong; just know your limits.'

'Of course,' she had told him, reminding herself that she probably needed to hire that cleaner sooner rather than later.

# FORTY-THREE

## MARK

Mark felt like he was walking in lead boots as he made his way along the magnolia painted hospital corridor with the stark strip lighting.

Lynn had called him that afternoon, telling him the hospital had called to tell her that there had been a rapid decline and their mother had developed pneumonia. They didn't think she had long left.

The whole place could do with a spruce up, that was for sure, the only hint of luxury being the coffee shop and M&S on the ground floor, thought Mark, trying to distract himself from what awaited him.

He had stopped outside the shop earlier, briefly wondering if he ought to take something for his mother, but then hadn't Lynn told him that she was barely conscious? Even so, he went inside and mindlessly bought some grapes and a magazine that she would never read.

Several times he had thought about turning back and walking away. After all, what was the point in being here after all this time? Especially if she was barely alive. There would be no resolution with his mother now, even if wanted it.

Just as he was seriously considering heading back to his car, he spotted Lynn entering the building through the glass door at the front entrance and striding towards him.

'I was just about to text you,' she said to him as she glanced at her watch. 'I thought we were meeting outside; I have been waiting for you.' She seemed mildly annoyed.

'Were we? Sorry,' he said, before giving her a hug. 'Maybe I was considering doing a runner?' He raised an eyebrow.

'Were you really?'

'Not sure. Probably. Anyway, I am here now, so I might as well get this over with.' He exhaled deeply, his stomach beginning to turn over with nerves.

He knew it must have sounded heartless as he uttered the words, yet he was unable to suppress his inner thoughts. But if Lynn wanted him here, then he would be. For her.

'Come on,' she said gently, taking her hand in his as they took the lift to the second floor. 'And it might actually be good for you to see Mum.'

'You mean give me some closure?' He looked at her doubtfully.

'I'm not sure what I mean.' Lynn sighed. 'It's just that I know you, and I imagine you would always regret not being here. I read somewhere that the person who cuts another person off goes through a lot of pain themselves, despite the decision they make,' she said as they headed upwards in the lift. 'Although maybe I am completely wrong.'

Was she right? It hadn't been easy when he first kept his distance, that was for sure, but lately? These days he hardly thought of his mother, although sometimes she would appear in his dreams. Di would have said it was a sign that there was unfinished business between them.

Lynn curled her brother's large hand in hers and found his palms to be slightly clammy.

As the lift doors opened and they walked into the corridor,

they passed a porter pushing a patient on a trolley, and Mark felt his heart rate increase. Was it too late to back out now?

As they entered the ward, that was silent apart from the exchanges of a couple of nurses at a workstation, Mark inhaled the distinctive odour of a ward full of old people, despite the efforts of cleaning staff and their disinfected mops.

They both applied some hand gel from a wall-mounted bottle, and one of the nurses turned and smiled at Lynn, before she approached her and Mark.

'Your mum has deteriorated very quickly,' said the nurse with a kindly tone. 'It's good that you are both here.' She patted Lynn's arm, glancing at Mark. 'Please let me know if you need anything.'

As they entered the side ward, Mark took an intake of breath when he took in the sight of the old woman sleeping. She seemed shrunken somehow, almost like a child, lying there in a blue cotton gown, her grey hair pulled back in a band. How could this frail old woman have made him feel so bad?

'Is she conscious?' he asked a different nurse, who was about to leave the room having checked his mother's vitals.

'In and out,' she said softly. 'I don't think she has long left. But talk to her. We believe the hearing is always the last thing to go in a person.'

Mark sat on a blue plastic chair beside his dying mother, his sister on the other side.

An hour or more went past, and Mark sat not really knowing what to do. He watched Lynn grasp his mother's hand, and talk to her about this and that, but he never felt inclined to do the same. What on earth would he even talk about? Maybe he would tell her what a terrible mother she had been to him, and how she had made him feel, so perhaps he was right to stay silent.

She would utter a few clear words here and there, but she was mainly incoherent.

He felt a stab of regret that he had not had a conversation with his mother whilst she was still able to answer some of his questions. Would she have taken accountability? he wondered. Perhaps even given a reason why she had shut him out so coldly? Maybe it would have at least provided him with some understanding, but now it seemed fate had denied him that opportunity.

Mark decided to head off for coffee for himself and Lynn, and when he returned Lynn was dabbing at her face with a tissue.

'Are you okay?' he asked as he handed her a coffee.

'I am.' She nodded. 'Maybe I just didn't want to cry in front of you,' she said, gratefully accepting her drink. At least the coffee chain in the entrance hall downstairs sold decent coffee, rather than the unpalatable stuff from the machine.

'You never did, as I recall.' He smiled.

Mark remembered a time she had fallen from her bike and later needed stitches in her knee, when she was around nine years old. He had been playing football with his friends nearby in the park, and she held in her tears until she had got home, racing to her bedroom with Mum in hot pursuit brandishing a strip of plaster, before she sobbed loudly.

Mark resumed his seat beside his mother, as her hand slowly slid towards him.

'Mum?' he asked, wondering if she could hear him. The nurse did say a person's hearing was the last sense to go. If she answered him, what would he say next?

'She was talking a little when you went for the coffee, but I couldn't quite make out her words. I know she said your name,' said Lynn, looking at her brother.

Mark slowly curled his hand around his mother's, when she suddenly gripped it with the strength of someone much younger and stronger. The action was so unexpected, he had to catch his breath.

No words were exchanged, but in that moment as she continued to grip his hand, he felt something. It was something that he had not felt from his mother for as long as he could remember, although he did recall moments of affection when he was very small, he supposed. He was about six years old when he was hospitalised with whooping cough, his mother torturing herself for missing his vaccination. She had been there every time he opened his eyes after sleeping, and there were hugs. He remembered the hugs.

He was suddenly blindsided by a surge of love. Maybe his mother was merely demonstrating a desperate attempt to cling to life, holding on to his hand like that, but he liked to think there was some remorse there. Or at least regret. Maybe even some love. If he believed that, then he could move forward.

'You okay?' asked Lynn softly, and he nodded, not trusting himself to speak.

They sat, hands entwined as her breathing became shallow and Lynn held on to her other hand.

When she finally slipped away, Mark felt something he could not quite explain, but at once he felt a little lighter. Was it forgiveness? Some sort of spiritual awakening maybe? Whatever it was, Mark suddenly felt at peace. He hadn't even realised he was carrying anything inside of him, until the stress left his body like a river bursting its banks and flooding the nearby streets.

His mother had slipped away quietly on a bright Monday afternoon, whilst the world kept moving around them.

His final goodbye to his mother had not been as traumatic as he had feared. He hoped she would rest in peace.

He thought of a scripture then relating to death. He could not recite it exactly, but it was something about finding peace as we slip away. He was starting to think of Alice as family too, especially after this. He wanted to be there for her, his neighbour – also, his new friends, his sister and nephew.

So, later, when they had dealt with the formalities at the hospital, and Mark felt like losing himself out on the water in his boat, he thought better of it. His sister needed him now.

'Fancy a drink?' asked Mark as he gestured to a pub across the road.

'Maybe a soft drink, as we are both driving,' she reminded him. 'Besides, I need to speak to Kyle later, although I don't want to ruin his long weekend.' She sighed. 'He's gone on a fishing trip with a few friends.'

'When is he back?'

'Tomorrow. Maybe I will leave it until then.'

'Probably best. There is nothing he could do now anyway,' said Mark wisely. 'I will be in touch about the funeral arrangements, then I would like to take you and Kyle out on Sunday for lunch, if you are free.'

He was determined not to let his sister disappear from his life again.

'I will be.' Lynn smiled. 'And I will make sure Kyle is too.'

# FORTY-FOUR
## DECLAN

Declan screwed up the third sheet of paper and tossed it into the bin. He was hardly Shakespeare and, as he recalled, English was just about his worst subject at school. He had barely scraped a pass in his exams. He preferred logic and order, so accountancy was a perfect career choice.

Maybe Alice was right about the power of the written word, but he preferred to talk to someone face to face.

So what was stopping him? As soon as Jess arrived home from work, he decided he would knock on her door and apologise for his behaviour on Saturday night. He wondered whether he should have spoken to her yesterday but recalled her saying that she would be spending the day with Maisie and her mum. Maybe after she heard what he had to say, though, she would never want to speak to him again.

There was only one way to find out. Declan told himself to man up, as he grabbed his key and headed next door. After knocking for several minutes, he gave up. It was a pleasant evening, so perhaps Jess and Maisie had headed to the park, or to feed the ducks at the pond. He would catch them later.

He was about to head inside his flat, when Jess called him from across the hall.

'Sorry, I was getting changed,' she told him. 'Maisie was playing on her iPad. I tell her never to open the door if I am busy.'

'Of course.' He smiled as he walked over.

'Did you want something?' asked Jess as politely as she could.

'I did.' He nodded. 'I wanted to talk about Saturday night.'

'Right,' she said, glancing down at her toes. The dusky-pink polish on her toenails was all but chipped off and she wished she was wearing her slippers.

'I probably should have called yesterday, but I knew your mum was staying,' he explained. 'And I also might have lost my bottle,' he admitted, just as Maisie appeared in the doorway. 'Maybe we could go for a walk or something?'

'Well, I have to dry my hair and get dressed, so if you can give me half an hour,' she told him.

'Of course, I'll call back then.'

'Where did you lose your bottle?' Maisie asked Declan, which put a smile on the face of both Jess and Declan. 'Because Mum always says to retrace your steps, and you should find what you are looking for.'

Jess and Declan exchanged a glance.

'I will remember that, Maisie.' He smiled at the adorable little girl.

Inside his apartment he made himself a cup of tea, then sat down and thought about what he would say to Jess later.

He at least needed to apologise for his shift in mood on Saturday night. Jess deserved that at least.

# FORTY-FIVE

## ALICE

Alice had enjoyed the most wonderful day.

She had chatted to two sisters, both in their eighties, at the cinema and felt a little stab of regret that she could not enjoy a day out with her own sister these days.

Still, she was thankful that they had a lot of memories to look back on.

One day in particular stood out in her mind, when they had taken a day trip when she was eighteen years old, and her sister fifteen.

They had gone to Soho and giggled at some of the shop fronts that advertised topless shows.

That night they giggled about it in the kitchen, and when their mother asked them to share the joke, they had made something up about recalling a comedy act they had watched performing in a street. Or some such excuse. She could not quite remember now.

She did remember them furtively sipping a cocktail in a bar, though, her sister looking much older than her fifteen years, and no one asking for identity cards in those days. They both looked like sophisticated young women of the world, with their carefully applied make-up, pencil skirts and high heels.

It had probably been quite risky when she thought about it now, especially when two men had approached them and invited them to a party. She dreaded to think what might have happened had they accepted, but thankfully Alice had the sense of duty to look after her younger sister, despite her mild protestations and calling Alice a spoilsport.

Alice thoroughly enjoyed her video calls over her tablet with her family, especially her sister. Her nephew had shown her what to do on his last visit, and it had been a godsend what with the miles between them. She would tell her all about her cinema trip next time they spoke.

The sisters at the cinema had been great fun, and afterwards they had invited Alice to join them for a bite to eat at a café on South Road, which she had gratefully accepted.

When they had cheerfully said, 'Same time next week?' before they departed, Alice confessed that she was a little particular when it came to films. Even so, they swapped numbers, and agreed to hopefully meet up somewhere else, or at the cinema if she found a film she was keen to watch.

It had proved to Alice yet again that if you were able to get yourself out into the big wide world, then you would probably end up having a chat with someone. She felt dreadfully sorry for those people who were unable to do so.

When she called her sister later that evening she was pleased to learn that the weather had also been fine down south and that she had spent the day at the seaside.

'It was even warm enough for an ice cream.' Her sister had smiled, and it had made Alice smile too. Her sister would refuse an ice cream on anything other than a really warm day, saying it always left her feeling cold otherwise.

Alice felt cheered that they had both enjoyed a pleasant

day, when her thoughts turned to Declan. She hoped that he was feeling better, and that he had managed to sort things out with Jess. They really would make the loveliest couple, she thought to herself as she went to make her supper.

# FORTY-SIX

## JESS

'We were actually thinking of going to the park as the weather is so nice,' said Jess, when Declan knocked at her door.

'Yay! Park!' said Maisie, jumping up and down.

'Just for an hour, as you have homework before bed, remember.'

Jess thought that maybe Maisie ought to have done it when she was in the shower rather than playing a game on her iPad but never mind.

'Homework at her age?' said Declan.

'I know. It is literally only writing a sentence, though. Handwriting practice,' she told him. 'And actually, I think it's a good idea if habits are formed early. I was traumatised by the amount of homework we were given in high school.' She laughed.

'True enough,' said Declan, remembering the same thing, along with the excuses he gave when he had forgotten to do it.

The still warm sun at six thirty bathed Jess's arms as she walked along in her sleeveless dress.

It seemed to be the beginning of a heatwave according to the weather reports, so tomorrow evening, if the weather was fine, she would walk the fifteen minutes down to the beach with Maisie and maybe have an ice cream. It was the beginning of summer, and soon enough, the beach would become their regular haunt.

Maisie loved the beach and would often bump into some of her school friends during the summer months. Jess enjoyed it too. Plus, it hardly cost anything. Jess would take a bucket and spade in a rucksack, along with a sandwich and some water. The only outlay would be an ice cream, and maybe a coffee for herself from the van that was a permanent fixture throughout the summer months, near the usually crowded beach.

They would return home before sundown and Maisie would sleep like a baby. It was so different in the winter months, when the evenings would often drag. She wished the summer could go on forever.

Jess and Declan fell into step as they headed towards the park, chatting about their respective day.

Declan told Jess that he had taken a day off but never went into details.

'Did you do anything nice?' she asked as they neared the park that was already busy with people enjoying the sunshine.

'Not really.' He shrugged. 'I went for a bit of a walk this morning, but mainly I just felt like a day chilling. It's days like this when a garden would be nice, though,' he mused.

'I know what you mean.' Jess smiled. 'I don't know what we would do without the park.'

As soon as they arrived at the play area, Maisie dashed off to an empty swing, thrusting her legs high into the air until she gained momentum.

Declan and Jess took a seat at a nearby bench, and Jess watched Maisie, her hair flailing behind her as she enjoyed herself, without a care in the world.

'She's really good,' observed Declan. 'I thought she would have been asking for a push by now.'

'Give it time,' said Jess. 'Although she is quite independent.'

Her daughter had dressed herself as soon as she was able to, and often resisted Jess's help, especially when it came to brushing her hair, but Jess would insist. There was no way she would allow her into school with tangled hair, despite her protestations.

A couple of minutes later, Maisie spotted a friend from school and made a beeline for her.

She waved over at Jess, before ascending the steps of the wooden climbing frame that had a rope bridge running across it, and a slide on the other side.

'I'm sorry about Saturday night,' said Declan, as Jess kept half an eye on her daughter.

It hardly seemed five minutes ago that Maisie had fallen from the very same frame, yet determinedly attempted it again the next time they had visited. Jess realised how much her confidence had grown as she now negotiated the rope bridge with ease.

'I won't lie, I was a bit puzzled by your sudden change of mood,' Jess admitted.

'I can explain that,' he said, his heart rate beginning to increase. If there was to be any future for them, he would have to tell her the truth.

'And just so you know, I really enjoyed our date,' he told her.

'I did too,' said Jess.

She wondered whether he would tell her about the woman she spotted him with in Southport.

It was not the meeting with his cousin in Southport he was about to explain, though, but rather his reaction to the two blokes in the street, when he heard someone call Jess's name.

'I thought it was you.' She smiled at the woman in the jeans and white T-shirt, with a young boy in tow.

Jess introduced her as a friend from work, and the two

began a conversation. After a minute or two the boy tugged at his mother's hand and pointed to an empty swing.

'I'll have to go.' She smiled, as the little boy raced off. 'See you in work sometime. Bye, Declan, nice to meet you.'

'She seems nice,' said Declan.

'Oh, she is, we used to work together but do opposite shifts now. We have a catch-up on our works nights out.'

Which Jess realised were not as often as they once were, although even then they were maybe around once a month. She would never leave Maisie with anyone other than family, and her mum did not live locally anymore. At least not at present.

She supposed she should have asked her dad to be a little more involved in his granddaughter's life, although last time she had mentioned visiting his new place, Maisie had shaken her head. Jess was not sure why, as his new partner had treated her well by all accounts, even buying Maisie some little toys and a new hairband, yet she had not been keen to return.

They had ended up meeting at the beach for a walk, which seemed to be the pattern of things, although less frequently these days, she realised with regret. She wanted her father to be a part of her and Maisie's life, yet deep in her subconscious it felt like a betrayal to her mum. She would never forget witnessing her mother's raw grief when her long marriage came to an unexpected end. Or the guilt she carried after seeing her father out with the other woman.

'It's nice that you socialise with your work friends. My colleagues don't do that so much,' Declan told her. 'Although I do play Sunday football with a couple of the blokes and go for a drink now and then.'

He had lost touch with some of his friends from his younger years when he had moved away from his old neighbourhood.

He was about to talk to Jess about the evening they had gone out, when Maisie come haring towards them asking politely if she could have an ice cream from the nearby van.

'I'll get these,' said Declan, standing. Her little friend joined them, and after sending her to check with her mum if it was okay to have one, the two children sat on the grass enjoying their ice creams with flakes poking out.

Maybe the park was not the place to discuss personal matters, he considered, especially as Maisie was having such a good time. He did not want the mood to change.

'Anyway, back to Saturday night,' said Declan. 'I just need you to know that I had a great time. And I would love to do it again.'

'Would you?' she asked him. 'I felt like you regretted it at the end of the evening,' she told him honestly, remembering how disappointed she had felt when he never moved in for another kiss.

'I'm sorry.' He exhaled deeply. 'I didn't mean to confuse you like that.'

'Did it have something to do with the blokes who walked past us near the station?' asked Jess. 'You seemed a bit unsettled after that as I recall.'

'In a way, yes,' he admitted. 'Look, I was wondering, could I call over once Maisie is in bed and explain properly. That is all I want to do,' he said, holding his hands up. 'Nothing else. I really enjoy spending time with you, Jess. And I owe you an explanation.'

'Okay.' She nodded. 'I will text you when Maisie's asleep, although with these light nights, it seems to get later.' She rolled her eyes.

'Fine.' Declan nodded, just as Maisie reappeared and asked him to spin her and her friend on the roundabout.

'Not too fast after that ice cream,' said Jess. 'Unless you want to deal with vomit.'

'Noted,' said Declan as they all strolled towards the roundabout.

# FORTY-SEVEN

## DECLAN

Maisie had flaked out just after eight, so Jess sent Declan a text to tell him so.

She looked in on Maisie in her bed, mouth open sleeping soundly after all her running around in the park and felt a rush of love. She could imagine a time when Maisie would not be a small child and idly wondered whether she would ever have any more children.

Jess instinctively plumped up the cushions on the sofa, when she heard the doorbell ring ten minutes later.

'Hi.' Declan stood on the doorstep, and looked almost nervous, compared to how he had appeared earlier.

'Come in, then,' said Jess, opening the door wide.

'Fancy a drink?' she asked once they were seated in the neat lounge.

Declan felt like downing a stiff whisky but thought he had better keep a cool head.

'I am afraid I only have white wine, or maybe you would like a coffee?' she asked brightly.

'Coffee is fine.' He smiled as he felt the nerves in his stomach roll. Was there anything to be achieved by telling Jess why he had been shaken by the appearance of those guys? He could invent a story about not feeling well at the end of the evening, he thought, as he steadied his breathing.

Once more, he told himself that the events of the past had nothing to do with his present, or his future. And with each day that passed, he realised that he wanted his future to be with Jess.

'So,' said Jess, sitting at the end of the sofa after she had made his coffee and got herself a white wine. 'You said you wanted to talk.'

'That's why I am here,' he said as he took a sip of his coffee. 'The thing is I had a great evening, as I have already told you,' he said, placing his cup down onto the nearby table.

'But?'

'But you were right, I thought I recognised the two guys near the train station.'

'Right,' said Jess as she took a sip of white wine. 'I knew something was up.'

She met his eyes. 'So who were they?'

'I'm not sure they were who I thought they were.' He sighed. 'But let's just say that if they were someone from my past, I would not have wanted them to know I lived around these parts.'

'Surely if they recognised you they would have said something?' She frowned.

'That's what I had been thinking,' he admitted. 'So I arranged to meet my cousin in Southport to ask her a few questions.'

*The lady entering the restaurant with him*, thought Jess.

'She kind of put my mind at rest, reminding me that allegiances change, and in fact the guys I thought I saw had moved away from the area.'

'What guys?' Jess frowned.

'They used to be drug dealers, bottom feeders for a drug

lord in my old neighbourhood,' Declan explained, his heart hammering.

'And what does that have to do with you?' she asked uncertainly.

'Have you ever heard the name Tony Callaghan?'

'I have, yes. It was all over the local news when he died. Hit-and-run, I believe,' she said, recalling the incident.

'I heard it was an accident,' said Declan. It had been an accident, there was no doubting that.

'Well, whatever, I hate to say it, but he was no loss to society,' said Jess. 'I think whoever did it probably did the police a favour.' She shook her head. 'Would you believe I ended up at his wake,' she told him, recalling the day she and a friend had met for lunch, and finished up in the pub.

'You knew him personally?' asked Declan, shocked.

'No of course I didn't know him.' She shook her head. 'We had no idea the wake was going to be taking place at the pub. We headed off as soon as it filled up with his cronies,' she explained. 'We thought the mourners would not be the most savoury group to be around, especially after the drinks started flowing.'

There was a pause.

'So why exactly are we talking about Tony Callaghan?' she asked him, as he stared into space and wondered why on earth he had ever started this conversation.

'Declan?' she repeated, a frown crossing her face.

'Because I killed him,' he replied, not daring to meet her eyes.

Jess felt like all the air had vanished from the room. She thought of little Maisie fast asleep in her bedroom, whilst she was sharing her sofa with a killer.

'You killed him,' said Jess, when she finally found her voice.

'It was an accident,' he told her as he met her gaze. 'You must believe that.'

'But I remember reading about that,' she said as the realisation dawned that Declan had been all over the regional news more than five years ago. 'The person did time in jail. That was you?'

Declan could see the colour drain from her face.

'The police thought I had motive, which to an extent I guess I did. But I swear on my own life and everyone I know, that was not the case,' he said calmly. He could feel his hands trembling as he reached for his coffee. 'But, yes, it was me. I was handed a five-year jail sentence for causing death by dangerous driving, reduced to three years for good behaviour,' he confessed, with a mixture of shame and a pleading look flitting across his face.

'You killed Tony Callaghan?' said Jess, her mouth gaping open, hardly able to take it in.

'By accident.' He sighed. 'I can explain if you will hear me out.'

Jess found herself nodding, not trusting herself to speak.

'I remember the day as if it was yesterday,' Declan told her. 'There was a low autumn sun in the sky, and it was blinding. As I drove along the street just outside the town centre my vision was blurred. Tony walked out between two parked cars with his phone stuck to his ear. Neither of us saw each other until it was too late,' he explained, before putting his head in his hands.

Jess took a glug of wine as her thoughts whirred around in her head. He had to be telling the truth. Declan was no cold-blooded killer. Was he?

'So why did the police think you might have had motive?' asked Jess, her head all over the place.

Declan told Jess all about his sister's problems with drugs.

'Tony was the kingpin, so I guess the police thought I had deliberately targeted him after what happened to Kelly.' He still caught his breath at the mention of her name.

'Oh, Declan, I am so sorry,' said Jess, instinctively taking her hand in his. 'Did she...?'

'Die? Yes.' He nodded. 'Ketamine. She reacted badly. I hadn't even realised she had moved on to that kind of stuff.'

He shook the picture from his mind of her lying in a hospital bed hooked up to machines.

'So you see, when I told the police about what happened, even though every word of it was true, I had a really hard time getting them to believe me. The jury too.' He sighed. 'In the end, I didn't get a more serious prison sentence, but if I had, I'm not sure I'd have blamed them, given the circumstances.'

'I take it there was no CCTV or dashcam footage?' asked Jess. She could not begin to imagine what Declan and his family must have gone through.

'There was a camera further along the road that captured nothing. Dashcam wasn't such a big thing back then. Maybe if it was, the jury would have seen Tony talking on his phone and not looking where he was going.' He pushed away the picture of Tony falling to the ground. The one that had given him nightmares.

It all felt like too much to process. Declan had served time in prison for killing someone. Could Jess be certain he was telling her the truth about it being an accident? She thought once more of Maisie lying innocently in her bed, oblivious to the evils of the outside world.

She prayed that she would be a happy teenager and not remotely interested in drugs. All she could do as a parent would be to advise her daughter and be there for her, as she imagined Declan's mother was. It was hard to imagine the pain Declan's mother must have endured, losing a daughter and a son too when he served his prison sentence.

Jess needed to get her head around the news that Declan had just imparted.

'I know this is a lot to take in,' said Declan, reading her thoughts. 'So I will go now. I just thought you deserved the truth,' he told her as he stood to leave.

At the door he stopped and searched her eyes. 'I like being around you, Jess, and I hope I haven't screwed things up. But I don't want any secrets between us,' he said, and despite the revelation she still felt something stir inside her when he stood close.

'I appreciate it.' She smiled.

'Well, I will leave you to it. I know it's a lot to get your head around, but I promise you it was an accident. Anyway, goodnight, Jess. Thanks for giving me a chance to explain,' he said, wondering if she would ever go out with him again.

'Goodnight, Declan.'

After he left, Jess topped up her glass and sat staring into space from the sofa, until the sky outside darkened and she stood to close the curtains. Declan's secret was huge, but how many of us harboured secrets, however small?

# FORTY-NINE

## JESS

Jess supposed she ought to have spoken to her mother first, but she knew she would only have worried about her. Besides, she had enough going on in her own personal life right now.

Instead, after mulling over Declan's bombshell all week, she dropped Maisie off at a school friend's party on Saturday afternoon and invited Alice over for a cup of tea. She would have suggested a walk to a local café but did not want anyone listening in on their conversation.

'This is a nice surprise,' said Alice, taking a seat on the sofa in Jess's stylish lounge.

She felt momentarily guilty at having one of the garden flats as Jess was living here with a young child, but maybe that would change in the future.

It occurred to Jess that it was the first time Alice had been inside her flat and vowed to do it again. Alice had become a good friend.

'I probably should have asked you over before now,' she told Alice truthfully, as she placed some tea and shop-bought fruit cake down in front of her. 'And I will do in the future, but today I need your advice about something, whilst Maisie isn't here.'

'Well, whatever the reason, I am pleased to be invited.' Alice smiled. 'And your flat is beautiful. You certainly have an eye for décor,' she said kindly as she glanced around the cosy room.

'Thank you.'

'So what is on your mind?' asked Alice as she sipped tea from a chunky grey mug, rather than her usual bone china cup.

'I hardly know where to start.' Jess sighed, taking a seat on a chair opposite her. 'It's about Declan.'

'Declan?' Alice frowned slightly. 'Has something happened?'

'You could say that,' said Jess. 'We were getting along really well, and our date was fantastic.' She smiled briefly. 'But then he went cold on me. I thought it was strange when he said a quick goodnight, and it seemed he couldn't get away quick enough.'

'I see,' said Alice, giving no indication that Declan had already mentioned the disastrous ending to their date. She wondered whether he had written Jess a note, as she had suggested.

'Did he say why?' enquired Alice.

'He did. He came to see me and explained everything.'

'And?'

She told Alice all about the men near the train station, and how they had unsettled Declan. She went on to tell Alice all about Declan's sister.

'How dreadful,' said Alice sympathetically.

'And then he dropped a bombshell,' she told Alice as she took a deep breath. 'He told me he had killed someone.' Jess could barely believe the words that were coming out of her mouth. It had thrown her into turmoil.

Alice's face was expressionless as she placed her cup down onto the coffee table. Perhaps it was just as well Declan had spoken face to face with Jess.

'He killed someone?' Alice asked.

'Accidentally apparently. The guy was a local drug baron,' explained Jess. 'Anyway, Declan swore it was not deliberate, and was eventually convicted of causing death by dangerous driving rather than something more serious. Which is pretty miraculous, given the circumstances around his sister's death.'

'And you don't believe it was an accident?' Alice raised an eyebrow.

'That's the trouble. I don't know what to believe,' said Jess, a faraway look in her eyes. 'I want to believe him, of course I do, but...'

Alice picked up her slice of cake from her plate and silently chewed. It was very good cake that Alice suspected had come from the M&S Food Hall.

'Then I can imagine that to be a very difficult position you find yourself in,' said Alice. 'And I am afraid there is not much advice I can give, if that is what you were hoping for.'

It was exactly what Jess had hoped for. Alice's wisdom seemed to know no bounds, but of course she was right. How could she advise her about something like this? Jess would need to figure out for herself if she believed Declan or not, if there was to be any kind of a future together.

'But what I will say is this,' said Alice. 'Do you really believe Declan is capable of mowing someone down in cold blood?' she asked candidly.

'No, no I don't.' Jess shook her head. 'But then emotions can tip people over the edge, can't they? Maybe he saw red and stepped on the accelerator when he spotted Tony.'

'Perhaps that is the case. Or maybe he was blinded by the sunlight and did not see him until it was too late. Call it a freak coincidence. Some may even call it karma,' she said. 'But whatever it was, Declan has paid the price for his crime. Should he be made to pay for it forever?' she asked gently.

'No, of course not.' Jess sighed. 'And maybe if he had been

imprisoned for something else, I might find it a bit easier to accept. But he was convicted of killing someone. I have Maisie to think of,' she told Alice. 'What if I make a terrible mistake, inviting him into our lives?'

'Oh, Jess, I am afraid only you can decide,' said Alice, placing her teacup onto the table. 'But what I see in Declan is a fine young man and I am not usually wrong about people, I will say that.'

'I see that too,' admitted Jess. 'And he is so lovely with Maisie.'

She thought of how he always had a joke or a ready smile for her daughter, who appeared to be pretty taken with him too.

'Then if I were to give you any advice, it would be to take things slowly,' advised Alice. 'People's true colours do not usually take too long to shine through. Go on dates, get to know each other. I believe people move in together far too quickly these days,' said Alice.

Jess was inclined to agree and she thought of her mother and Pete Riley.

'And as you rightly say, you have Maisie to think of,' continued Alice. 'Trust your instincts. And if you need a babysitter, I am available.' She winked.

Jess went and threw her arms around Alice, unable to stop herself.

'Thanks, Alice. You are right, Declan has paid the price for his crime, and I will take things slowly. Perhaps we all need someone to have a little faith in us.'

'And to invite us over for tea and cake, which is quite delicious, thank you,' said Alice.

'M&S Food Hall's finest,' Jess said with a grin. Just as Alice had suspected.

As they finished their drinks and continued their chat, Jess realised that true friends came in all shapes and sizes.

During their chat, Jess told Alice all about the time she had spotted her father in the café with the employee he ended up leaving her mother for.

'Sorry to burden you with all my problems,' Jess said with a deep sigh. 'I suppose I have been carrying a bit of guilt around with me.'

'You are not burdening me whatsoever,' Alice assured her.

'Thanks. I guess I don't have an awful lot of people to confide in,' she admitted. 'I just keep thinking that if I had said something they might have made a go of things. I still haven't told Mum to this day,' confessed Jess.

'Now that is something I may be able to offer an opinion on,' said Alice. 'The fact is, he saw you that day, so if anything was going to make him feel guilty and reconsider his relationship with the other woman, then surely that would have been the turning point.'

'I suppose.' Jess shrugged. 'So do you think I should ever tell Mum?'

'I'm not sure there is any point, other than getting it off your chest,' advised Alice. 'Your father chose his own path. Besides, he was only having coffee with a colleague, as far as you were concerned. There is nothing unusual in that. I am sure your mum would understand if you did ever decide to bring it up. But it is up to you.'

'Thank you, Alice.' Jess was comforted once more by her words of wisdom. Tea and cake were the least she could provide for a wonderful friend like Alice. What a godsend her moving into Wisteria House had been.

# FIFTY

## ALICE

Alice had returned home after spending a pleasant couple of hours with Jess and was sitting in her wicker rocking chair, beneath a cherry tree and listening to the trickling waters of a water feature.

The tree had been delivered from a garden centre, after she had ordered it online. When she mentioned it to Mark, who seemingly now had a taste for gardening, he had kindly come along and planted the tree in the ground.

Sometimes, when she sat beneath it, she wondered how many more spring blossoms she would live to see. But then she didn't really mind. She hoped future tenants would enjoy the tree growing in all its glory and not rip it out if they remodelled the garden.

She also wondered who had chopped down the oak tree she and her sister had planted as a child. Unbelievably, it had been planted from an acorn, lovingly nurtured in a pot before planting it in the ground. When they left the house, it was already two foot high.

As a young woman, she thought of knocking on the door and asking if it was still there but never managed to do so before she headed off to London. Maybe the tree had been destroyed during the blitz, even though the house had remained. Who knew?

Jess had told Alice that she should probably ask her over for tea more often, but then, perhaps Alice ought to do the same. Especially as she had one of the garden flats. It did not have to be a grand affair like the dinner party, but a cup of tea and a chat was always nice.

She would invite them over soon. She was sure Maisie would enjoy sitting in the rocking chair and looking at the garden ornaments that included pretty toadstools and little fairies dotted around the borders of the lawn.

She could feel the sun warming her face, and almost lulling her to sleep, when she heard her telephone ring. It was her oldest nephew, Callum, telling her he would be in Liverpool on Monday, and was she free for lunch.

'But, of course! How wonderful.' Alice could barely contain her excitement. She loved both of her nephews dearly. Callum was such fun to be around, and she always left his company feeling completely invigorated.

Callum told her he would be visiting a prospective client in the city to discuss the refitting of floors in the large music arena.

'It's a huge job,' he told her excitedly. 'I could probably pay off my mortgage with this one job alone,' he confided.

Callum was the sales director of a large flooring company and often earnt generous bonuses.

She often thought that Callum, unlike his brother, was a little frivolous with money. She knew that he often threw lavish parties and seemed to be constantly jetting off somewhere on holiday. 'Splashing the cash,' as her brother-in-law would say. Maybe she would pay for their lunch, she decided.

They chatted for a while longer, after which Alice rustled herself up a simple tomato pasta supper before settling down to watch a film.

She had recently discovered a TV channel that showed black and white movies and was thrilled to find a Bette Davis film that was due to start at six o'clock. It might also distract her from the house sale that dominated her thoughts. Maybe she would have a little glass of wine to go with her dinner. It was Saturday evening after all.

# FIFTY-ONE

## DECLAN

It was early evening when Declan bumped into Mark as he was making his way in through the sliding glass doors of the Co-op.

'Hi, how are things?' Declan asked Mark amiably, his cheerfulness hiding the knot of tension he felt in his stomach after his conversation earlier in the week with Jess.

'Good, thanks. Actually, I am pleased I have run into you; I was about to give you a knock later,' said Mark.

'Oh right, what's on your mind?'

'Actually, do you fancy a pint?' asked Mark.

It was a warm Saturday evening, and Declan had no other plans.

'Sure, sounds good.'

They walked the short distance to the pub on the corner, and sat in the outside beer garden, a pleasant area with blue painted fencing and pot plants bursting with colourful blooms.

Nursing their pints of draught beer and cold lager respectively, they sat in the warm sunshine at a wooden picnic-style table and chatted.

'I got talking to a guy at the marina a week or so ago, but it completely slipped my mind till today,' said Mark as he sipped his beer. 'He mentioned he was looking for a new accountant.'

'Oh yeah?' said Declan with interest. He could probably fit another part-time client around his hours, but only just. As well as the café on Liverpool Road, he had recently started doing the books for a small painting and decorating firm, owned by one of his football friends. Still, the more clients on his books, the closer he would be to setting up himself.

'Have you heard of Sanctuary Bathrooms?' Mark asked Declan.

'I have,' said Declan. 'They have a shop in town, don't they?'

He had browsed the huge showroom just outside the town centre that catered for every taste in bathrooms with his mum one Saturday afternoon. She had bought a new shower, and he had dreamt of the day he would own his own place, and have a huge bath, like the one displayed on a granite floor in the corner of the room.

'And another two showrooms across Merseyside,' Mark informed him. 'As well as a huge warehouse. Ken told me the business has grown massively over the years.'

Declan felt a tingle of excitement. This was a massive deal. Sanctuary Bathrooms was a huge organisation, and the director was looking for a new accountant.

'So, what's the deal with his current accountancy firm?' asked Declan. His thoughts had already turned to the office in Liverpool Road, just waiting for him to set up shop.

'Cooking the books seems to be the essence of it. Embezzlement of some sort,' Mark told him. 'He's up in court next month.'

Declan gave a low whistle. 'Wow, so I am guessing he wants someone sooner rather than later?'

'I would imagine so. Anyway, I told him to hang fire until I had a chat with you,' explained Mark. 'Are you still thinking of setting up by yourself?'

Declan had told Mark all about Alice's offer of some office space when they had chatted on the evening of his BBQ.

'I would love to, for sure. I just haven't had a big enough account to pack in my job with the council,' he told him as he sipped his drink.

'Until now,' said Mark. 'Anyway, I told Ken I would give you his number, so you can at least arrange a meeting with him.'

Mark pinged Ken's number to Declan, and they tapped their pint glasses together.

'Hope it all goes well, mate,' said Mark. 'It seems a shame to let that office space go to waste.'

Declan could not agree more.

'Fancy another?' Declan offered when they had finished their drinks.

'Why not?' Mark smiled. 'It's been a bit of a week. I might just lose myself in a few pints,' he told Declan.

'I'm so sorry to hear that,' said Declan when he had returned with their drinks, and Mark told him of his mother's passing.

'Do you want to talk about it?' he asked Mark, although he sensed that was doubtful. All the same, he knew how important it was for men to talk about their problems and open up. One of the lads at Sunday football had been in a dark place a year ago and often spoke of how the football and the chats with his friends in the pub afterwards had saved him.

He hadn't really reached out to anyone when his sister died. Running had become his saviour. But at least there had been solace in that. If only everyone could find that something.

'Thanks, but we weren't close,' Mark told Declan candidly as he sipped his beer. 'I was with her at the end, though, and I am glad I was. It was more for my sister really, but it seems to have given me some peace of mind,' he admitted.

The two men sat silently for a couple of minutes, before Declan lifted his pint in a toast to Mark's mum.

'May your mum rest in peace.'

'Cheers, mate,' said Mark as he clinked his pint glass against Declan's.

'And you know, I am here if you ever do feel like you need to talk,' reinforced Declan.

They talked about the football, and this and that, and after a final drink, walked back to the apartments together, feeling relaxed and happy.

'I'm glad I ran into you; it was just what I needed,' said Mark, patting Declan on the back. It was the first time in a while he hadn't missed the presence of his wife. 'Although I think I might leave these for another day,' he said about the scotch he was carrying. 'I can't take the pace at my age. Unless, of course, you fancy one?' he offered.

'No, thanks. I will call it a night too.' Declan smiled. 'I have football in the morning.'

'In that case, goodnight,' said Mark.

'Night.'

Declan glanced over at Jess's apartment as he put the key in his front door but thought it best to leave her be for a while. He could only hope she would believe he was telling the truth about the accident.

For now, his thoughts turned to the call he would make to Ken Watson first thing on Monday morning, as he didn't want to bother him over the weekend. He dared to hope that it might be the start of something he had only dreamt about. And so much of it was thanks to the friends he had made at Wisteria House.

# FIFTY-TWO

## MARK

They had such a small family, and his mother had few living friends, so the internment at the crematorium was small and brief.

Afterwards, Mark took Lynn and his nephew, Kyle, out for a meal.

He barely recognised his nephew, with his long hair. He was wearing a black T-shirt and jeans and was attending a local music college.

'So do you get any local gigs?' asked Mark as he tucked into his fish and chips.

He felt ashamed he knew so little of his life these days. Three years could mark such a change in a teenager's life. He was determined to make up for lost time.

'A few,' said Kyle. 'At the uni mainly.'

As his nephew sipped his pint, Mark realised that the last time he saw him he had only been allowed soft drinks. Never again would he waste a second of spending time with loved ones. Losing Di should have taught him that.

Kyle told Mark a little about the music his band played, when he had asked, but he was reserved with his answers.

'Do you mind if I get off?' asked Kyle an hour later after he had taken a message on his phone. 'A couple of my mates are going into town.'

'No, you go,' Lynn said, giving her son a farewell hug. It hadn't been easy for him today. Making conversation with an uncle he had not seen in a while. He had always loved Mark, and when he had gone quiet on them, Kyle felt abandoned.

Not that Lynn was blaming Mark. He had been dealing with his own grief. And she supposed she could have reached out to him a little more too and met on neutral ground. She knew how difficult it was for him to visit her when their mother had been staying. Her nursing job had all but drained her, though, so anything else was put on the back-burner.

It amazed her how adults could lecture their kids on how to behave when they were often so screwed up themselves.

'He's a good lad,' said Mark after Kyle had departed. 'You have done a good job.'

'Thanks.' She smiled. 'And so have you.'

'Me?'

'Yes, you. Kyle adored you and Diane. He still talks of those walks in the Lake District fells when he was little. And how you taught him how to drive.' She laughed.

'Ssh, that wasn't strictly legal, that.' He pulled a face, recalling a time he had let Kyle take the wheel on a deserted stretch of beach when he was about thirteen.

'And that time you took him to the Grand Prix at Silverstone. He was the envy of his whole class that year. Not many kids his age got to do stuff like that.'

'I suppose so.' He grinned. 'Thanks, Lynn.'

'What for?'

'For those memories. Maybe I shouldn't be so hard on myself.'

'You shouldn't,' she said kindly. 'He's busy as all twenty-one-year-olds are. I barely get a look in myself these days.' She smiled. 'Which is how it should be. But I know he is thrilled at the thought of you being around a bit more.'

'Do you think?'

'I know so,' she assured him. 'Oh, and I want you to know that there is a spare room at my place,' she offered. 'Should you need it.'

'Thanks, sis,' he said gratefully.

When they said their goodbyes, Mark felt a mixture of optimism for the future and regret for the past. Never again would he waste a second of his time being estranged from his loved ones. Losing Diane should have taught him that.

As he headed home he thought about Alice's wise words. She had often talked about communication, and how love could conquer all. Her words had seemed a little idealistic when he thought about it, yet he did feel a kind of peace at his dying mother's bedside. He was glad he went.

He would miss Alice when she was no longer here, which was something he did not like to think about. In the meantime, he would drive her to Sefton Park some time to take that trip she had often talked of doing.

# FIFTY-THREE

## JESS

'Mum!' exclaimed Jess when she glanced at the customer approaching her till on Monday morning. 'What are you doing here?'

'Thought I would surprise you.' Her mum smiled as she placed her basket down at the end of the conveyor belt.

'Well. You have certainly done that,' said a delighted Jess.

'I thought I would make you and Maisie my spaghetti bolognese tonight. I know how much you like it,' she said. 'What time is your lunch break?'

'Literally in fifteen minutes,' said Jess as she scanned the items in her mum's basket.

'Great. Meet me in the Costa over the road,' said Carol as she unfolded a tote bag from her handbag and packed some mince, spaghetti and garlic bread into it. She knew Jess had a cupboard full of herbs and tins at home.

Jess thought her mum looked a little red eyed and wondered whether she had been crying. She didn't have time to think too much about it, though, as a steady queue was building at the checkout.

When she got to Costa, Jess squeezed her mum in a hug before taking a seat opposite her in the café with the red walls.

'So when did you get here?' asked Jess as she took a seat opposite her mum.

'About an hour ago,' said Carol. 'I parked the car outside your apartment. I got the train in, as I hate driving in town,' she said as she dropped a sachet of sugar into her flat white coffee.

'Will you be going back to the Lakes?' asked Jess as she took a sip of the cappuccino her mum had ordered for her.

'No,' said Carol, shaking her head. 'It's over between me and Pete. I am going to look for something to rent, and you and Maisie can come with me, if need be.'

'Oh, Mum.' Jess reached over and squeezed her mum's hand. 'And are you okay?' she asked her gently.

'Oh, I'm fine.' Carol gave her a brave smile. 'Actually, I feel like a weight has been lifted from my shoulders,' she admitted. 'More than anything, I just feel like a fool.' She sighed.

'Don't be silly,' said Jess.

'And guilty,' said Carol as she sipped her coffee. 'Running off like that and leaving you and Maisie.' She shook her head.

'Oh, Mum, don't do that to yourself. You are entitled to a life of your own,' said Jess. 'We did miss you, though,' she added quietly.

'And I missed you both too,' Carol said, her voice cracking with emotion.

'So what did Pete have to say?' asked Jess.

'Not a lot, truth be told.' Carol sighed. 'I think he knew things weren't right between us. He never tried to persuade me to stay.' She shrugged.

'You looked like you had been crying earlier,' said Jess. 'Are you sure you are okay?'

Just then a toddler threw a soft toy snake from their pram that landed at Jess's feet. She stood and passed it back to the child's young carer, who she presumed to be the boy's mum, who thanked her.

It reminded her of when she would take Maisie out in the pram and people would coo over her as she was such a cute baby. How quickly the years had passed.

'Do I look okay now?' asked Carol as she fished her compact from her bag. 'I bet I look a right show,' she said as she dabbed some concealer beneath her eyes.

'Of course you don't,' Jess reassured her. 'I was just worried you had been upset, that's all.'

'I was,' Carol admitted. 'I bawled my eyes out on the drive over here.'

'Oh, Mum,' said Jess, feeling saddened at the thought of her mum doing that all alone.

'But don't worry.' Carol held her hands up. 'Really, I am fine. I think things had built up and I just let it all out,' she told her daughter. 'A few slushy songs on Smooth Radio and I was gone.' She smiled. 'It was actually quite therapeutic.'

There was no need to tell her daughter that the break-up with her and Pete had dragged up all of the memories of the split with Jess's father. She felt like a failure somehow. Or at least a poor judge of character, but then she supposed Pete had given her a confidence boost when she needed it most. All the same, she could not help but feel that everything was her fault. She would be fine, though. Being back here with her daughter and granddaughter was exactly what she needed.

'I'm glad you're okay,' said Jess as she fished her front door keys from her bag and handed them to her mum. 'Let yourself in; I will be home about five thirty.'

'Shall I pick Maisie up from school?' Carol offered.

'Yes, that would be great. She is meant to be in after-school club, so it will be a lovely surprise,' said Jess, imagining the look on the face of her daughter when Carol arrived to collect her.

'So I am okay to stay? I will be looking for a place of my own, though, obviously,' said Carol.

'As if you need to ask.' Jess rolled her eyes. 'I have already told you, you can stay for as long as you need to.'

'Thank you, darling. I will get another key cut on the way back to the train station,' said Carol. 'Oh, and I saw Declan this morning,' she added. 'He was just heading in as I pulled up. I don't think he saw me, though.'

Jess wondered why he had taken time off work, but then it was none of her business.

'Right,' said Jess just as her cheese panini for lunch arrived at her table.

'Is everything okay between you two? You never said much when I spoke to you last,' said Carol.

'Oh fine,' said Jess, waving away the question. 'Both busy working I guess, we are bit like ships that pass in the night.' She smiled.

'So you still haven't been out on another date?' asked Carol, looking puzzled.

'No.' Jess took a bite of her panini. 'Look, I will fill you in properly later, Mum. I promise.'

'Okay,' Carol said, taking the hint not to ask any more questions.

They finished their lunch and chatted about the price of property in the area, and soon enough it was time for Jess to head back to work.

'See you later, Mum,' said Jess, giving her mum a quick hug. 'We will have a good chat when Maisie is in bed this evening.'

'We will,' said Carol. 'I will pop a bottle of white wine in the fridge to chill.'

'Looking forward to it.' Jess smiled, wondering how many more evenings they would be spending at Wisteria House. She was also not looking forward to revealing to her mother what she had discovered about Declan.

# FIFTY-FOUR

## DECLAN

Declan was not surprised that Jess had not been in touch. What did he expect? There could not be many women out there who were prepared to give a chance to an ex-convict. Not without giving it some serious thought. And she had Maisie to think about after all.

He shook his head at the thought of her just seeing him as a criminal when nothing could be further from the truth.

It had been a relief when he had secured the job with the council, although he supposed they had to be seen to be fair in their selection process. He had explained at the interview all about his having no previous involvement with the police, and how the tragic fatality of the pedestrian had been the result of an accident.

It seemed to take forever for the closing date for applications, and Declan took a driving job and applied for other positions in the meantime, but eventually he had been contacted. To his utter shock he had been selected for the appointment in the accounts department.

Declan missed talking to Jess. Even her morning routine seemed to have shifted a little, as he had not seen sight nor sound of her and Maisie. Not that he saw her regularly in the morning as he probably left before they did, but the evening was a different matter, when they would often arrive home at the same time and have a little chat.

He looked at himself in the mirror in his suit and wondered whether he should go for a more casual look for his meeting today.

Ken Watson had invited him to his home for the interview, rather than an office, explaining that he liked to get a 'feel' for someone in a more relaxed atmosphere. Did that mean he should ditch his suit, though? He took a deep breath and decided to keep the suit. Then changed his mind again. He had to get this right.

He eventually settled on a pair of chinos and a smart polo shirt, with a jacket thrown over the top. He still wasn't sure he had got it right, though, as he stepped outside and headed to his car. Did he look like he was about to play a round of golf? But then Ken did say he wanted to see someone in a relaxed atmosphere. Declan's doubts went around in his head, until he arrived at the address he was given, and decided he had made the right choice.

Pulling into the curved driveway of the huge white painted house that had space for several cars, Declan clutched his CV and knocked at the highly polished black front door with two buxus plants either side that contrasted perfectly with the exterior of the house.

A young woman of around his age opened the door, before warmly inviting him inside. She shouted for her dad, then disappeared with a gym bag slung over her shoulder.

'Declan, glad you could make it,' said Ken Watson, shaking his hand firmly as he emerged from another room.

Declan had booked the morning off work, preferring to get the interview done first thing, rather than thinking about it all day.

'Please come through,' said Ken.

Declan followed him along a hallway with a block wooden floor to a spacious lounge. Ken gestured for him to take a seat on a huge expensive-looking fabric sofa.

'Drink?' Ken gestured to a wooden sideboard with a silver tray containing an assortment of spirits.

'Or some tea, or a coffee?' asked a smiling woman of around Ken's age who had just appeared. Ken introduced her as his wife, Sally.

'I wouldn't mind a coffee, if it's no trouble,' said Declan, thinking it too early in the day for a proper drink, even though it might settle his nerves. Besides, he had come in his car.

'We will be in the conservatory,' said Ken to his wife, gesturing to the room at the end of the lounge.

It surprised Declan that Sally had offered to make coffee. The house was so impressive a housemaid would not have seemed out of place here.

A few minutes later, Declan was sitting in the conservatory with Ken, a tray of drinks and a delicious-looking carrot cake, that Ken informed Declan his wife had made, set in front of them on a coffee table.

Sitting in an easy chair and surrounded by large plants, and with the black and white chequered floor, Declan might have been sitting in a bar or café somewhere. It was a far cry from the disastrous interview he had attended last time in the offices of Jarvis and Green. The conversation flowed easily, and Ken seemed impressed by what he saw in Declan.

'So much nicer having a chat this way, isn't it?' said Ken as he sipped his coffee. 'I don't think formal interviews bring out the best in people as they are often so nervous.' He smiled.

'I agree,' said Declan, who felt completely at ease as Ken ran his eyes over his CV.

It was hard to put an age on Ken Watson. Lightly tanned, and with a thick head of greying hair, he could be anywhere between fifty-five and sixty-five years old. His wife was similarly well groomed, with perfectly styled hair and stylish clothes. It was so difficult to tell a person's age these days what with all the cosmetic treatments, thought Declan. Every time he switched his radio on in the car there were ads for some beautifying treatment or other.

'So why would you want to leave a secure job with the council?' asked Ken as he helped himself to a slice of his wife's carrot cake.

Declan knew he would be asked that. He had wondered how he ought to answer the question, without appearing greedy for money.

'I think I would like to challenge myself,' Declan eventually replied. 'I am hungry to grow a business. There is no opportunity for that working for the council, despite the job security,' he explained.

'That's true.' Ken nodded. 'I started with the same ambition. I was a salesperson originally, then one day I thought, why I am selling stuff for someone else? I literally started out by selling sinks and taps from a shed in the garden,' he divulged.

'That's impressive,' said Declan, as he thought of the size of the Sanctuary Bathrooms empire now.

'Thank you,' said Ken. 'But I believe if you have the drive and determination you can achieve pretty much anything.'

Declan could not have agreed more. Sure, it was easier if you were given a monetary handout to start up but he believed the desire to achieve something could override anything. Along with a little bit of luck. Alice was offering him premises, a gesture he was keen to take advantage of.

Once more he found it easy to visualise himself in the office, and he felt the familiar tingle of excitement. He could do the accounts for Sanctuary Bathrooms, and along with the other small accounts it would match his wage from the council, if not more.

There would hopefully be more clients, and maybe even staff one day, he thought with excitement. He realised his thoughts were running away with him again. He had not even been offered the job.

They chatted easily, and when the interview appeared to be over, Ken asked Declan the question he had been dreading.

'I notice there was a gap in your employment a while back. Any reason for that?' Ken asked.

Declan had thought about doctoring his CV, but what would have been the point? What if any prospective employers had insisted on references? In the end he had decided to leave things as they were.

'I could lie to you,' said Declan, facing Ken, 'but as you have just discovered a crook has been looking after your accounts, I don't think you would appreciate that,' he told him.

'Go on,' said Ken, a slight frown crossing his face.

*Sod it*, thought Declan. If the job was meant to be his, then it would be. He took a deep breath.

'I was in prison,' he found himself saying. 'I was convicted of dangerous driving. Someone was killed.'

'I see,' said Ken. He stood silently for a second, thoughtfully chewing his lip.

'There were no drink or drugs involved, in case you were wondering,' Declan added. 'It was a tragic accident.'

He went over the story he had recounted so many times about the blinding sunlight and Tony Callaghan not looking where he was going as he stepped out into the road. Only he never felt the need to mention his name.

'Obviously you will need to go through the books with a fine-toothed comb,' said Ken. 'Could you manage that whilst you work your notice with the council?' he asked.

Declan would work twenty hours a day if he needed to. Was Ken Watson really going to give him a chance?

'Absolutely. I have no family or commitments,' Declan told

him, and for a second, he thought about Jess. 'And that determination you mentioned,' he told Ken enthusiastically. 'I have tons of that.'

'Then in that case, I won't keep you wondering,' said Ken. 'I am very impressed with what I have seen.' He nodded slowly. 'And I am not the type of man to hold someone's past against them. You have paid your dues.'

'So?' said Declan, holding his breath.

'So, if you are interested, I would like to offer you the position.'

Declan had not realised his shoulders had been up to his ears, until he felt them relax.

As Ken shook Declan's hand firmly, Declan might as well have been told that he had just won millions on the National Lottery.

Sanctuary Bathrooms was a huge account. He would literally work every hour of the day if he had to. Opportunities like this didn't come along every day of the week. He would make a success of his new position. He could not afford to fail.

At least there was a bit of positivity in his life at the moment, what with all the worry over losing his home.

'I won't let you down,' he promised.

'You'd better not,' said Ken, with the raise of an eyebrow.

# FIFTY-FIVE

## ALICE

Alice felt a slight coolness to the air as she walked home from her appointment, pleased she had worn her red cashmere scarf tucked inside her trench coat. The cooler weather was fast approaching, and Alice looked forward to it.

Autumn had always been her favourite season. She loved how the countryside gave up its crops that had been growing in the soil throughout the summer, and how forests turned from a blanket of green to a kaleidoscope of burnt orange and amber. She relished the early nights at home, with soft lighting that reminded her of cosy evenings spent with George.

Sometimes, during the winter months, they would wrap up and take a beach walk in the afternoon before darkness fell. They would return to a hearty casserole that had been gently cooking in the oven. Even now, the thought of them doing such things together gave Alice a little pang in her heart.

'Oh my goodness,' gasped Alice when both of her nephews arrived to collect her to go out for lunch. 'You never said Liam was coming too.'

She hugged both of her nephews tightly.

'Thought I would surprise you,' Liam said with a smile.

Callum, who was approaching fifty, was thinning slightly on the top of his head, but Liam, who was a couple of years younger, still had a good head of light-brown hair.

'Well, you have certainly done that,' she said, thrilled that both of her nephews were standing in front of her. 'Are you coming in?' she offered. 'Or are we heading straight out?'

'We will get going if you like,' said Callum, clutching some keys in his hand.

Once outside, Alice was surprised to find Callum pressing a key to unlock the doors of a shiny-looking Porsche.

'You are driving? I assumed we would be getting the train,' said a perplexed Alice. Especially as the train station was just around the corner.

'I thought you might enjoy a spin in my new motor,' said Callum proudly.

'It is very smart,' said Alice as she eyed the car with the new number plate. It seemed Callum really was doing well for himself these days.

She settled into the journey, passing the familiar sights along the Dock Road as she had so many times.

One of the city teams had recently had a new stadium built, the huge outline visible in the distance. She imagined the supporters descending trains and heading there on match day. She had done the same thing herself with George, once upon a time, who had been a keen football supporter. She only went the once out of curiosity, though, as she preferred to watch the horse racing.

Soon enough they had headed down towards the Liver Building and parked up at a car park not too far from Water Street.

'I thought I would treat you both,' she said as they arrived outside the restaurant with the impressive entrance. 'I know you both enjoy a good steak.'

'You don't have to do that,' said Liam.

'I know I don't, but I insist. If I can't treat my own nephews, then who can I?' She smiled.

'You forget how many marvellous restaurants there are around the city these days,' said Liam as he glanced around the beautifully decorated restaurant.

The grade II listed building was inside a former banking hall, and boasted high ceilings, marble pillars and original timber panelling.

Their server quickly and politely showed them to their table and handed each of them a menu.

'I hope you enjoy it,' said Alice.

'This is some place,' said Callum, glancing around. It reminded him of a place down south near the river that he took his wife to on special occasions.

'The décor is beautiful, isn't it?' said Alice. 'Apparently the inspiration for this restaurant came from tango clubs in Argentina. They serve the best quality steak too.'

Alice recalled the evening she came here with George, not long after it had opened. They had sipped mojitos beneath the soft lighting and listened to Latin American music in the background. She remembered how George had loved its mixture of flamboyance and intimacy, and they had enjoyed the most magical evening. Six months later he had died but she would cherish that evening in her heart forever.

'Gaucho is a chain of restaurants now, but they still manage to retain that personal touch, I think,' said Alice. 'And, of course, they serve the best food.'

'I bet not many of them are housed in such a stunning building,' said Liam.

'I agree,' replied Alice. 'Did you know this restaurant was recently featured in a BBC series?' she informed them.

'No, but I am not surprised,' said Callum.

'So, Liam, are you still enjoying being a teacher?' she asked as they placed a drinks order. 'I imagine it must be quite a challenging job these days.'

'It can be,' agreed Liam. 'And some days, I won't lie, I dream about early retirement,' he revealed. 'But I love seeing how some of the kids can succeed, given the right guidance,' he told her. 'One of my ex-pupils is studying to become a doctor, against all the odds. There is no greater feeling than seeing that happen.'

She knew that Liam was head of the maths department at a school in a not-so-great part of town. She was impressed that he still felt the passion for his career after so many years. It was important to be happy in the workplace.

'The lad just had a real talent for maths and science,' Liam continued. 'But also a very unstable home life. I helped him to gain a scholarship to a good private college, and it opened up a whole new world. He just soared,' he said, feeling a moment of pride.

'How wonderful,' said Alice, thinking once again how everyone ought to be entitled to a good education regardless of your postcode. Thank goodness for teachers like Liam.

'And, Callum? Your job is going well, I take it?' she said as she perused the food menu.

Callum was the UK head of sales for a global flooring company.

Surely it must be, she thought to herself, taking in his expensive clothes and wristwatch. Not to mention his car. She was sure he had a different model when he had visited last time.

'Pretty good,' he said as their drinks arrived. 'Although there is always room for improvement. Or should I say more profits.' He rubbed his hands together and smiled.

The sideways glance Liam gave his brother did not go unnoticed by Alice.

'If we get the arena refit, I am looking at a great bonus,' he said hopefully.

They talked of their families and Alice smiled at a stack of photos her nephews brought up on their phones. She was pleased to learn that Liam had recently paid off his mortgage, having paid extra over the past decade.

She beamed at photos of her great-nieces and great-nephews, in their late teens and twenties now, and she supposed it would not be too long before they started having families of their own.

There was a time when Alice had considered having a social media account herself, but she preferred to have her occasional calls over a telephone, or via a tablet where she could talk to someone face to face. No wonder people chatted less to each other these days when there were so many alternative ways to communicate, she thought to herself.

Talk turned to Callum's meeting tomorrow, as well as Alice's new life in the apartment block.

'I feel truly blessed to have met so many wonderful people.' She could not help but smile when she thought of how the group had become such firm friends.

A waitress arrived then and took their orders for steaks.

Callum ordered a selection of sides that seemed a little excessive to Alice, but maybe he had a large appetite. She was eating much less herself these days, which she supposed was normal at her age.

'I'm glad you have made some new friends,' said Liam. 'Mum worried about you a bit after Uncle George died, living in that big house alone.'

'I know she did, but I am perfectly fine,' she assured him. 'But I must admit I feel much safer in the apartment, as well as more connected to people. And I love the easy access to the city on the train.'

'There is that, I suppose,' said Liam. 'You should be careful out there, though; there are some not so nice people around these days,' he cautioned her.

'Oh, don't worry, I don't go out with anything valuable. If a mugger grabs my bag they can have it.' She shrugged. 'They would find some mint imperials, a packet of tissues and a lipstick. I always keep my phone and bank card in an inside coat pocket,' she revealed, tapping the side of her nose, much to the amusement of her nephews. They could imagine the look on the face of a mugger going through the contents of the bag. Hopefully she would never find herself in that situation, though.

When the food arrived they eyed the delicious-looking steaks and huge bowls of side dishes that included mashed potato, Tenderstem broccoli, Latin mac and cheese, as well as a huge mixed salad.

Alice and Liam opted for a peppercorn sauce with their steaks, whilst Callum opted for the chimichurri.

He piled his plate high with a generous serving of mashed potato, and a wedge of mac and cheese. He was still quite slender, although her sister had once mentioned that he was a member of a gym that charged extortionate fees. Apparently, the gym provided everything from ice baths to 3D body scans.

'It is so wonderful spending time with you both today,' said a delighted Alice. 'At my age I just never know if and when I will see someone again,' she said as she cut into her butter-soft steak.

'Don't say that,' said Liam. 'I am pretty sure you will get a telegram from the king on your hundredth birthday.'

'Hmm, maybe. Although I am not sure living to be a hundred is something desirable, unless you are still able to enjoy life.'

'That's true enough,' agreed Liam.

'And I will be back up this way soon. At least, hopefully,' said Callum. 'So you needn't worry about not seeing me for a while.'

'I shall look forward to it.' Alice smiled.

She thought about her house near the sea, the proceeds in the bank for her nephews' future.

She could also not help thinking that if she had not sold up, her friends at Wisteria House would have somewhere to stay, at least temporarily. It had got her mind working overtime.

As their conversation continued, Callum talked of all the things he had recently acquired, including a new kitchen with granite worktops.

'Pay no attention to Callum,' Liam advised her when Callum had nipped to the toilet. 'He has always been materialistic,' he said, with a shake of his head. 'Always upgrading everything in his house when it isn't necessary.'

'That is rather wasteful, I must admit,' said Alice.

'Honestly, he could have paid his mortgage off ten times over with some of the massive bonuses he has earnt over the years,' Liam divulged. 'But what did he do? Only go and buy a bigger house. And he is constantly upgrading his car. He is never satisfied. He will probably be paying out for a hair transplant next,' he said, with a mischievous grin, and Alice suppressed a laugh.

She wondered if Callum was secretly mad that his brother had inherited his mum's healthy thick locks. 'Well, he has no need to worry about his inheritance,' Alice told Liam as she speared some broccoli onto her fork. 'The proceeds of the house sale on Marine Terrace are to be split between you both. It is all in my will.'

'Which is more than generous, Auntie Alice, really. In fact, I wouldn't mind if you want to donate all of your money to a cats' home, should you wish to. I have always rather liked cats.' He grinned. 'I don't see why either of us should feel entitled to anything.'

'Thank you for understanding,' she told Liam. She reached over and patted his hand.

She could not help but feel disappointed with Callum. She

thought of a frequently misquoted Bible scripture that tells us that the *love* of money is the root of all evil. It seemed a shame that so many people chose to worship at the altar of riches these days.

Alice had enjoyed a thoroughly lovely afternoon with her nephews, and when Callum dropped her off at the apartments, in his impressive-looking car, she wished him well over the contract for the refit of the flooring in the arena.

'Thanks, Auntie Alice,' he said, placing a kiss on her cheek, as did Liam. 'I will let you know how it goes. See you again soon.'

As he drove off she felt a brief pang of sadness. She envied those people who had family on the doorstep, who would drop in regularly for a cup of tea and a chat. How wonderful must it be to never feel truly alone, knowing you could call on someone if you needed to. But she felt grateful to have made some wonderful new friends. And they were quickly becoming like family to her.

# FIFTY-SIX

## DECLAN

Declan was dying to tell Jess the good news about his job but thought he would call his mum first.

Besides, he still did not know whether she would want to bother with him again. He had thought it best to give her space but was not sure for how long. Surely she would have made contact with him by now if she was interested? Should he knock at her door or take her silence as a sign he should stay away? he wondered, his mind a jumble.

'Your own office? That sounds fancy,' said his mum when he called her. 'Well done, love.' She paused for a second. 'But do you think it's sensible walking away from a job with the council?'

She had a point, of course, and she was only looking out for him, but it was the opportunity of a lifetime. And he did have a modest amount of savings he could fall back on.

'I'll make it work,' he told his mum confidently.

'Well, if anyone can, you can,' she told him proudly.

He had picked himself up from the most terrible situation after all. Being imprisoned whilst still grieving his sister would have sent many people under, but Declan had battled on bravely and focused on the day he would have his freedom once more.

His mother had not been quite so courageous and sought comfort in alcohol. Thankfully she was now living a life that although not exactly filled with joy, at least brought her some contentment.

They chatted for a while, and he told her he would call over one evening after work.

'Will you be bringing the new girlfriend with you? What's her name, Jess?' she asked and his heart sank.

'She's not exactly my girlfriend, Mum,' he said. 'But I will explain that when I come over.'

'Alright, love. I have something to tell you too,' she said. 'And don't worry, it isn't anything bad. In fact, it is something nice.'

'Come up on the bingo, have you?' he joked.

'Something like that.' She laughed. 'Anyway, see you soon.'

'Wednesday after work, then. Bye, Mum.'

Declan wondered what good news his mum would be sharing when he went to visit. He hoped it was something nice. She deserved it.

# FIFTY-SEVEN

## JESS

'I still can't believe you are here,' said Jess to her mum as they settled down with a brew when Maisie was in bed. 'Are you sure you are okay?'

'Don't you worry about me,' said Carol. 'I am exactly where I need to be.'

Carol had wondered how she had ended up here, when two years ago she had been living in her cosy terraced house with her husband. She had envisaged a comfortable retirement until Jess's dad had decided he wanted the exact opposite.

She would never reveal to Jess how much her father had hurt her. She did not want to influence her decision to have a relationship with him, although it appeared things between them were less than perfect.

Just recently her ex-husband had lost weight, bought an open-topped car and was travelling up and down the country with his new love each weekend. That was according to one of her old colleagues at the Co-op. She wondered if it was the real thing between the two of them. Or just one last-ditch attempt on her husband's part to try and recapture his youth. At sixty, he was far too old for a mid-life crisis.

She wondered if she had become boring and that was why he had strayed. She still enjoyed having fun, although maybe her conversations had revolved around her part-time job and the comings and goings of the staff. Perhaps if he had helped with the housework a little more, she might not have felt constantly exhausted.

Still, it was all in the past now and she had gotten over him and accepted the situation. She had no choice. She just felt sad that her ex would not be around to be the grandad Maisie deserved. Especially as Maisie did not seem keen to visit him at his new place. Surely that must hurt him? Some might say he deserved it, but Carol was never one to think that way.

'You are too soft, Mum,' her wise daughter would sometimes tell her when she put herself out for others. She believed what went around usually came around, though.

'Actually, while you were in the shower, I have been looking at rentals in the area,' Carol told Jess as she sipped her tea.

'Gosh, Mum, there is no rush. You have only been here five minutes,' said Jess.

'Yes, but I don't want to get too comfortable here,' she told her daughter. 'Besides, you don't have much storage and most of my stuff is taking up space in your cupboard in the hall. And let's not forget the sale of Wisteria House.'

It was true that Jess had had to move things about a bit, and some of Maisie's toys and games were now on the floor of her spacious wardrobe, Maisie's room already overflowing with her things. Time to do a charity shop donation, thought Jess. Especially as Christmas was only a few months away, when more toys would arrive.

She didn't want to think about the sale of Wisteria House, though.

'Anyway, I have spotted something on St Nicolas Road. A ground-floor apartment in an independent living facility that is well within my price range.'

She turned the laptop to show her daughter the apartment with the communal garden. It looked in good order, apart from the décor that needed some updating.

'That looks nice,' said Jess. She quite liked the idea of her mum being in a place with a community room, even though she was only in her sixties and still fit and active. 'And it is close to the beach.'

'That's what I thought.' Carol smiled. 'Literally a five-minute walk to the sand dunes. And the leisure centre.'

Maybe she would take up swimming again, thought Carol, something she had once loved to do. She suddenly felt excited for the future.

'I think I will arrange a viewing,' said Carol positively. 'I will call the estate agent tomorrow. But for now, I want to hear all about what has been going on in your life,' she said to her daughter.

'Shall I grab that wine from the fridge and a couple of glasses?' suggested Jess.

'Oh, go on, then,' said Carol, collecting their half-finished cups of tea and taking them into the kitchen.

Jess decided that she would talk to her mum about Declan. There would never be a right time to have the conversation, so she might as well get it over with and hear her thoughts on it.

She still hadn't spoken to Declan, although she had thought of him every day, unsuccessfully trying to push away the thoughts of the kiss they had shared. His past was behind him. He had served his sentence. Yet a tiny part of her brain could not seem to shift the possibility that he had mown a man down in cold blood.

What if he possessed a rage when provoked? She could never take that risk. Especially not with having Maisie.

'I can picture that apartment looking really cosy,' said Carol as she clutched her wine, feet curled up on the sofa. 'And Maisie can have sleepovers.' Carol frowned for a moment. 'I hope children are allowed to stay in an over-sixties apartment block. Anyway, it will give you the chance to go on an evening out now and again,' Carol suggested. 'And I can always stay at yours if children are not allowed,' she said, already imagining herself living in the apartment. 'So have you made plans to go out with Declan yet?'

'About that,' said Jess as she swigged down a large glug of her wine.

# FIFTY-EIGHT

## ALICE

Alice had found a writing set in a charity shop in the village on her last visit there.

It had been a steal at two pounds and included six good-quality sheets of paper and pink envelopes, with a swirl of flowers around the edge. It had also included a pen, so she had dropped an extra couple of pound coins into the charity box on the counter.

She thought of Liam then, and his comment about her giving her money to a cats' charity if she desired.

Her nephews really were polar opposites, she thought to herself, as she slid the handwritten notes into the pink envelopes that she would post through the doors of her friends and neighbours. Thankfully they were both good people. Callum had always desired the best of everything even as a child, whilst Liam preferred to have his nose in a good book, when she thought about it.

Just then, as if breaking into her thoughts, her phone rang and Callum's face appeared on the screen.

'Press the camera,' he instructed her when he could hear her voice but could not see her face.

'Oh right, there we are.' She laughed when her face appeared in the corner of her screen. 'I am not sure I will ever get the hang of this.'

'You are getting better,' Callum assured her. 'Anyway, I just thought I would ring and tell you that we got the flooring contract for the arena.' He smiled broadly.

'That is wonderful news,' said Alice. 'Really it is, well done.'

'Thanks. So, it means I will see you again soon. And next time dinner is on me.' He grinned.

'I shall look forward to it,' said a delighted Alice.

'So what are you up to today, then?' he asked breezily.

Mark had knocked earlier and surprised her with the offer of a day out to Sefton Park. She told Callum this.

'Sounds good. I remember going there with you and Uncle George. Did we go on a boat on the lake?' he asked her.

'Probably yes, although I am not sure if that is still a thing. The Palm House is still there, though.'

These days the Victorian glass building was hired as a venue for all kinds of things, including weddings and concerts by candlelight. When Callum and Liam were young it had merely been a botanical conservatory, filled with exotic plants. They were removed in the nineteen eighties, and the Palm House had fallen into disrepair and been closed.

Thankfully some community fundraising had seen the building fully restored almost ten years later, much to the delight of Alice. As well as the plants, the Palm House also displayed bronze statues of famous people, including the explorer James Cook.

Callum told Alice about his forthcoming weekend plans, that included going to watch a show in the West End. 'Top-tier tickets. We have booked a meal for Nobu afterwards too,' he told her.

'Is it a special occasion?' asked Alice, wondering whether she had missed a birthday or wedding anniversary.

'No, not really. But it is the weekend, and I guess I am celebrating the new contract,' he explained.

Alice suspected the bonus paid from securing the flooring contract would not remain in his bank account for very long.

'Well, have a wonderful time,' she told him genuinely.

'Thanks, Auntie Alice. I am sure we will.'

Alice had come to realise that life was far too short to live it any other way than how your heart desired.

# FIFTY-NINE

## ALICE

The memories came rushing back to Alice, as they always did when she entered Sefton Park.

If she closed her eyes she could see herself and George on the lake, him rowing and her sitting back doing her best to look glamorous, wafting a fan in front of her on a hot day. *Poor George doing all that work*, she thought to herself with a smile on her face.

The park was busy with joggers, dog walkers and couples strolling along enjoying the autumn sunshine. The only children in the park today were toddlers, or babies fastened into prams as older children would have been in school.

They strolled along the Victorian park, enjoying the serpentine paths and open lawns. They passed a fountain on a lake and Mark asked Alice if she wanted to sit down on a bench nearby.

'I'll tell you what, let's make it to the café and I will treat you to an ice cream,' said Alice good-naturedly.

'If you're sure, then let's do it,' said Mark.

Taking a seat at the café, Alice felt the muscles in her legs ache, even though they had only been walking for around fifteen minutes. It was another reminder that Alice was old in years, but she didn't dwell on it. Every day was a gift, and today she was pleased to be in her favourite place with good company.

'I can see why you love this park,' said Mark as he tucked into a tub of vanilla ice cream. Alice opted for her ice cream in a cone.

'I remember coming here with Di, but only once or twice as I recall,' he told her. 'I remember going for a bite to eat on Lark Lane. I believe it's changed a bit now,' he said as he scraped the last of his ice cream from the tub with a wooden spoon.

'Oh, it has,' said Alice. 'Very fashionable these days. It was once the hang-out for artists and writers, with a much more Bohemian vibe.'

She had partied there once in an apartment above one of the shops and stayed until the dawn had broken the next morning.

After their ice creams, they slowly made their way to the Palm House.

The iron and glass architecture of the domed building took Alice's breath away every time she saw it, its appearance always reminding her of a large white birdcage.

Today there were no events taking place, as they frequently did, so they were free to wander around and enjoy the lush vibrant plants with their scented foliage. It always felt to her like stepping into a tropical oasis in the heart of the city.

Alice had thoroughly enjoyed her time in the park but turned down Mark's invitation for a bite to eat on Lark Lane as she felt a little worn out.

'I hope you don't mind, Mark,' she said as they headed back towards the car park.

'Of course I don't,' Mark told her. 'Whatever you want, it's your day today.'

'Thank you, Mark. Although if you have no other plans, perhaps I can make us a sandwich and a cup of tea when we get home?' she offered.

'Of course, Alice, that would be lovely.' He smiled.

It was yet another reminder of how fortunate she was to be back at Wisteria House.

# SIXTY

## MARK

Mark spotted the 'sold' sign one morning as he was leaving the apartment.

Carol had just returned from dropping Maisie at school when she ran into him.

'Morning, Carol. So it looks like that's it, then,' he said, glancing at the 'sold' sign that must have appeared last night.

'I guess we knew it was coming.' Carol sighed. 'Jess will be devastated. Hopefully I will have a place soon, though.'

'So, have you moved back to the area?'

'Yes. I'm staying here with Jess and Maisie, at least for the time being.' She squinted in the autumn sunshine, wishing she had brought her sunglasses.

'Oh right,' said Mark in surprise. Her life in the Lake District had sounded idyllic when she described the surroundings at the BBQ evening. But then maybe she had missed her family.

'Do you have time for a coffee?' she found herself saying.

'I have all the time in the world,' said Mark. 'Actually, I don't suppose you fancy a walk as it is such a lovely morning?

We could walk through Alexandra Park, then grab a drink from a café somewhere.'

'Yeah, I'd like that,' said Carol. 'I don't suppose we will have many more days like this, before the weather turns cold.'

She found herself wishing she had applied some make-up before she had headed out this morning. Still, she could at least put some lipstick on when she popped inside for a moment.

'Just let me put this in the fridge first,' she said, lifting the milk she had just purchased from the Co-op.

She quickly checked her hair in the hall mirror, before sliding some lipstick over her lips and grabbing a light cardigan.

Alexandra Park, a small park favoured by dog walkers, was quite busy this morning with the usual occupants of the neighbourhood. Park walks had become a bit of a thing for him after spending the day with Alice, he thought to himself.

An old lady was sitting in her usual place on one of the memory benches, a plaque dedicated to her husband. She had informed Mark of this one morning, when they had got chatting.

They wished her a good morning as they passed by, and she returned their greeting.

A group of teenage girls, bags slung over their shoulders, were making their way to school, chattering loudly as they went.

'Oh, to be that age again,' commented Mark, who had always been popular with girls.

He watched a small group of boys from a neighbouring school turn and glance at the girls as they walked past.

'I wish I had had a few more adventures at that age,' Carol found herself saying.

'Do you?' asked Mark. Carol was such good company now, and he imagined her being a bundle of fun in her youth.

'Yeah, I do,' she confessed. 'Don't get me wrong, I had a lot of fun with my friends, I just wish I had been a bit more adventurous,' she reflected. 'I had a friend who went off and worked abroad as a nanny. I wish I had done that.'

'I imagine that was quite an adventurous thing to do, back in the day.'

'Oh, it was,' agreed Carol. 'Everyone thought she was really daring, going off like that on her own. Not like me, married at twenty-one and still living in the place I grew up,' she told him.

As they approached one of the exits at the far end of the park they passed an elderly gentleman who wished them a cheery good morning as he threw some nuts and seeds from a plastic supermarket bag to a flock of birds on the nearby lawn.

'Let's hope the birds eat all that food or the rats will,' Mark whispered to Carol as they walked past, not wishing to offend the old man, who regularly fed the birds in the park.

Some of the leaves on the trees already had a soft yellow bleeding through the green, and at some point the trees would become a mixture of red, gold and green, thought Carol as she walked. As she did so, the line of a well-known eighties song popped into her mind, and she smiled.

'Something amused you?' asked Mark.

'"Karma Chameleon",' she said, explaining her thoughts.

'That song was number one when my daughter was born,' he said.

He told her all about his daughter, who lived in Australia.

'Wow. I didn't know that. You must miss her,' said Carol.

'We both did at first,' he told her, referring to himself and his late wife. 'But when we went out there and saw the life she was living, we knew it was right for her. We would go out at least once a year, and she and her husband would come over here,' he told her. 'She came over after Diane died and tried to persuade me to go and live with her.'

'And you didn't fancy it?'

They had stopped for a second on a path to allow an enthu-siastic young boy to ride past on his bike.

'I felt too old to make a new life on the other side of the world,' he said as they strolled along. 'Besides, my life is here, along with my memories. We are still close, though. There are lots of FaceTime calls.' He smiled. 'In fact, she and her husband are actually coming over early in the new year, doing a bit of a tour, visiting old friends too,' he told her.

'That will be nice,' said Carol, hardly able to imagine how she would feel if Jess and Maisie lived on the other side of the world.

They eventually arrived at an exit on the right-hand side of the park and walked on until they reached Coronation Road.

There was another park on the road, that included a playground for children and a field for dogs to run around. The council had recently installed some new outdoor gym machines, as well as upgrading some of the equipment in the play area.

'Did you know Declan was instrumental in getting the funding for the upgrading of the park?' Mark informed Carol as they walked by.

'Was he really?' said Carol.

'Yes, and the gym equipment. He told me about it once. Only when I happened to mention something about the park, though,' he told her. 'I like Declan; he's a good bloke.'

Carol had replayed the conversation in her head this morning when she had dropped Maisie at school. Jess had insisted on taking the train into town as she knew how flustered Carol got driving into the city centre, despite her mum offering.

Along with most people in the city, Carol remembered reading about the downfall of Tony Callaghan. To hear that Declan had been the one who had killed him, though, had come as a huge shock.

She understood her daughter's concerns, of course she did. Yet something inside her told her that Mark's instincts were right. Declan was a good man. All the same, she thought this was something her daughter would need to figure out for herself, despite any advice she might give her. At least she was back here now, so could keep her eye on her daughter and granddaughter should anything change.

When they took their seats at a café in the village high street, on which there were more eateries and less shops these days, Carol considered talking to Mark about what Jess had told her, before deciding against it. What would be the point? Besides, it was up to Declan to decide who he should tell about his past, should the need ever arise. Whatever had happened in a person's life was no one else's business, thought Carol. Don't we all have a past?

Carol declined the offer of breakfast and popped the complementary caramel biscuit into her mouth that came with the coffee.

'So did you say you were back here for good, then?' asked Mark as he stirred his drink.

'I am, although I can't live with Jess forever,' she told him. 'In fact, I have already booked an appointment to view an apartment tomorrow. Not far from the beach. And given the situation with the apartment block, at least her and Maisie would have a roof over their head.'

'Sounds perfect,' said Mark. He surprised himself by feeling pleased that Carol would be moving back to the area. She really was so easy to talk to. He also tried not to think about his current home being sold. He did have his sister, though, although he wondered if he was too long in the tooth to be sharing a home with someone else, even family.

'It needs a bit of modernising, although nothing too drastic,' Carol said positively. 'A lick of paint, and maybe a more modern shower is pretty much all it requires.'

'Well, if you need a bit of muscle, I'm your man,' said Mark, who then felt the colour rise in his cheeks. God, he hoped he wasn't blushing at his age.

'I might just take you up on that.' She winked. 'Anyway, I

don't want to be getting my hopes up,' she told him. 'Although if something is meant to be, it will be. I am a firm believer in that.'

After his wife's death, and now his mother's, Mark did not want to sit with his grief any longer. His new friends were so full of life, maybe he ought to try and take a leaf out of their book. At least from time to time.

'Maybe you're right.' He smiled. 'And I mean it, if you need any help redecorating the flat, I would be happy to help.'

'Let's hope I get it, then,' Carol said with a wink as she tapped her cup against Mark's. 'And thanks for the coffee.'

'My pleasure,' said Mark with the warmest of smiles and a feeling of optimism for the future.

## SIXTY-ONE

## DECLAN

Declan was nursing his mug of morning tea and thinking about moving in with his mum. Mark had told him that he was viewing an apartment later and no doubt Jess and Carol were hoping that somewhere suitable would come onto the market soon.

The thought of the friends being scattered across the city broke his heart, but there wasn't an awful lot he could do about that.

'Hi, Mum,' said Declan as he walked into his mum's home clutching a bunch of her favourite yellow roses.

'Hello, love,' said his mum, who looked different. Had she had her hair done? 'Ooh thanks, love, let me pop those in a vase,' she said, gratefully accepting the flowers.

Norman appeared from the kitchen then, and pumped Declan's hand up and down with his usual strong handshake.

'Now then, young man, how are you?' He smiled.

'Good, great in fact.' The thought of soon being self-employed and taking occupancy of the Liverpool Road office had put a real spring in Declan's step.

'Have you found a new apartment yet?' his mother asked.

'No, I haven't, Mum.'

He would sleep in the office if he had to. On a temporary basis at least. There was a large storage room just off the kitchen.

'So what's your good news, then?' Declan asked his mum as he took a seat on the sofa.

'Let's have tea first,' said Norman. 'There's a bit of fruit cake too,' he said, bustling off back to the kitchen.

'Keeping me in suspense, I see.' Declan grinned. 'And you look nice, Mum. Have you had your hair coloured?'

'I have.' She smiled. 'Do you like it?'

'I do. It takes years off you,' he told her genuinely.

'I got a new cut too.' She shook her head, and the chin-length bob fell back into place. 'It wasn't cheap as I went to one of those salons in town, but Norman treated me.'

'You're worth it, love,' Norman called from the kitchen.

Declan thought that she looked like the mum he remembered before his sister died, always immaculately turned out.

He felt himself breathe an inward sigh of relief at the thought of his mum beginning to get some enjoyment from her life again. He knew she would never completely get over losing her daughter, of course she wouldn't, but it was lovely to see her feeling brighter and he had Norman to thank for that.

'Actually, Norman, leave the tea but bring the cake,' Declan's mum called through to the kitchen. 'I think we ought to open that Prosecco in the cupboard. I should have chilled it really.' She frowned.

'Good call,' said Norman, who shortly appeared with the Prosecco and three glasses.

'What's the occasion?' said Declan, glancing from his mum to Norman.

'The thing is, we have been getting along so well, as you know, these past couple of years, and well...' Norman paused for a moment as he glanced at Eileen.

'We thought we might move in together,' Declan's mum blurted out.

'That's brilliant news,' said Declan, standing to hug his mum, before Norman moved in for a hug too. They stood in a group hug for a second, and Declan felt an overwhelming surge of affection for them both.

'Really, I am glad you approve,' said Norman when they broke apart. He had looked momentarily nervous before Eileen announced the news.

'Not here, though. We have found some nice sheltered accommodation not far from the train station. We will sell our respective houses and bank some money for our future.'

'That sounds sensible,' said Declan. 'You could go travelling.'

'I'm not sure my knees are up to too much sightseeing,' laughed Declan's mum. 'Although I have always fancied a cruise.'

'So have I,' said Norman. 'We should definitely do it. I quite fancy the Caribbean.' He placed an arm around Eileen's shoulders and gave them a squeeze.

'Of course, you can stay here with us until we have sold, until you find something else, I mean, but I'm afraid it won't be a permanent solution,' his mum told him.

'Don't worry about me, I will find somewhere,' he assured her. 'I'm so glad you're happy, Mum. Are you sure about moving away from here, though?'

'Thanks, love. And yes, I am looking forward to moving away and starting a new chapter,' she assured him. 'I think it's about time.'

As he thought about Wisteria House he realised with a heavy heart that she was not the only person who would soon be moving on. He also realised that he would no longer have a reason to visit his old neighbourhood. It gave him mixed feelings of both sadness and relief.

# SIXTY-TWO

## JESS

Jess had been hoovering the carpet in Maisie's bedroom, and when she stepped into the hall, she spotted the pink envelope near the front door.

Tearing it open, she smiled when she realised it was from Alice. She loved her preference for popping a note through the door, even when she only had to knock.

She read the note then tucked it into her jeans pocket. It was an invitation for tea and cake on Sunday afternoon, and Jess wondered if everyone else in the apartment block had been invited.

With a sigh she realised that she still had not spoken to Declan after their last meeting and wondered if he would be there.

Her thoughts turned to the dinner party at Alice's, and how everything had changed since that evening. She recalled how the possibility of a romance between her and Declan had flitted across her mind, their chemistry obvious. When they had gone out on a date, she had been certain they were a potential couple.

Alice had been right in telling Jess that no one could decide if Declan was to be a part of her life, apart from Jess herself. But it was huge. Surely anyone would be right to think carefully about bringing a man with a past like Declan's into their child's life?

Carol had taken Maisie to the park, whilst Jess gave the apartment a good clean. It was helpful having Carol around, and she dearly hoped that the viewing of the apartment would help her to put down roots in the city once more. In the meantime, she was more than welcome to stay here with her and Maisie.

'Hello, Declan, how are you?' asked Carol when she ran into him outside the apartments an hour later.

'Hi, Carol. I'm okay, thanks. You?' he asked, wondering if Jess had spoken to her about their recent conversation.

Upon seeing him, Maisie had run to him and placed her arms around his waist and he pushed away a jolt of affection for the child. He would need to harden his heart if there was to be no future for him and Jess.

'Where have you been?' asked Maisie. 'Are you not friends with us anymore?' she enquired, with all the innocence of a child.

'Of course I am.' He smiled at Maisie. 'I have just been a bit busy, that's all.'

'That's okay, then.' The little girl smiled at him. 'You can come inside now if you like.'

He almost took her up on her offer and followed them inside, until Carol reminded Maisie that Mummy was busy cleaning up. She had probably finished by now, but she didn't like to impose Declan's presence upon her, without asking first.

Carol and Declan engaged in some small talk, before they went their separate ways. As Declan turned to leave, Carol whispered in his ear.

'Jess told me about your chat. Give it time,' she told him.

'I am.' He smiled, wondering if the distance between them would only continue to grow.

Inside his apartment, Declan picked up the pink envelope and read the invitation from Alice.

Sunday afternoon for tea and cake? Normally he would accept any invitation from Alice and it was after his football after all. Plus, it was highly likely that Jess would be there. It was just a shame he had a mountain of accounts to go through that he had planned on starting on Sunday.

It would be a mammoth task searching for discrepancies in Sanctuary Bathrooms' accounts over the last couple of years. But if he was to be a good accountant to Ken Watson, he needed to sort out the files and deliver what he had promised. And if there was one quality Declan possessed, it was being a man of his word.


'That looks yummy.'

Maisie eyed the delicious-looking strawberry drip cake that took centre stage on the table in Alice's lounge.

An assortment of sandwiches cut into triangles shared the space on the table, along with a selection of pastries and some fruit scones.

A large teapot was filled and carried through to the table, along with some china teacups and saucers. The set-up would not have looked out of place at Annie's Tea Rooms, a café a mile or two up the road, thought Jess.

'This is really lovely, Alice,' said Jess as she sat around the table next to Mark.

Alice glanced at her watch and noticed that it was five minutes past three. She was disappointed that Declan had not arrived, but then he had not actually confirmed.

'Are you sure it's okay Mum coming?' asked Jess. 'She should be here any second.'

Carol was still searching for a suitable place to live as the viewing on the flat had proved to be unsuccessful.

'Of course I am sure. It will affect her indirectly anyway I would imagine,' said Alice to a puzzled-looking Jess.

Right on cue there was a knock on the door, and Carol came rushing into the apartment.

'Sorry I'm late,' she said. 'I nipped into the village in the car, and someone took my parking space outside. Well, I say my space, but it isn't really, is it?' She rolled her eyes and laughed.

She handed a bunch of flowers to Alice that she had bought from Sainsbury's and Alice accepted them gratefully.

'Please sit down,' said Alice, who offered Carol a cup of tea.

Jess could not help feeling a pang of disappointment at Declan not being at the gathering, despite her confused feelings towards him. Maybe he thought it best to avoid her. Or perhaps he was just giving her space. It was what she had wanted after all.

They ate and chatted, and Maisie devoured a huge slice of the strawberry cake, after Jess insisted she at least ate a sandwich first.

'Right, well, it is a little disappointing that Declan is not here but never mind,' said Alice. 'I will catch up with him later.'

As she stood to walk to a dresser at the far end of the room, she felt a pain shoot through her hip.

'Are you alright?' asked Jess, getting to her feet. Alice had said nothing, but Jess had noticed her wince in pain.

'Oh, I'm fine, don't worry. A little sciatica, which is only to be expected at my age,' she assured Jess as she moved slowly across the room.

'You're sure?' asked Jess anxiously.

'Yes, yes, don't worry,' she assured her. 'I am just slowly falling to bits.' She managed a smile.

## SIXTY-THREE

### ALICE

Not for the first time, Alice cursed her increasing immobility. After her walk with Mark the other day, she had been completely exhausted and napped for an hour when she got home. Her body had ached when she woke. It seemed her age really was catching up with her.

Having retrieved the envelopes from the drawer, Alice stretched her back out in a move she remembered from her warming-up exercises as a dancer. She made her way back to the table as, thankfully, it seemed to ease the pain a little, maybe freeing a pinched nerve.

'Right, well, now that I have you here, I just wanted to bequeath you all a gift,' said Alice.

'A gift?' said Mark. 'Really, Alice, there is no need for that. Unless it's someone's birthday.'

He glanced at Jess and Carol, and they shrugged.

'My birthday is on the sixth of April,' piped up Maisie as she licked her fingers of cream from the cake, and Jess handed her a napkin.

'No, it has nothing to do with anyone's birthday,' said Alice. 'But I want you to have something.'

She slid the envelopes across the table to Jess and Mark and urged them to open them.

Mark's mouth dropped open when he slid the document from the envelope and glanced at the contents.

Jess was still too dumbstruck to say anything.

'Tenancy agreements? I don't understand,' Jess said, looking up at Alice.

'It's quite simple. I am your new landlord,' Alice said casually as she sipped her tea. 'Or landlady, if you prefer.'

'You have bought Wisteria House?'

'I have indeed.' Alice was thrilled to be able to impart the news.

Jess could feel her heart beating faster, and she wasn't sure she was hearing correctly.

'So we can stay here?'

'Well, that is the idea. Did you think I would buy the building, then turf you out onto the street?' Alice laughed.

'No, but I can't believe it,' Jess said, open-mouthed. 'And I don't understand; didn't we all have letters about two months' notice? I thought the place was sold to someone else?'

'Ah, about that,' said Alice. 'When I enquired about buying the apartments I was told a sale was already going ahead. I asked the estate agent to inform me if the sale was to fall through. And would you believe, it did. I believe someone up there was looking out for us,' she said, glancing up above.

'I can't believe you would do this,' said Mark.

'I don't have long for this world, so what use is my money lying in a bank when it could improve the lives of my dear friends, right here and now?' she asked them. 'You will never have the insecurity of fearing homelessness again.'

'But what if the building is sold again, when—' Mark broke off.

'When I am gone? Oh, don't worry, I know I am not immortal.' Alice smiled. 'But I have expressed in my will that you are allowed to remain here for as long as you choose to. My nephews will only inherit the building on the condition they honour the agreement. I'm sure that's a long way off yet, though.'

'I don't know what to say,' said Jess as she fought back tears.

There was a knock on the door then, and Alice stood to answer.

'It's a shame Declan could not be here, as I wonder what he might think about it,' she said as she strolled to the front door.

'Wonder what I might think about what?' asked Declan, clutching his pink letter as Alice opened the door.

'Sorry, I'm late, and I did mean to reply to your note,' he told Alice as he stepped inside. 'Then the time seemed to just run away with me, and I admit I forgot.

'Hi,' he addressed the group around the table, and Maisie, who was sitting playing with a couple of dolls on the sofa, said hello and that he ought to try some strawberry cake.

'I might just do that.' He smiled. 'So, what have I missed, then?' He turned to Alice. 'I thought I heard you say something about my reaction to something.'

'You heard that as I approached the front door? Oh dear, these walls really are paper thin,' said Alice.

'Which means you might have to be careful what you get up to,' Mark said laughing, and Carol laughed too. Declan's face flushed. 'Playing loud music and the like,' Mark quickly added, and Alice could not help but smile.

'Do come and sit down,' said Alice. Declan took a seat at the far end of the table, opposite Jess and Carol.

Alice filled him in on the news.

'Oh, and I forget to mention, I am halving your rent,' she told her friends.

'Alice, you can't do that,' said Declan. 'Being able to stay here is enough. I can't believe it.'

'But I insist. It will give you the option to save. In a few years, you may have a deposit for a place of your own. But whatever you decide, I know it will help you,' said Alice.

He shook his head, hardly able to take it in.

'Declan, it will give you some security as you are soon to become self-employed. And I hope you don't mind, but I wonder if you might take responsibility for the payment of the rent and the communal charge.'

'Of course,' he agreed, still feeling shocked.

'And, Jess, the reduction in rent means you could save for Maisie's future, or whatever you wish. You must have the garden flat of course, for Maisie, when I am no longer here,' she said matter-of-factly.

'Oh, Alice,' whispered Jess.

'And, Mark, I assume you will want to stay here? I know you have all become great friends.'

'There is nowhere I would rather be,' he said, his voice breaking.

The tears of gratitude that Jess had been holding in spilt over then as she stood and embraced Alice.

'You don't know what this means,' she said, wiping a tear away from her eye. 'Thank you.'

'Oh, I think I do.' Alice smiled, happy that Jess had had the good grace to accept the tenancy.

'Alice, are you absolutely sure about this?' asked Declan, but if he was honest, she was right. It was exactly the security he needed whilst setting up by himself.

'Why would you do this for us?' asked Jess, still teary.

'Ah, why. That is indeed the question,' Alice said as she leant back in her chair.

At Alice's request, Mark went to retrieve her favourite malt whisky from a cupboard.

'Many years ago, I was given a chance in life.' She sipped her whisky as she spoke. 'This was once our family home, as you know, but we lost it,' she told them.

'What happened?' asked Mark tentatively.

'My father had crippling debt.' Even after all these years she felt a lump in her throat as she spoke. 'Which was unbeknown to my mother for a long time.' She paused for a moment. 'Watching the horse racing was his passion. I went along myself as a young child,' she reflected. 'When the war broke out the racing stopped, apart from at Newbury Racecourse. He would often travel there, which he would explain away as a business trip. He invested a lot of money in a racehorse.'

It wasn't hard for the friends to anticipate what was coming next.

'It didn't perform as promised, and he lost everything. Including the house. We managed to find a rental a mile away. I don't think my mother ever got over it,' said Alice wistfully.

'That must have been hard,' said Jess, reaching over and gripping her hand.

'At the time, I was having dance classes run by a wonderful lady called Ida. It was one of the things that had to go, given our financial situation,' she told her friends, lost in memories from the past. 'I thought that was the end of my dancing career, but not so,' she explained. 'Ida spotted something in me. She gave me classes for free. She even sorted out some accommodation through a lady who ran a guest house in London when I trained as a Tiller Girl. I owe my career to that lady.'

'How wonderful,' said Jess, wiping away a tear from her eye.

'Indeed.' Alice smiled. 'So you see, I have always believed in helping others out wherever possible. You never know how it could change their life.'

'Gosh, Alice, look at the state of me,' said Jess, wiping her mascara-streaked face with a tissue.

The friends sat quietly digesting the news Alice had imparted. Declan was the first to speak.

'We can never thank you enough, Alice.'

'It is my absolute pleasure,' she assured them. 'Oh and

whilst we are all here, I just wondered what your plans might be for New Year's Eve?' asked Alice. 'And, yes, I know it is a while away, but I find at my age it is good to have a date to aim for.' She laughed. 'It keeps me going.'

'Nothing as of yet. I've never been one for New Year's Eve,' said Mark, still dazed by Alice's generosity. 'Even when Diane was alive, we had a quiet one. A glass of bubbly and Jools Holland on the telly at midnight. If we could stay awake that long.' He laughed.

'Same here,' said Jess. 'I can never be bothered waiting hours for a taxi home, even if I could get a babysitter.'

'Then how about a party here?' suggested Alice. 'Declan, do you have plans?'

'I've been asked out for a dinner with Ken Watson and some of the staff. It's an early meal, though; I could join you all later for drinks?'

'Perfect,' said Alice with a smile.

'A party sounds like a great idea,' said Mark.

'Wonderful. I will be happy to have you all here,' said Alice. 'I will get some caterers in for a special buffet and the finest champagne. I can't guarantee I will be awake at midnight, but it will be a double celebration as New Year's Eve just happens to be my birthday,' said Alice.

'Your birthday? In that case, I think that would be just perfect,' said Declan. 'But I insist on paying for the champagne.'

'I'll cover the cost of the buffet,' said Mark.

'Can we bring some balloons, Mummy?' said Maisie.

'Yes, Maisie, that's a great idea.' Jess smiled at her daughter.

As they raised their glasses and toasted Alice's good health they could hardly take in what had happened here today. Dear Alice had given each of them the security of being able to stay in their homes. Surely there was no greater gift.

# SIXTY-FOUR

## DECLAN

Declan entered the office building with his mum in tow and glanced around.

He had spent the last few weeks sorting the accounts for Sanctuary Bathrooms and he had worked his notice at the council offices.

His colleagues had had a collection and presented him with a bottle of champagne and a gift voucher for two hundred pounds. He had been truly touched by the gesture, as there were only five people in his actual office, but a work friend had let slip that a lot of people in the rest of the council offices were keen to chip in.

Ken Watson had been more than impressed with the work he had done so far, as Declan knew he would be. He had worked night and day to put things in order. He had also managed to secure a few more small accounts. If things continued to go well, he could maybe even think about one day hiring his own staff.

His work had kept him so occupied he barely had time to think of Jess, which in a way had been a blessing.

Then on Thursday, he ran into her on the landing, and he felt his mouth go dry.

'Jess, how are you?' he had asked.

'I'm okay,' she had told him. 'Still trying to get over the shock of Alice's gift.'

Declan had told her that he felt the same, despite him knowing it would have given Alice great pleasure.

'Anyway, I'd better go.' Jess was in her usual morning rush. 'We don't want Maisie being late for school.'

'And being told off by my teacher,' added Maisie.

'We can't have that, can we.' Declan had smiled. 'See you around, then.'

If Declan thought being busy with his accounts had somehow made his feeling towards Jess diminish, then he was wrong. His heart had felt heavy in the days that followed their meeting. As soon as his office was sorted, he would go and speak to her and ask her out on another date. He was desperate to know if there could be any sort of a future for them.

Jess had barely spoken to him the day Alice had shocked them with the news of the apartments. He had taken it as a sign that she was no longer interested in him, but he wasn't one to give up that easily.

'Right, let's get cracking,' said his mum as she set down her box of cleaning utensils.

Declan had carried the hoover up the staircase, and when she attempted to take it from him, he batted her away.

'The least I can do is vacuum the carpet, Mum.' He smiled. He did keep his own apartment in good order after all.

'If you insist. I will clean the sink and give the cupboards a good wipe down, then,' she said, marching off towards the small kitchen.

Norman had been around and touched up the paint around the door frames and skirting boards and had offered to paint the walls and ceiling but Declan had refused and hired a painter and decorator. He did not want Norman falling and ending up injuring himself.

Two hours later, with every inch of the office cleaned and his wooden desk polished, Declan sat on the black leather office chair with a feeling of excitement.

A few potted plants had been dotted about, looking good against the white painted walls, along with a couple of comfortable chairs.

'What do you think, hey, sis? Not bad for someone who left school with three GCSEs,' he whispered as he looked heavenwards, whilst his mum had gone to make them a cup of tea. 'I hope you are proud, kid,' he said as he felt himself choke up with emotion. 'Because I am.'

In the week that followed, Declan had been so busy with his work he had still not found the time to ask Jess out on another date.

He was mulling it over whilst leaving for work one morning when he spotted an ambulance outside the apartment block. As he drew nearer and noticed Jess chatting to one of the ambulance crew, he felt his heart sink.

He was told that Alice had taken a tumble, and it was feared she may have broken her hip.

Declan popped his head inside the ambulance to find Alice seated and sedated with heavy painkillers.

'Oh dear, what have I told you about going out on that skateboard,' he said with his usual humour, although his heart broke at the sight of Alice looking so vulnerable. He couldn't bear the thought of her not being around.

'Declan,' said Alice wearily, reaching out for his hand. He clasped her papery hand in his and willed her to receive some of his strength.

He thought of the day he had first encountered her outside

the apartments. He was not ready to say goodbye to her just yet. She had to be okay.

'I'll go to the hospital with her,' he told Jess.

'What about work?' Jess asked.

'My first appointment is not until eleven thirty.' He glanced at his watch. 'I will make sure Alice is settled first.'

'I will come after my shift,' Jess said to Alice. 'In fact, I will see if I can finish a couple of hours early.'

'Oh, don't you worry about me,' said Alice sleepily. 'You have Maisie to think of.'

'I have packed a bag with essentials,' Jess told Declan. 'Nightwear, toiletries, and her phone. Oh, and a bottle of water.'

'Does she have her phone charger?'

'Gosh no. I'll run and get it.'

Jess nipped inside and found the charger as the ambulance crew made sure Alice was comfortable for the journey to the hospital. Declan waved to her as they drove away.

# SIXTY-FIVE

## JESS

Jess was grateful that her mum had taken Maisie to school this morning. She would not have wanted her to see Alice in pain and being escorted into an ambulance.

Thankfully, Alice had managed to call Jess from the floor of her lounge, as her phone had been within reach on the nearby coffee table. Jess had been about to leave for work when she received the call and was with her in seconds.

Luckily, Alice had had the foresight to give her friends a spare key a while ago, following her last bout of illness. Thank goodness she had.

'What are you still doing here?' asked Carol when she had returned from dropping Maisie at school, as Jess was only just leaving.

'It's Alice,' explained Jess. 'She had a fall. I waited with her until the ambulance arrived.'

'Right, come on, let's get to the hospital,' said Carol.

'Don't worry, Declan has gone with her,' explained Jess. 'I will need to get to work as we have a couple of staff on holiday,' she told her.

'Let me give you a lift, then,' insisted Carol.

'But you don't like driving in city centre traffic,' Jess reminded her.

'Oh, come on, I will be fine driving,' said Carol confidently. 'Sometimes we just have to get out of our comfort zone. I have been quite good at doing that lately,' she said as they headed out to the car. 'And, oh yes, I have managed to get my old job back at the Co-op. I will tell you about it as we drive.'

'Gosh, poor Alice,' said Carol as she fastened her seat belt in the car. 'I hope she is going to be alright.'

'Me too.' Jess sighed. 'I know she is made of strong stuff, but a fall at her age, well...'

'Let's think positive,' said Carol firmly.

'Yes, we must,' agreed Jess. 'Anyway, tell me about your job.'

'Just part-time, three mornings a week,' Carol explained as they drove along. 'I called in and asked the manager if there was anything going, and it just so happened one of their younger part-time staff has gone off to university in Leeds, so it was perfect timing.'

'Ah, I'm pleased for you, Mum. I suppose it will keep you occupied.'

Jess had been worried her mum might be a little bored in her retirement, although she knew she had taken a couple of walks with Mark, and she had casually mentioned that he had invited her down to see his boat on the marina one day if she fancied it.

'It will. I always enjoyed working there, as you know. Much as I love collecting or taking Maisie to school, I miss the local gossip.' She winked.

'Did you know a new dance class has started up at the community centre on Coronation Road?' Jess asked her mum. 'Salsa, I believe, every Friday at six p.m.'

'Ooh I might have to check that out, then,' said Carol.

They chatted about how Christmas would soon be upon them, and how they ought to make a fuss of Alice and invite her over for Sunday lunch. Carol wondered whether she would still be living with Jess at Christmas.

The apartment on Nicholas Road had not quite been right for Carol, as the lounge had been north facing, and quite dark. The interior had also needed more work than she had first anticipated.

Still, there was something else on the market that she was going to view tomorrow.

'Mark has offered to come and view the flat with me tomorrow,' Carol told her daughter as they pulled into the car park near Liverpool One. 'I think he might lend a hand if any work needs doing. It will give him something to do,' said Carol.

'Are you sure that's the only reason?' said Jess, raising an eyebrow and Carol laughed.

'Right, see you later, love.' Carol gave her daughter a kiss on the cheek before they went their separate ways. She was going to call in at John Lewis and look at some new soft furnishings she had been browsing online.

She crossed her fingers that the apartment she was viewing tomorrow would be the right one. She was looking forward to making a new home for herself. It was time for her to get on with her life.

Jess seemed to always be haring off somewhere. In between her working life and trips to the hospital to visit Alice, there never seemed to be any time to do anything else. But she would do anything for Alice. She could never repay her for the security she had provided for herself and her daughter.

Her mum had fallen in love with the ground-floor apartment on Blundellsands Road East, that had a large lounge that would flood with light on bright days.

There was a communal garden too that was immaculately looked after. Carol had been worried she was a little young for over-sixties accommodation, despite her being in that age bracket herself, but her fears were unfounded. Most of the residents were a lively bunch, many of whom enjoyed an evening at the local pub for their quiz night. Several of them, including Carol, were heading to Manchester in the new year on the train to watch *Strictly Come Dancing* on tour.

Jess was pleased that Carol and Mark appeared to be growing closer too. He had helped her decorate the new apartment and fixed some new curtain poles to the walls.

It was a crisp winter afternoon when Jess popped around to her mum's after school with Maisie.

'We are really good friends,' Carol had answered when Jess asked her if she saw a future with Mark.

'Do you think that's all you will ever be?' asked Jess.

'I'm not sure,' Carol answered honestly. 'I love spending time with him. And he is very handsome,' she admitted.

'But?'

'I'm just not sure I could ever get involved with another man romantically. Look what happened last time that happened.' She sighed.

'Oh, Mum. That was different,' said Jess as Maisie was engrossed in building a Lego model. 'You were probably in a bad place after you and Dad separated. Maybe you felt flattered by the attention.'

'That's true enough,' said Carol, when she thought about how Pete Riley had swept her off her feet. 'Besides, I'm not sure Mark even sees me that way.'

Jess doubted that very much. She had seen the way he looked at her mum.

'We went to watch a band his nephew was in at the pub last week, as you know. We had a lovely evening, and when he dropped me off, there was not even a peck on the cheek,' she said. 'I think he is strictly in the friend zone, as you young ones say.'

Carol recalled feeling relieved and disappointed in equal measure when Mark had not kissed her goodnight.

'Well, I think you would make a lovely couple, that's all I am saying,' said Jess as she stood to get Maisie a drink.

'Thanks, love, it's nice to know I would have your blessing,' she told her daughter. 'But I will tell you this for nothing. Even if Mark does become my boyfriend, if I can even call him that at my age,' she said, with a roll of her eyes, 'I will never live with another man as long as I live,' she finished firmly. 'I've spent most of my life sharing my home with a man. It's time to get to know myself and have a few adventures along the way.'

'Never too old to show some girl power, hey, Mum.' Jess laughed.

'Don't you forget it,' said Carol. 'Even if I did need a bit of help with that curtain pole.'

## SIXTY-SIX

## DECLAN

When Declan took a call from the hospital regarding Alice, he was prepared for bad news. Despite the doctors saying Alice was doing well, she had looked tired when he had visited her yesterday.

Thankfully, she had not broken her hip but rather sustained a small fracture in her pelvis that would not require surgery, but plenty of rest.

The doctor informed him that Alice was to be discharged later that morning.

'She has made remarkable progress for a woman her age,' the doctor told him. 'I feel she would progress further in her own environment, and, of course, she will be discharged with a care package, involving a carer popping in until she is completely stable on her feet.'

'That's great news,' said Declan. He agreed that her continued recovery would improve back home. He, Mark and Jess had been regular visitors to the hospital, but it would be easier for them to keep an eye on her at the apartment, as they had done following her chest infection.

Alice's nephews had been to visit her in hospital a couple of weeks ago, whilst Declan had been there. He thought they seemed like nice enough blokes. They had expressed regret that their own mother had not been well enough to visit her sister. Still, they kept in touch via Alice's tablet, as they always did.

'I would offer to collect her,' Declan told the doctor. 'But I won't be free until late afternoon,' he said, thinking of a couple of meetings he had with potential clients. The way things were going, he would probably need to employ a part-time accountant sooner rather than later.

'Don't worry about that. It is probably a more comfortable ride in the ambulance,' the doctor assured him. 'Is it possible there would be someone to be at her home when she returns, would you know?' the doctor enquired.

Declan thought of Mark, or perhaps even Jess, and hoped they might be free. He would give them a call.

'I will make sure someone is there to greet her,' he told the doctor.

If they were unavailable, he would get away as soon as he was free.

He was so grateful that Jess and Mark were there to look after Alice, but he was determined not to let work overshadow the rest of his life. He had come to learn that friends were everything. Especially friends like his.

# SIXTY-SEVEN

## ALICE

Alice's friends had been astounded by her progress in the weeks that followed. Perhaps being in her own home had helped as the doctor had thought, as it wasn't long before Alice had told the carer she was no longer required. Even so, Jess always checked on her before she left for work to ensure she was up and dressed.

Alice had shown the determination of someone half her age and was now walking largely unaided, apart from using a walking stick if she needed to get to the local shop.

'If I don't get out for a daily walk I think I shall go mad,' she told Jess one day when she met her in the lobby downstairs. Sitting watching daytime television all day was enough to drive a person to drink, thought Alice. Thankfully, she had discovered some interesting podcasts to listen to.

'Okay, but be careful,' said Jess, who thought Alice probably needed a walking frame rather than a walking stick, but never said anything.

Even if her friends and family had tried to advise her otherwise, there was no way Alice would give up. Her hip had healed nicely thankfully, without needing any major surgery, which she had attributed to her strong bones. Being a dancer in her younger days and a lifelong healthy diet had almost certainly helped. Still, she knew she had been lucky. And she was not so foolish as to venture outside if there was any ice on the pavements.

The weeks had quietly bled into December now, and the shops were busy with people buying gifts for their loved ones. Darkness fell over the city around five, when the Christmas lights would add some festive cheer to the gloomy weather. The sight of the decorated tree in the village centre cheered up Alice immensely every time she walked past.

Jess had been kind enough to invite everyone to her place for Christmas lunch. Carol would bring an additional folding table to accommodate everyone, as well as preparing and bringing some of the food.

Alice had a feeling that Carol was someone who would be instrumental in keeping the group together and it gave her some comfort. She could rest easy knowing that the house was safe and that the friendships would continue. Soon enough it would be time to pass on the baton.

# SIXTY-EIGHT

## Christmas

Declan had politely declined Jess's invitation for Christmas, explaining that he would be spending it with his mother.

'It's always difficult for her at this time of year,' he had explained.

'I understand,' Jess had told him, even though she could never begin to comprehend how it must have felt for his mother to lose her daughter, or Declan his sister. At least they would get together on New Year's Eve.

Jess had suggested a lucky dip for the Christmas lunch table, rather than people feeling the pressure of having to bring gifts for everyone else. Not that she expected them to, of course, but even so a lucky dip was always rather fun in work, so she was pleased when everyone was on board with the idea.

Although Jess completely understood Declan's reasons for not attending Christmas lunch, she could not help feeling it would not be the same without him there.

She had quietly come to the realisation that she no longer

wanted to deny her feelings towards him. And could only hope that she had not left it too late.

Christmas Day was a lot of fun, and Maisie had been overjoyed to receive the latest toy that had sold out in almost every outlet in the country.

Her father had returned from working abroad, where he had managed to purchase one of the most desired toys on Santa's list. He had also taken Maisie to the Lego store in town, and treated her to a new Lego set, before a slap-up lunch at her favourite pizza restaurant.

Thankfully, Maisie had been just as overjoyed with her bicycle that Jess had saved up for and surprised her with.

Maisie had become accustomed to her father's infrequent appearances, without it causing her too much distress. At least Jess hoped that was the case. She could only hope that she was surrounded by enough love from the people in her life to compensate for her father's absence. She tried not to think about when Maisie was older, and whether she would have a reliable male role model in her life.

Alice had enjoyed her Christmas lunch immensely, and laughed at her lucky dip prize, a pair of knee-high stripy socks.

Once home, she had changed into her nightwear and slipped into bed to read. It felt strange not spending Christmas night in the house she once shared with George and she hoped the new family would enjoy their first Christmas in their new home.

'I have been very well looked after today,' she said to another framed photograph of her husband. 'In fact, my friends have been wonderful looking after me for some time. I managed to survive a nasty fall, which was my own fault, but perhaps you already know that.' She smiled, thinking of how she had forgotten to place her jigsaw box under the coffee table, and stumbled right over it. 'Such a silly thing to do, but I am getting on in years.'

She felt her eyes become heavy, as she began to yawn. She wondered how many more Christmases she would have on this earth, but when the time came, she would be ready. In the meantime, she would enjoy every minute.

'Goodnight, my love. Merry Christmas.'

It wasn't long before she had drifted off to sleep and she dreamt of Christmases past in the house she once shared with her husband. She was in a room filled with singing and laughter, as her family and friends sang along to a tune George was playing on a piano in the drawing room.

Beside it was the huge real Christmas tree that George always insisted on. Alice would grumble about the needles dropping onto the floor, but as it was George who would decorate it so beautifully, going over the top with lights and bows, she did not complain for long. It was the season of goodwill after all.

Jess had deliberated for so long over what she should wear for the party. She had spotted a gorgeous black dress in town but thought it might be a bit much for a house gathering. Then again, it was New Year's Eve.

'You look beautiful,' Carol had told her when she had tried the dress on in the shop. 'Wear the dress for the party. I would, if I still had your figure,' she joked.

'Do you think I should?' Jess asked doubtfully as she gave a little twirl in front of the mirror. She had to admit it did look good on her.

She was torn between the dress, and a fashionable trouser suit, that had a more relaxed look.

'Definitely. I'm wearing a dress. My trusty red wrap over

that I have had for years. It's very forgiving.' Her mum had laughed. 'Especially after some food and drink.'

Declan had insisted on paying for the quality buffet that would be delivered to Alice's in the late afternoon of the party. He had also ordered champagne for the celebration. He would never be able to pay Alice enough for her generosity.

When Mark found out, he had purchased some outdoor lights to drape along the fence, as well as a couple of patio heaters, should the party spill over outdoors.

Jess and Carol had taken over the purchasing of balloons and banners to decorate Alice's flat, as well as a celebration cake from the food hall at M&S.

'I am so looking forward to the party,' said Alice to Declan as they chatted one morning on the landing.

'Me too,' he told her. Declan realised that Jess would be there, and the thought of it gave him a warm feeling inside.

'So where are you off to?' he asked Alice, who informed him she was heading to the church opposite the Co-op.

'Hop in, then,' he said. 'I'll drop you off, unless you want to be all independent,' he teased. He was heading into the office a little later today, as things were quiet in between Christmas and New Year.

'You know me so well.' She smiled. 'Although on this occasion, I will accept a lift. It is rather cold out there.'

After Declan had been into the office and checked a few emails, he would pop into town and buy himself a new suit.

He had decided to splash out on something of quality that would serve him well in his new role meeting up with clients, as well as for New Year. And maybe even something to wear at a top restaurant in the city if he got up the courage to invite Jess.

SIXTY-NINE

.

## The Party

Alice's garden looked stunningly beautiful. Mark had hung the lights along the fence and set up the patio heaters.

He had found something online that turned the water in the fountain different colours, and gold banners had been attached to the fence, bearing words of congratulations that shimmered beneath the lights. Along with Alice's selection of garden fairies and ornaments, the whole space would look magical when darkness fell.

Once more, Maisie's friend had been invited for a sleepover, after Jess's friend had mentioned she could not find a babysitter for New Year's Eve. The two little girls would keep each other occupied, so Alice was more than happy for her to attend.

Carol had offered to take them to Jess's flat before midnight, but Jess had been one step ahead and bought a wigwam and two sleeping bags for them to settle in.

She would not expect Alice to look after the girls overnight at her advanced years but wondered vaguely whether Declan might help her get the girls back to her flat.

Jess felt the butterflies in her stomach when she thought of Declan being at the party.

'I think that's a wrap,' said Carol as she glanced at the impressive buffet that had arrived twenty minutes ago that she had laid out on the table.

The white iced cake at the centre of the table looked impressive too and had been adorned with some edible gold glitter. The room was festooned with balloons, and two banners were displayed on opposite walls, one bearing the words 'Happy Birthday', the other 'Happy New Year'.

Alice had been banished to her bedroom to change, and when she emerged wearing a beautiful silver dress and her favourite red lipstick, she gasped.

'It all looks wonderful,' she said. 'How have you managed to do all this so quickly?'

'Well, the balloons were already inflated and in bin bags,' revealed Carol. 'The rest took two minutes.'

The buffet had been uncovered whilst Alice had changed, and she took in the platters of delicious-looking food.

'And you look sensational,' said Jess. 'Like a movie star.'

'Thank you kindly.' Alice smiled. 'And you both look beautiful too. Isn't it wonderful to dress up for a party?'

'It is,' agreed Jess, who still felt a tad overdressed, but she had to admit she looked and felt great in her fitted black dress.

Ten minutes later, Maisie and her friend Libby had arrived. Libby's mum had taken them to a pantomime in town, and they ran in excitedly with flushed cheeks.

'Thanks for this,' whispered Libby's mum. 'To be honest, I don't even feel like going out, but the restaurant has been booked for months.'

'No problem. The girls always love a sleepover,' Jess assured her.

Both girls squealed when they spotted the wigwam behind the sofa and headed straight for it.

'Thanks. And happy New Year for later,' Libby's mum said. 'Happy New Year.'

'We just need to wait for Mark and Declan, then you can have your present,' said Carol to Alice.

Just then Mark arrived. He was wearing a smart blue shirt and a pair of black jeans that made him look years younger, thought Carol.

'Present? But I told you not to bother with a present; all of this is more than enough,' said Alice as she glanced around the room.

They had already presented her with cards that were lined up along a shelf, along with the ones from her family down south.

'As if we would not buy you a gift,' Jess said with a laugh.

A few minutes later, Mark heard the sound of a car pulling up outside.

Looking through the window, the friends spotted the sleek Bentley, and out stepped Declan. The car belonged to Ken Watson, who had provided his chauffeur to drop Declan off after the meal.

'Oh, how marvellous!' exclaimed Alice. 'I haven't ridden in a Bentley for more years than I can remember.'

As Declan headed up the path, the sight of him made Jess's heart beat wildly. He had never looked more handsome in a gorgeous dark-grey suit over a white shirt. She could hardly wait for the celebrations to begin.

'Right,' said Mark, clapping his hands together after everyone had enjoyed a drink and sampled some of the delicious buffet. 'It's time for your present, Alice.'

'A present? Really you shouldn't have. You all being here is enough.'

'You really thought we wouldn't buy you a birthday gift.' He raised an eyebrow as he presented Alice with her birthday present.

'What on earth can this be?' asked Alice as she tore off the sparkly silver wrapping paper. 'I do love a surprise,' she said excitedly.

When she opened the box and peered inside, her hand flew to her mouth.

'Oh, my goodness. Is that what I think it is?' she asked as she lifted the white metal structure, that looked like a birdcage from its box.

'An exact replica of the Palm House at Sefton Park,' Mark informed her. 'I had it especially made. One of my friends down at the marina is a metal worker. Look inside; the roof comes off,' he instructed Alice, who was so shocked she could barely speak.

Mark recalled how much Alice had enjoyed their day out together at Sefton Park.

Inside, a selection of tiny plants and rocks were nestled on a bed of soil. It reminded her of a bottle garden or terrarium she had once owned.

'It's perfect. Simply beautiful,' she said. Never in her life had she received such a thoughtful gift.

'Oh, and there is one more surprise,' said Mark as he pulled the curtains back from the patio doors.

He slid open the doors to reveal the garden in all its glory.

'I'm not sure my heart can take any more of this,' said Alice as she stood open-mouthed, taking in the scene outside.

Libby and Maisie raced outside and ran to the colour-changing fountain surrounded by the fairies.

Jess sorted some music and the drinks flowed as everyone gathered outside.

A little after ten, Alice was certain she would not make it until midnight as she was already feeling a little tired. Maybe she would settle in her favourite wicker garden chair with a blanket near the patio heaters. It seemed her friends had thought of everything.

# SEVENTY

## DECLAN

A short while later and with the girls snoozing in the wigwam, Declan approached Jess with a drink.

'You look beautiful tonight,' he told her. 'I haven't been able to take my eyes off you.'

Their fingers touched when he passed her the glass of champagne, and once more she felt the tingles through her body.

'You scrub up well too,' she told him, feeling light-headed by his nearness. He smelt of woody cologne and wore his expensive-looking suit perfectly.

'Thanks.' He smiled. 'Maybe we can have a dance later, if things slow down,' he suggested.

'I'd like that,' said Jess.

A while later, everyone had drifted back inside, apart from Alice, who was snoozing gently in her chair. It seemed a shame to wake her, thought Declan, although maybe he would in a little while.

True to his word, he invited Jess outside and slid the patio door behind them. He searched for a slow number to dance to on Spotify and drew her close to him.

As they gently swayed to the music, Jess could feel her heart hammering inside her chest. When the music stopped, he pulled her even closer, and his lips came down on hers. It brought back memories of their kiss at the bar that evening, but it felt so much sweeter as they had waited so long to be together again.

When they finally pulled apart, they glanced across at Alice.

'Seems a shame to wake her,' said Declan as an early firework shot through the sky somewhere.

They hadn't noticed Alice opening one eye and smiling when she saw them kissing. Seeing two of her favourite people finally together felt like being handed another birthday gift.

Carol and Mark were still going strong, and Carol was showing Mark how to jive. She told Jess she would be staying over at Mark's 'as friends' as there would be no chance of a taxi after midnight, and Jess had given her a knowing look.

'I think it's time we got those two to bed,' Jess said to Declan, after peeping in at the two girls asleep inside the wigwam. 'Do you think we could lift them without disturbing them?'

'Hopefully. They look cosy inside their sleeping bags. I could carry them up,' he offered.

'We can both do it,' suggested Jess.

Everyone helped to do a quick tidy up, with the promise to return and do it properly in the morning.

In the end, hardly anyone made it to midnight, but Jess had a feeling that her mum and Mark might. With Alice settled in bed, everyone began to drift off.

'Night, Mum. Night, Mark. Happy New Year, even though it is forty minutes away,' said Jess, as Declan said the same, and Carol and Mark returned the greeting.

'Are you any good at cards?' Jess heard Mark ask her mum

as they walked to his door and she wondered where they got their energy from.

With the children settled in bed, Declan said goodnight and headed for the front door of Jess's apartment.

'Do you have to be anywhere in the morning?' asked Jess.

'No, it's New Year's Day,' he reminded her.

'Then stay,' she said as she led him to her bedroom.

# SEVENTY-ONE

## ALICE

The winter had quickly turned to spring, and Alice was grateful to have made it into another year. She wasn't sure she would do following her illness and subsequent fall, but it seemed the Good Lord had other ideas.

Declan's business was going well, and he and Jess had quietly become a couple, which was more than Declan dared to dream of.

The fall last winter had taken its toll on Alice, there was no doubt about that. It took her twice as long to get out of bed these days, and her lack of energy was beginning to frustrate her. But then, she was ninety-two years old.

'Morning, Alice.' Mark knocked on her door on an unusually warm Saturday morning in late April.

'Do you fancy coming for a bit of lunch later?' he asked. 'Thought we might eat outside. Carol is coming, and I will see if Declan and Jess are free.'

'That sounds lovely.' Alice smiled. 'We must make the most of these sunny days.'

'That's what I thought,' said Mark. 'Shall we say one o'clock?'

'Perfect,' said Alice, who loved nothing more than spending time with her friends. She felt a rush of affection for them every time she glanced at her terrarium that she had lovingly cared for.

The friends spent the loveliest afternoon, delighted to be enjoying some sunshine and enjoying a BBQ.

'Who would have thought we would be doing this in April?' asked Mark as he flipped a burger over.

'Global warming,' said Declan, and a discussion about that had ensued.

'I'm so happy you are settled, Mum,' said Jess to Carol as they poured some drinks. 'I never imagined you and Dad would break up, but it's good to see you finally happy.'

'Thanks, love. I think deep down I knew we would separate,' said Carol to a shocked Jess.

'You did?'

'Yes. Oh, I kidded myself that things were fine, but we had been going through the motions for a long time,' she admitted. 'If I am honest, I was just scared of being on my own. Even though I often felt lonely in the marriage, which is not how you should feel,' she confessed.

'You have never told me that. I always assumed you and Dad were happy.'

'Well, you never let your kids know such things, even when they are adults.' Carol smiled.

Jess wished she could have confided in her, but it was typical of her mum not to want to burden her with her marriage problems. Maybe she was right about shielding your children from worry. She imagined she would be the same with Maisie.

'I saw him once,' Jess blurted out. 'And I'm sorry I never said anything to you, but it seemed innocent enough. He was having a coffee at lunchtime with a colleague,' she told Carol. 'He wasn't a bit fazed when he saw me. I'm sorry, though, Mum; I should have said something.'

'Oh, love, don't worry,' said Carol. 'I saw him once too, you know, with that woman.' She could hardly bear to mention her name. 'Getting out of a car together near the shopping precinct.'

She dropped a slice of lemon into her gin and tonic.

'Did he know you saw him?'

'No.' She shrugged. 'And I never mentioned it. I thought if it was a fling, then it might fizzle out. Stupid, I know.'

'Oh, Mum.'

'Don't worry, really.' She patted her daughter's arm. 'I am actually happier than I have been in years.' She winked. 'And if I can give you any advice, it would be to not rely on anyone else for your own well-being,' she told Jess wisely. 'Your father wasn't responsible for my happiness; I realise that now. We have to create that for ourselves.'

Not for the first time, Jess realised that she was indeed responsible for her own happiness, and of course that of Maisie. But she was pleased that she had decided to take a chance on happiness with Declan. Especially knowing she would always survive on her own.

When it was time to leave, Declan and Jess escorted Alice back to her apartment.

'Fancy a cup of tea?' Jess offered once they were inside.

'Ooh I do. And I think I will take it outside in my favourite chair,' said Alice. 'And make the most of this lovely weather.'

'Coming up,' said Declan as he followed Jess to the kitchen.

Jess brought the tea out to Alice, along with a throw for over her legs as the afternoon grew a little cooler.

Alice heard the voices of Declan and Jess grow distant as she felt her eyes grow heavy on that bright April afternoon, sitting in her favourite chair.

She began to dream of herself and George dancing together

at the Tower Ballroom at Blackpool, a place they would frequent in their younger years.

As they took to the floor, a band played their favourite song and a spotlight shone down on them. She was wearing her favourite red dress, and George was wearing a navy suit. She felt like Ginger Rogers dancing with Fred Astaire as a mesmerised audience looked on.

Bathed in the light, Alice felt a warm glow wash over her body. As George twirled her around, a slow smile spread across her face and she felt at peace.

'I'm coming to see you, my darling,' she whispered as she closed her eyes. 'I think my work here is done.'

There were ten people in the church for the funeral of Alice Bennett, but there was more love in the room than if there had been a thousand mourners.

Jess had choked back tears when she watched Alice's sister being pushed along in her wheelchair by one of her sons to the front of the church. The family had travelled up for the funeral and would be staying at a hotel overnight.

They listened to the words of the vicar in front of the light-oak coffin, laid with a wreath of Alice's favourite lilies.

Declan had decided to write a eulogy, and as he stood at the pulpit and began to read, Jess felt a surge of pride.

He talked of how Alice had brought them all together, and how he would never forget her.

'I knocked her off her feet when we first met,' he told the small congregation. 'Luckily she forgave me.' He smiled. 'In fact, she invited me inside. I had been in a bad mood that day,' he said, recalling the disastrous interview. 'But I left with a smile on my face,' he said, his voice breaking. 'But that was Alice all over. She had a knack of making you feel better. She was wise, kind and beautiful. And she loved her family, who she often spoke of,' he said, directing his gaze at her loved ones. 'We may be few in numbers here today, but Alice was truly loved.'

He talked a little more of her character, as he glanced towards the framed photo of her on the coffin.

Alice's sister quietly sobbed as Jess felt the tears roll down her cheek.

Jess thought of one of Alice's sayings then. 'Less is more,' she would say if something seemed a little overdone. Never more so than today with the quiet, dignified service, befitting of such a gracious lady. She could hardly bear the thought of never seeing her again.

'So today, in this stillness we honour you, Alice Bennett,' said Declan. 'You meant the world to those that mattered. You were seen. You were heard. You will never be forgotten.'

'Never.' Jess sniffed as Mark gave her hand a little squeeze.

As they filed out of the crematorium to the strains of Alice's favourite hymn, chosen by her sister, Jess was sure she would not be the only one who would miss having Alice around. A light had gone out in all of their lives. They would make sure her memory lived on.

'Are you sure you have never been salsa dancing before?'

'I swear,' replied Mark as he passed some garlic bread to Declan. 'I guess I must just be a natural.'

The friends were in Alice's old apartment enjoying a late lunch and raising a glass to Alice.

Mark and Carol had been dancing at the community centre the previous evening, and it seemed Mark really did have a natural talent. Carol was thrilled at how much he had come out of his shell of late. She was certain that if he had gone alone he would have had a line of willing female partners to dance with.

They all raised a glass to Alice as they enjoyed their meal.

'To think this is where it all began,' said Declan. 'We might never have got together had Alice not invited us to dinner.'

'I'm not sure we would have,' agreed Jess. 'It makes you think, though, doesn't it? Sometimes it only takes one person to change your life.'

'True enough,' said Declan as he also thought about Ken Watson and the chance he had given him. He could never thank him enough.

It was Saturday afternoon, and Jess had just returned from

doing a bride's make-up a couple of miles away. She had recently attended a refresher course at night school and now spent the occasional weekend mornings doing wedding make-up. Thankfully she had not encountered any Bridezillas up to now. She was grateful that her mum had watched Maisie, and prepared a tasty lunch with the help of Mark and Declan.

'Living here feels like the greatest gift from Alice,' said Jess as she enjoyed her delicious pasta. 'I feel her presence is all around. And Maisie absolutely loves the garden, don't you?'

'I love it more than anything. I am going to have a bouncy castle at my next birthday party, aren't I, Mummy?' she said excitedly. 'And my friends from school are going to come.'

'You are indeed.' Jess smiled lovingly at her daughter.

'Typical of Alice to think about you and Maisie having the garden flat,' said Carol.

'Isn't it just,' said Jess. 'She was always thinking of others.'

'Right, let's clear these plates, then who fancies a walk to the beach?' suggested Declan. 'I need to get some steps in.'

'Great idea,' said Mark, and Carol and Jess agreed.


On their walk, the group passed through Alexandra Park and stopped at a memorial bench.

'What do you think, Alice? I reckon he is telling me porkies about not dancing before.' Carol nodded towards Mark.

She glanced at the plaque on the bench, after placing a posy of white flowers into a plant holder.

The memorial bench had been Mark's idea as he recalled Alice's affection for parks. It may not have been Sefton Park, but it was so close to the apartments and they could visit it regularly. Jess and Declan thought it a fitting tribute too.

Mark and Carol were a couple now, although Carol was still adamant about never living with a man again. And what was the need? They had their own space, something they both relished, and enjoyed their time together when they did meet up.

'I'm so glad things are working out with the bridal make-up,' said Carol to Jess as they exited the small park.

'Me too. I'm really enjoying it. The bride this morning went for a natural look, which was a bit different than what I usually do,' she told her mum. 'She said something about not wanting to look like a drag queen on her big day, which made me chuckle.'

'What's a drag queen?' asked Maisie and Declan could not help but smile as Jess tactfully explained it as an entertainer who liked to wear bright clothes.

Jess was enjoying doing wedding make-up, and had recently booked driving lessons as she hated relying on anyone else. It was awkward carrying her huge cosmetic case on public transport but hopefully it would not be forever. She would never have been able to afford the lessons without the generosity of Alice.

She wondered if Alice knew the impact she was having on all of their lives. Declan was doing well in his business and enjoying it immensely. He was in the middle of organising a ball for a charity evening to support a local children's hospice, inviting other local businesses along. He would never forget to heed Alice's words and look after others whenever possible.

Mark was grabbing life with both hands, and in the process discovered that he was a good dancer. He was no longer locked in his grief, although he did still relish his alone time, something Carol understood completely. He was no longer estranged from his sister and nephew, who he regularly enjoyed leisurely Sunday lunches with.

'Do you ever wonder if Alice is watching us?' said Carol as a white feather swirled to the ground in front of them.

'Who knows?' said Declan. 'Although surely you don't think that is a sign.' He laughed. 'It's probably just come from a nearby seagull.'

'But you never know,' said Jess. 'Alice had a deep faith. So perhaps she really is smiling down on us from somewhere. I like to think so anyway.'

They walked quietly as they pondered Jess's words.

'Right, come on, let's get a move on,' said Mark, patting his stomach. 'I need to work off that third slice of garlic bread and a slow stroll is not going to do that.'

'We can jog if you like,' suggested Declan.

'A brisk walk is fine at my age.' Mark smiled.

'Can we feed the ducks at the pond on the way?' asked Maisie.

'Of course we can.' Jess lifted the bag of seeds from her bag that she had remembered to bring.

They may live in an apartment, but it was such a lovely part of the city there was nowhere else she would rather live.

'Then can I go on the swings near the beach?'

'You can,' said Jess.

'And get an ice cream?' asked Maisie hopefully.

'Whatever you like.' Jess smiled.

As she strolled along with her friends, she felt a feeling of contentment that she had never known. Life was for living after all. And she owed it to Alice to live it to the full.

# A LETTER FROM SUE ROBERTS

Dear reader,

I want to say a huge thank you for choosing to read *The Last Dinner at Wisteria House*.

I so enjoyed writing this book, as it was such a departure from my usual beach reads. I hope it was just as enjoyable!

If you did enjoy it, and want to keep up to date with all my latest releases, just sign up at the following link. Your email address will never be shared and you can unsubscribe at any time.

*www.bookouture.com/sue-roberts*

I hope you loved *The Last Dinner at Wisteria House* and if you did I would be very grateful if you could write a review. I'd love to hear what you think, and it makes such a difference helping new readers to discover one of my books for the first time.

I love hearing from my readers – you can get in touch through social media.

Thanks,

Sue Roberts

# KEEP IN TOUCH WITH SUE

facebook.com/Suerobertsauthor
x.com/SueRobertsautho
instagram.com/suerobertsauthor

# ACKNOWLEDGEMENTS

I would like to thank every single one of my readers, and those who have reached out to me via social media, and continued to purchase my books. Also, all of you book bloggers and reviewers who help recommend our books to others. Your support is much appreciated.

Of course, it goes without saying that huge thanks go to my wonderful publisher Bookouture and ALL of the wonderful team. A special thanks to Natalie Edwards, who has helped me so much to make this book the best it can be. I am truly grateful.

We lead such busy lives that sometimes we do not have enough hours in a day to speak to even our neighbours. This book touched on the fact that even saying hello to someone can brighten their day. Sometimes it can even be the start of a friendship, if we open ourselves up to the possibility.

Finally, I would like to thank all of my friends and family for stories they tell me, and things they remind me of (that often go in my books!). I have such gratitude to have you all in my life.

PUBLISHING TEAM

**Turning a manuscript into a book requires the efforts of many people. The publishing team at Bookouture would like to acknowledge everyone who contributed to this publication.**

**Commercial**
Lauren Morrissette
Hannah Richmond
Imogen Allport

**Cover design**
Lynn Andreozzi

**Data and analysis**
Mark Alder
Mohamed Bussuri

**Editorial**
Natalie Edwards
Imogen Allport

**Copyeditor**
Jane Eastgate

**Proofreader**
Becca Allen

## Marketing

Alex Crow
Melanie Price
Occy Carr
Cíara Rosney
Martyna Młynarska

## Operations and distribution

Marina Valles
Joe Morris

## Production

Hannah Snetsinger
Mandy Kullar
Nadia Michael
Charlotte Hegley

## Publicity

Kim Nash
Noelle Holten
Jess Readett
Sarah Hardy

## Rights and contracts

Peta Nightingale
Richard King
Saidah Graham

Dear Reader,

We'd love your attention for one more page to tell you about the crisis in children's reading, and what we can all do.

Studies have shown that reading for fun is the **single biggest predictor of a child's future life chances** – more than family circumstance, parents' educational background or income. It improves academic results, mental health, wealth, communication skills, ambition and happiness.

The number of children reading for fun is in rapid decline. Young people have a lot of competition for their time, and a worryingly high number do not have a single book at home.

Hachette works extensively with schools, libraries and literacy charities, but here are some ways we can all raise more readers:

- Reading to children for just 10 minutes a day makes a difference
- Don't give up if children aren't regular readers – there will be books for them!

- Visit bookshops and libraries to get recommendations
- Encourage them to listen to audiobooks
- Support school libraries
- Give books as gifts

There's a lot more information about how to encourage children to read on our websites: **www.RaisingReaders.co.uk** and **www.JoinRaisingReaders.com**.

Thank you for reading.